RIDDLES
OF THE
SPHINX

Riddles of the Sphinx

Meagan Cleveland

First published 2023 by Meagan Cleveland

ISBN: 9781738145508

Cover, typesetting and illustrations by Holly Dunn.

HEL

DELPHI

CORINTH

MYCENAE
ARGOS

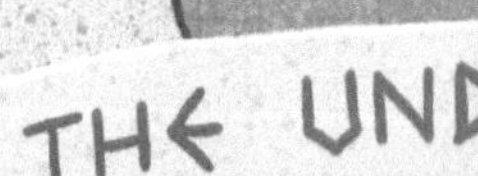

THE UND

ΛΔΣ
THEBES
ATHENS
RWORLD

1

THE PATH OF LIGHTS

All my life, I knew one thing to be true: outside was dangerous.

Outside, the plague ravaged the city, taking the lives of hundreds of Thebans. No one was safe, not even the King and Queen—my parents. Or so Pyrrha, my nurse, told me.

I had never been outside the palace. For sixteen years, I had been kept within the walls of the women's quarters with only my sister Antigone and Pyrrha for company. There, in those small rooms, the plague did not bother us. And as princesses, we never wanted for anything.

But there was one thing we did long for—excitement. Pyrrha remedied this by feeding us a steady diet of stories.

Pyrrha sat in her usual corner atop a small stool, carding wool to prepare for spinning. Her hands worked the white tufts, her eyes fixed on us.

Antigone sat at Pyrrha's side, watching her as she worked, committing her movements to memory so she could take on the task herself.

I hovered behind them, always on the outskirts, waiting to find my place among them. Antigone caught my eye and gestured for me to come sit. I sank beside her, casting a smile her way. She smiled in return.

Pyrrha's hands stilled and we looked at her expectantly.

She set her work down and leaned forward in her seat. The flames dancing in the braziers behind her cast flickering shadows around her face.

"So what will the story be tonight?"

"A story about the gods," Antigone demanded.

"Have you ever heard the story about how Delphi was founded?" Pyrrha asked.

My sister and I shook our heads.

"In the days after the Great Flood, Python the serpent was born from the slime," Pyrrha began. "Hera, queen of the gods, learned that her husband Zeus had impregnated a young woman named Leto. Furious, Hera sent Python after Leto, chasing her across the earth to prevent her from giving birth.

When Leto found a place to rest she gave birth to twins, Artemis and Apollo. Once he was grown, Apollo went in search of the serpent who was said to have made its home at Delphi. Apollo slew the serpent with a hundred arrows and it died in a pool of its own poison. The god named the spot Pytho because of the smell of its rotting corpse. In honour of his victory, the god established the Pythian Games.

Every four years, men from all across Hellas went to Delphi to attend the Pythian Games. There, they would compete in footraces, chariot races, boxing and more."

"Has anyone from Thebes been to Delphi to compete in the games?" I asked.

Pyrrha smiled sadly. "In the past, yes. But Thebes hasn't participated in the games since the plague befell the city."

At that, she turned back to her work, humming as she

dropped her spindle and began to spin wool for us to weave the next day.

"We should go," I whispered to Antigone.

"What?" she said, startled.

I knew she heard me.

"We should go," I repeated, leaning closer to her.

"Ismene, you know as well as I do that we can't leave."

She was right, of course. Who knew what horrors awaited us outside the safety of the palace walls?

And yet, that night as we settled down to sleep, my mind raced with thoughts of the sacred mountain, the shining god and the monstrous serpent he had slain. As I drifted off to sleep, I could swear I heard a voice whisper in my mind.

Ismene.

I did not weave the next morning. The voice in my head wouldn't let me.

Usually, my fingers itched to touch the brightly-dyed threads, an image floating in my mind's eye to trap in cloth. When my fingers brushed the crimson thread, the voice called my name.

Ismene.

The sensation was like an internal itch I could not scratch. An irritation that would not go away. I tried to ignore it. I'd been hearing the voice all morning at the back of my mind. A soft whisper drowned out by the rhythm of my hands at my loom. Now, the voice was insistent.

Ismene.

My fingers caught in the thread.

The more I tried to ignore it, the louder the voice grew inside my head until I became pale and trembling from resisting its call. The itch began to feel more like pain.

Ismene!

"Leave me alone," I mumbled through gritted teeth.

"Are you alright?" Pyrrha asked. She rose to her feet from her stool and rushed to me, leaving the ball of wool in her *kalathos.* "You are as pale as a ghost, child," she said, her palm on my brow. "Come lie down."

Pyrrha led me away from the standing loom, a large wooden frame that sat in our quarters so we could spin and weave like fine aristocratic young women.

Antigone did not look up as we passed where she sat with a small handloom, the size allowing her to do more delicate work on smaller bands of cloth. An *epinetron*, a ceramic covering to protect her leg, balanced on her knee. Though she did not turn her head, I could feel her eyes following me across the room.

I let Pyrrha tuck me into my bed. Even though as a girl of sixteen I was old enough to be married with children of my own, my nurse still coddled me as if I was a child.

"There now, love." Pyrrha leaned down and kissed my temple. "You'll feel better after a rest."

If anything, I felt more restless. The voice rose to a crescendo in my head, my name a steady rhythm beating in my mind like the beat of the shuttle of the loom.

Ismene. Ismene. Ismene.

Later that night, when I thought I had found some peace at last, the voice took up its plea in earnest, an unseen force drawing my limbs towards the doors to the women's quarters.

Time to go, Ismene.

I was too tired to resist.

I found myself at the threshold to the women's quarters. My whole world. In the innermost part of the Cadmeia, there were no windows to let in light or air. The rooms were dark, the air was close and thick with smoke and the other bodies that spent their time in there. But it was familiar, it was safe.

Go on, the voice coaxed, invisible hands pushing at my shoulders. *It will be alright.*

I looked behind me, past the looms, to where the sleeping forms of Antigone and Pyrrha lay. Safe in their beds, rooted to reality without bodiless voices luring them into the unknown.

I'm not luring you anywhere. The voice was amused. *I want to show you something.*

"Then, will you leave me alone?" I whispered, trying not to wake the others.

For now.

I took a shuddering breath and slipped out of the women's quarters.

It was late and the palace was still. The light of the braziers in the hallway left long and flickering shadows on the walls, a crowd of trembling ghosts watching my nervous progress. There was no sound but the slap of my leather sandals across the well-worn stone.

Those invisible hands rested softly on my shoulders, steering me to the *megaron*—the large hearth surrounded by four pillars, the epicentre of the palace where the King and his advisors met and held ceremonies and feasts.

I had only been to this room a handful of times, on sacrifice days and my brother's coronation. On these occasions, the clamour of the crowds was always overwhelming after so long with only two other souls for company. In the dark of the night, it was eerily silent save for the crack and hiss of the fire. The embers of the *megaron* gleamed crimson, a steady pulse flickering in the golden light at their centre like a heartbeat.

"What now?" I asked the voice in my head.

It did not reply but I felt an insistent tug that led me around the four pillars and the brightly-painted frescoes on the walls behind them. As I passed the hearth, I glanced towards the walls and thought I saw the shadow of a young man walking beside me. I looked ahead and realised I was heading towards the entrance to the palace.

My heart began pounding, thoughts of the plague racing in my mind.

"Wait," I said, forgetting to lower my voice.

Still, the hands tugged at me.

I couldn't go outside. What about the plague?

It is safe. The plague has not infected these streets for years.

"Why should I trust you?" I demanded, holding onto the post of the doorway with white-knuckled hands. "You could be a monster, for all I know. Some fury coming to torment me."

I'm not.

"That's what a fury would say," I muttered.

I assure you I am not a fury.

I scoffed. "And I should take your word on that?"

Yes.

The hands lifted from my shoulders.

I just want to show you.

"Show me what?"

Come see.

Slowly, I pried my fingers from the door. I let out a shuddering breath and crossed the threshold.

Inside, the air was thick and heavy. Outside, the air was light and cool.

I felt as if a weight had been lifted from my shoulders.

An invisible hand took one of my own in its grasp and led me across the acropolis. I could see nothing in the darkness and I reluctantly relied on the voice to show me the way. It kept a commentary in my head noting places as we passed.

Over there is the birthplace of Herakles.

There, Cadmus sowed a dragon's teeth into the earth to become men.

Even though I couldn't see the places it spoke of, I drank in the stories it told, the stories my nurse had raised me on. It was one thing to hear the great hero Herakles was born in my city, another entirely to walk by his birthplace.

And here is my father's house.

I stumbled.

My foot was caught in the uneven cobbled path. My sandal flew off and I knelt clumsily, scrambling for it. Soon, my fingers found the leather sole and I slipped it back onto my foot.

We had stopped beneath some great building, a towering black mass, its braziers glowing dimly in the night. I couldn't get a good look at the building.

"Who is your father?" I demanded. "Who are you?"

The voice did not answer. Instead, phantom hands helped me up and led me away. I desperately wished I could see beyond the flickering shadows of the braziers at the doors to the building. If I was brave enough to go out in the daylight, maybe I could go to the house and learn to whom the mysterious voice belonged.

We continued on our way in silence.

Finally, the darkness receded, lit by the rows of lamps at the base of a great wall. Understanding dawned on me. I was walking along the defensive wall that surrounded our city.

We had stopped at the base of one of the seven gates of Thebes.

"Which gate is this?" I asked the darkness around me.

The Neis Gate, the voice replied. *Now, up you go.*

I climbed the stairs until I stood atop the ramparts. I noticed the wind first. It tugged playfully at my unbound hair, tendrils of dark curls tickling my cheeks and my nose. The cool night air was like a gentle caress on my skin. A startled laugh bubbled from my lips at the sensation.

Then, I noticed the lights. In the darkness of the night, the lights glowed as steadily as the stars in the sky. They dotted the landscape, a golden current flowing northwest.

A river of stars.

I breathed. "It's beautiful." The phantom hand around mine squeezed. "Is this what you wanted to show me?"

Yes.

"It's beautiful," I repeated, "but why do I need to see it?"

It is the path to me. Follow the path of light and you will find me.

Phantom lips whispered and I could almost feel their touch upon my cheek.

I did not immediately return to the women's quarters. I left the famed seven gates and headed into the city itself. As the sun began to rise, the city roused itself. The streets, which had been empty and eerie during the night, bustled with people by morning.

As I wandered, my pace was slow and unsteady and angered those around me. Shoulders clipped mine and people snapped at me to hurry up or get out of the way. I tried to quicken my pace.

I let the crowds direct my path, following the throngs of people heading toward the *agora*.

The *agora* was so much more than just a marketplace. It was an open space where people assembled to talk politics, to sell their wares, to meet old friends and new. The space was surrounded by public buildings, shops and *stoas* to protect the crowds from the sun or rain.

I had never seen anything like it.

So many people, so many faces and voices laughing and arguing, smiling and grimacing. The air was thick with the smells of roasting meat that street vendors proffered from their stalls. Other stalls held glistening sweets and figs, drenched in honey, that made my belly rumble. There were vintners, cloth merchants, jewellers, shoemakers and dressmakers and shops selling knives and spears. I had never seen so many colours and textures, soft wool, glimmering gems, lustrous pearls and cold bronze. Craftsmen glowered from under the shade of the porticoes while *kapeloi*, traders, waved customers over to admire their wares.

I looked back towards the Cadmeia, worrying whether Antigone would miss me, but no one else took heed of my concern as they went about their daily business. They had no idea that while I stood there watching them, I felt my entire world shifting. Changing.

The *agora* was alive in ways that the palace was not. I saw the same faces of my sister and nurse every day in the women's quarters. Here, there were so many faces I had never seen, each one a possibility I wanted to explore. For all I knew, the owner of the voice could be among the crowd.

I circled through the marketplace, my eyes fixed on the figs glistening with honey. I stepped forward and grabbed one of the figs I had been eyeing. I took a bite. Warm honey flooded my mouth.

I strolled throughout the *agora*, browsing the wares. I noticed a group of people surging all in one direction. I began to follow them until we came to an open space near a hillside, rings of seats arranged to nestle among the hills around them. It was a theatre.

Scores of people were already sitting on the wooden seats, all eyes were on the stage.

An actor in a painted mask emerged from behind the *skene*, the tented backdrop behind the stage. He spoke the prologue, the mythological background for the play we were about to see. He spoke about the hero Perseus, slayer of the gorgon Medusa and saviour of the princess Andromeda.

At one point, the prologue spoke of the birth of Perseus. His mother Danae, of the beautiful hair, was the daughter of king Acrisius of Argos. When the oracle declared his daughter would bear a son that would defeat him, Acrisius imprisoned his daughter and left her to wither away. But Zeus was enamoured with her beauty and came to her in a shower of gold. Later, she bore him a son.

The prologue ended and the chorus emerged and began to sing the *parodos*.

I did not pay much attention after that. I could not stop thinking about Danae and how the men in her life locked her way without a thought. Until that morning, I had never even ventured outside of the prison my quarters had become. Did Danae even realise she was being imprisoned? Or did they say they were protecting her, too?

The crowd around me cheered as Perseus emerged on stage, triumphant. He had just vanquished the monstrous Cetus and received Andromeda as his prize. Andromeda began to speak and I was struck by the sound of her voice. She wasn't a woman at all, but a boy, his voice cracking and booming with the first signs of youth. He was dressed as a girl and no one batted an eye. If only I could dress as a boy and go out in plain sight and do all the things I wanted.

But why couldn't I?

After the play finished with tremendous applause I made my way back to the Cadmeia. I was silent most of the way, a plan unfurling in my mind. I imagined myself dressed as a boy, finally doing all the things I never could do before. All I had to do was find the right clothes—

I stumbled.

The cobbles beneath me were uneven and I had lost a shoe. With a start, I remembered earlier that night. I had lost a shoe then as well, before the house the voice claimed was his father's. In the black night, I could not see what lay before me but now, in the light of the afternoon, I could.

I looked up.

The sun blazed white in my eyes and I lifted a hand to shield them.

In front of me was the temple of Zeus.

The voice belonged to a god.

2

THE FEAST

"Zeus is your father?" I gasped aloud, staring up at the temple from the dusty road.

Yes.

"Who are you?" I whispered.

Think about it. Again, amused.

I thought of the river of lights. The voice said the lights would lead me to him.

Of course. "Apollo," I murmured.

The sun blazed brighter in the sky, its rays trailing across my skin like idle fingertips.

Apollo, the son of Zeus, was one of the twelve Olympian gods. He was also the vengeful god from Pyrrha's stories—the serpent slayer.

"What do you want from me?"

Follow the path of lights and you will find out.

My thoughts turned to the night before. The current of golden lights swam behind my eyes. But I did not head back to the Neis Gate to follow the path of lights. It was time for me to head back to the Cadmeia.

My decision was made and the voice was gone. His absence felt like stepping into a shadow—all at once, I felt dark and cold. I had to find my own way back to the palace. Alone.

Sunset painted the sky in reds and golds and I took one last lingering look at the lower city, watching as lights flickered from the windows in the dim early evening. Ducking into the palace, I noticed the labyrinth of workrooms where women spun dyed wool and wove tapestries and fine cloth, where Cretan craftsmen painted clay pots, and smiths worked bronze into beautiful ornaments and sturdy weapons. I passed the storerooms where large *pithoi* held olive oil and wine, wheat and barley, olives and figs and other necessities. The scribes did not look up from their clay tablets as I passed, too immersed in recording our stores. I marveled at all I had seen, realising what I had missed over the years as I was kept hidden in my quarters like a treasure in a box.

Finally, I stood before the door to the women's quarters.

I crept inside. The rooms seemed smaller now. I felt as if I had grown too large to be contained within them, bursting with the knowledge that there was more outside these walls.

I nestled into my bed beside my sister, savouring her warmth.

As the bodies stirred around me my only thought was of when I would go outside again.

When we began our work at the loom the next morning, the voice was silent. I had not done what he wanted. I had not followed the path of lights. Perhaps only then would I hear the god's voice again.

Pyrrha rose from her place in the corner.

"Is it time?" Antigone asked.

"Time for what?" I watched Pyrrha bustle to our sleeping quarters and come back out again with bundles of clothes.

"Time to get ready for the feast," she replied.

I looked at her blankly.

"The feast being held for your brother. Haven't you been listening to me at all?"

I hadn't paid much attention to Pyrrha or Antigone that morning, especially after the revelation that outside the palace was safe after all. After the revelation that a god had some plan for me.

But what?

Pyrrha gestured for me to stand up and come over to her. Antigone left her place at the loom and stood beside me as Pyrrha dressed us.

In the stories she told us, Pyrrha always described how the hero would be armed for battle by some goddess or other—usually Athena—each piece of armour delicately placed to protect him from the dangers he would face in battle.

As Pyrrha dressed us, I felt as if she were arming us in her own way. As if the love with which she dressed us could protect us from the dangers of the world. She moved like the goddess. The *peplos*, the squares of cloth she wound around our bodies and fastened at our shoulders with golden pins, was our armour.

Instead of arming us with weapons, Pyrrha strung strands of Egyptian glass beads around our necks, and slipped slim bands of gold around our wrists. She dressed our hair in braids, plaiting the hair like hemp rope and coiling the braid around our heads. She placed a veil atop our curls and lowered the light fabric over our faces, a shield against harm.

She dabbed precious oils along the inside of our wrists, the base of our throats. The sweet scent of basil was comforting and familiar.

Once we were presentable, she led us down the twisting corridors to the central hall, the jangling of our golden bands and necklaces announcing our arrival. We followed the same path the voice led me on the night before to the *megaron*.

The halls of the Cadmeia were startlingly different by day. Last night, I walked through the shadows with only flickering lamplight and the voice in my mind for company. Today, scores of people passed us in the halls, eyeing us curiously. Separated from the rest in the women's quarters, we were a mystery to the young men who made up our brother's court.

When our parents died of the plague, Thebes had no ruler. My brothers were the rightful heirs but they were too young. Our uncle Creon called the five founding families of Thebes to the Cadmeia and installed a regency where he and the heads of these five families ruled until my brothers came of age. The *megaron* now clamoured with the sons of the families called the *Spartoi*, the Sown Men.

It was a story Pyrrha told us often. The founder of our city, Cadmus, came from over the wine-dark sea and fought a monstrous serpent at a holy grove. The serpent had killed all his men and he had no one to help him build his city. Athena came to him and bade him to sow the teeth of the serpent into the ground and these were to become seeds of men. Cadmus watched as the men sprouted from the ground to slaughter each other until only five remained. Together, Cadmus and the five Sown Men founded the city of Thebes.

These boys were said to be the descendants of those men, grown from a serpent's teeth. There was something serpentine in the way they watched us make our way through the hall. As they circled us, it felt as if their pressing bodies were the coils of a serpent closing in tighter and tighter until they stole our breath.

With scores of eyes upon us, Pyrrha deposited us beside our brother Eteocles, the king of Thebes.

When my brothers came of age our uncle suggested they rule in turns, with one brother as king one year and the other the next. To decide who would rule first, Creon had them draw lots, like the gods. It was common knowledge that Zeus became the lord of heaven by lot and it did not seem out of place to decide the king of Thebes in a similar fashion.

By right of birth, the throne belonged to our elder brother Polynices. But he drew the wrong stone. To avoid unpleasantness, they agreed that Polynices should leave the city and return in one year's time to assume his place as king. Eteocles' first year of rule was coming to an end. He had a month left.

Eteocles ignored us as we settled in beside him, nestled along the blue walls with frescoes of beautiful women standing in a procession, their white arms bearing goods to present to the gods. But from where I stood, it seemed as if the women were lined up to present their gifts to my brother, the very walls themselves bending to his will.

Our brother looked past us, to our uncle.

"Is everything ready?" Eteocles demanded.

Creon gave my sister and me a warm smile before turning to our brother.

"Yes, you'll set out at first light in two days. You'll take the chariot, of course, and the others will ride on horseback."

Eteocles groaned. "It will take forever to get there, what with the crowds blocking the roads. You could see their lanterns glowing all the way to Delphi."

I thought of the river of lights I had seen last night. That must be where the voice wanted me to go. To Delphi.

Yes.

The voice whispered so quietly I wasn't sure I had even heard it.

My uncle smiled.

"You forget, you are a king. The crowds will move out of your way."

Eteocles eyed him as he adjusted the golden circlet that sat atop his dark curls.

"I never forget."

"Good. Remember why you are going," Creon urged, lowering his voice until I had to lean in closer.

"To consult the oracle," Eteocles replied.

"You must speak to her, we need to know what the god thinks of your decision."

I wondered what decision they could be talking about. Eteocles must give the crown to Polynices and go into exile for one year. Perhaps he was going to ask the oracle where he should go. I waited impatiently for them to continue but the voices of my brother and our uncle were drowned out by the crowds in the hall.

"Who do you think will win this year?"

"One of us! Thebes is back. Finally!"

"Ismene, are you listening to me?" Antigone's voice cut into my eavesdropping.

"What?" I turned to her. I could see a frown tugging at the corner of her mouth through the thin material of her veil.

"I was saying," Antigone repeated, "how funny it is that Eteocles is planning a journey to Delphi after we had just spoken of it."

"You said we can't leave."

"Yes, we can't but they can." Antigone sighed, as if I should have known that already.

"That's not fair." It really wasn't. I was growing tired of the restrictions on my movement now that I realised the outside world was a safe place to go.

"There are different rules for us, you know that," Antigone answered, an edge to her voice.

I turned from Antigone to glance wistfully at the young men discussing their journey and I felt the sharp pang of jealousy. I longed to go with them.

There were many things I didn't know I wanted until the voice led me outside to see a river of stars and all that life had to offer.

"Why—" I began to ask, turning back towards Antigone, but she cut me off as silence descended upon the hall.

"It's starting."

The sacrifice was about to begin.

A young heifer was brought into the hall, its small horns were gilded gold, a necklace of flowers strung around its neck. I looked down at my own finery. They had also dressed up the sacrifice.

My brother rose from his throne to perform his duties. A bowl of lustral water was brought to him by an attendant, a braid of flowers wrapped around its rim. Another attendant brought a basket of barley and behind them stood one of the *Spartoi* with a broad axe. Creon stood aside with a bowl to catch the heifer's blood.

Eteocles poured the lustral water and sprinkled the barley, singing his prayers to Hermes for the journey ahead. He stepped towards the heifer and gently cut a section of its forelock and then cast it into the flames of the *megaron*. The heifer lowered its head to the barley scattered before it and the axe rose and fell.

The first portion went to the god. Thighbones wrapped in fat went into the fire with a hiss, the smoke going up to the heavens. The rest went to us. Wine was poured and the meat was prepared, taken off in strips to cook over the fire. A feast of roasted meat for all those assembled in the hall. Wine sloshed around in golden cups as the men cajoled and sang as they feasted.

Antigone and I sat with our brother, silently savouring our food. It was not often that we dined on beef.

It was not often we got to go outside our rooms either. All this time, I thought we were in there for our protection, to guard against the plague. But my brother and his court were preparing to journey through the city to get to Delphi. The city was safe, after all. Just as the voice had said. What else was he right about?

Sipping at my mixed wine, I mustered my courage.

"We should go with them. The plague isn't the problem anymore—"

"Ismene, the plague hasn't been a problem for years."

I stared at her. All this time, a cluster of small rooms had been my whole world because I was told it wasn't safe to leave. And all this time, that had been a lie?

"But Pyrrha said..."

"Pyrrha's job is to keep us in that room," Antigone snapped. "She keeps us ignorant and compliant. You thought we weren't allowed outside because of the plague? We aren't allowed out because of who we are. We are princesses, Ismene. Pieces in a game for power. And they keep their pieces locked up until they are ready to play. They are never going to let us go anywhere unless they will benefit from it."

I had never heard such venom in my sister's voice.

"Why wouldn't they want us to go anywhere?" I asked. "Why would they benefit from us staying locked in the women's quarters?"

"We are princesses, Ismene," she repeated. "If we were married, our husbands would also have a stake at the throne. Do you think for one moment that the *Spartoi* have forgotten about us all these years? The heads of the five families would give anything for our hands in marriage for their sons. But there are five families and only two of us. It wouldn't do for some of the *Spartoi* to have an advantage over the others. So they keep us hidden away."

"But who is keeping us in there? Eteocles?"

Antigone laughed. There was no humour in the sound.

"You think Eteocles actually has any power? The *Spartoi* control everything he does. That's why they made him king over Polynices."

"No, that was decided by lot."

She shook her head, necklaces jangling.

"It was decided by *them*. They made sure Eteocles had the right stone."

I was silent. Everything I knew was falling apart around me.

Antigone leaned in to place her hand atop of mine.

"It is all a game to them, Ismene. And only cheaters win."

3

THE WORLD OUTSIDE

I sat in shocked silence for the rest of the feast.

The *Spartoi* had sent our oldest brother away because they couldn't control him and they backed our impulsive younger brother in his stead.

Did our uncle know about this? I thought of the way Creon whispered urgently to Eteocles before the feast started. No, Creon must be trying to help him, to help us. When our parents died, Creon became the only parent I knew. I had to trust in him.

I looked down at my plate, my appetite gone. How could I eat, how could I celebrate when the world I knew was falling apart around me? Beads of white fat formed on the slices of beef as it cooled. I pushed it around my plate, my fingertips slick with grease.

I saw that my cousins were striding across the room to come to join us. Haemon was tall and he moved with a dancer's grace whereas Menoeceus was rather short, his brash personality making up for what he lacked in height. Haemon and Menoeceus were the same age as Antigone and I and were raised in the nursery with us. Sometimes, I felt they were my brothers just as much as Eteocles and Polynices.

Haemon went over to his father and his king to pay his respects. Menoeceus came over to us.

"What's the matter, Ismene? You look as if you found a fly floating in your wine." He grinned down at me.

"Ismene just realised the plague is over," Antigone said.

Menoeceus' eyes flickered over to where Eteocles sat.

"Sorry, Ismene. It would have been better if you kept living in blissful ignorance."

Antigone scoffed. "Ignorant is a good word for it. She thinks she can go with you to Delphi."

Haemon left his place beside his father and came to join us, catching the last of the conversation.

"I'm sorry, Ismene, but you can't." Haemon was Creon's eldest son and always acted as a prince. "It isn't fitting for an aristocratic woman to go out in public."

Menoeceus grimaced in sympathy behind his brother's back.

"That's the only reason? I can't go out because of who I am?" I was a fool to think that the plague had been keeping me indoors all this time. A fool for believing my nurse. She always said it was too dangerous, but she was only feeding me lies to keep me in line. Was it better to live in ignorance or know that the world outside was safe but I was still unable to leave? "It's not fair." I thought of the river of lights and how I could never follow it.

"Life isn't fair, Ismene," Antigone said, turning to talk to Haemon.

"If the rules aren't fair," I muttered. "It's time to change the rules."

Pyrrha appeared, reminding me of her betrayal. She had come to take us back to our quarters but she was in no hurry.

She cooed over the two boys who were once in her care, gnarled hands raised up to cup their cheeks. The boys bent down to her with smiles.

I tried to keep the anger off my face.

Antigone rose from her chair and motioned for me to follow. I kicked the chair back from me. Pyrrha's head snapped towards me.

"Are you alright, love?" She reached for me, but I shook her off. "Are you still feeling ill? Careful now, let's get you two to bed." She made her way out of the hall and I trailed behind her, looking down at my feet as I went. I was so angry I couldn't look at her.

I did not sleep much that night. I tossed and turned, unable to stop thinking about my predicament.

A god wanted me to leave my home, to find him in his temple and do...what exactly?

I didn't know if I could trust him. So far, he had turned my world upside down. He had made me mistrust my family, made me question everything I knew. Was that someone who had my best interests at heart?

But.

I had seen too much, I knew too much to go back to being that scared girl locked away in the palace. Perhaps the god had done me a favour.

I still wasn't sure if I trusted him but I knew I had to go find him. If not for him, for me.

The next morning, it seemed Pyrrha had a bad night's

sleep as well. She still lay in bed, her knees drawn to her chest.

When we approached her bed, she looked up with a start. She straightened and began to rise off the bed, but she doubled over in pain.

"I think you need to stay in bed today," Antigone murmured, gently pushing the older woman back down. "Ismene, find me some water and a cloth."

I went and found a square of cloth and dipped it in water, wrung it out between my hands and brought it to Antigone. Still angry with her and Pyrrha, I slammed it down on the bed. The cloth slapped wetly beside Pyrrha's face, droplets of water beaded on the lines that seamed her cheeks.

Antigone looked at me cooly. "What's the matter with you?"

I shrugged and turned to leave.

I did not expect Antigone to follow me. She grabbed my arm and spun me to face her. She stared at me, her arms folded in front of her chest. "What's going on with you?"

"Nothing—" I struggled to think of a lie to tell her but she cut me off.

"Don't lie to me. I know something is going on. Where were you yesterday? I couldn't find you for hours."

"I went out."

Her eyes narrowed. "Out where?"

All my anger, my frustration and hurt and shame at being lied to rushed forth, my words gathering like a flock of birds within me and taking flight.

"Out! Out of here, out of this prison! I wanted to get out of the Cadmeia so I did."

Antigone watched me in silence for a few moments, giving me time to calm down. "So, where did you go?"

"I went out to the Neis gate, the *agora* and the theatre."

Antigone frowned. "The Neis gate? Why?"

I bit my lip, wondering if I should tell her. If I should trust her. I waited for the voice, the god, to tell me what to do. But he was silent.

I gathered my courage.

"The voice told me to."

I told her everything. I told her how the voice had called my name, had led me into the night and ordered me to find him. I told her who the voice belonged to, and what he wanted me to do next.

After I finished, I waited for her to reply, my stomach in knots.

"So, this voice belongs to a god? Apollo himself wants you to go to Delphi?"

Relief washed over me. She understood and I felt I could trust her again. I reached for her hand.

But she pulled hers away. "Do you think I'm stupid? The other night you said you wanted to go to Delphi with the others and now you expect me to believe that a *god* wants you to go there? You shouldn't use the gods to get what you want, Ismene."

"You think I'm making this up?" A lump formed in my throat. "I'm not lying."

"Of course, you are! You think I'd believe that a god would need *you* to help him? You are nothing! *We* are nothing!" she shouted, her pale face red with anger.

She didn't believe me. She couldn't. All this time she knew the truth but she didn't do anything about it. She accepted her lot in life. It was the fate of a princess to be locked away until marriage or death.

I would not accept that fate.

"You can believe me or not, but you aren't going to stop me from going to Delphi. It is what the god wants."

"Stop using gods as an excuse to get what you want!" she hissed back.

The lamps around us guttered and went out, darkness flooding the room.

Antigone grabbed my arm. I shook her off.

"What happened?" She groped for me in the dark but I stayed out of her reach. "Ismene?"

Behind us, a lamp flickered to life, the flames grew as we drew closer.

"What is going on?" Antigone whispered.

The light disappeared and the lamp nearest the door began to glow.

"I think he wants to show you, too." I let her take my hand and we walked out into the night.

Lamps blazed to life as we passed, their light guiding our way. We followed the same path I had taken that night. Then, I had been blind, shaking with fear of the unknown. Now my eyes were open and I shook with excitement.

Though it was a black night, I could see the buildings we passed in my mind, memories of my afternoon in the city centre. We trailed past the temple of Zeus, the braziers flaming. I savoured the look of astonishment on Antigone's face.

Soon the shadow of the wall loomed above us and we began to climb. When we stood atop the ramparts of the Neis gate, I turned my sister around until we stood facing northwest, facing the river of light that led to Delphi.

"Oh," Antigone breathed.

"That is what I came out to see the other night. Apollo wants me to follow the path of light to him."

"But why? What does he want?"

"I don't know," I answered. "But I can't refuse a god, can I?"

"No, you can't." Antigone closed her eyes. When she opened them, she faced me. "I am sorry I didn't believe you."

"You believe me now?"

The braziers along the wall flared brighter.

"Yes, yes I do." She looked around. "But that doesn't mean that I like it."

I opened my mouth to argue but she placed her hand over my lips.

"*Think*, Ismene. When has anything good ever come out of a god's interference? Think of all the stories Pyrrha told us. When the gods come to mortals, it never ends well for the mortals. The god leaves them dead or mad. I don't want that to happen to you." She let her hand fall from my face.

"I won't go mad."

"You can't promise that."

"Don't worry so much about me. I can take care of myself."

Standing atop the ramparts, I told my sister my plan. I expected her to interrupt but she listened quietly the entire time.

"What do you think?"

"It might work," Antigone responded. "But I have some ideas of my own."

Back in our quarters, Antigone went in search of some clothes. I peeked my head into the bedroom, peering at our nurse.

Pyrrha was sleeping soundly on her bed, her arms wrapped around her middle. She looked so small and frail. I felt a flash of guilt at my anger towards her. I considered her responsible for my imprisonment in these rooms all these years when really, she was stuck in here, too.

It would have been too easy to resent the ones she was charged with keeping inside, but Pyrrha loved us and cared for us like her own children. Perhaps, to her, keeping us locked up was her way of keeping us safe. I padded softly towards her, took the warm cloth from her forehead to wet it again. I placed the cool, damp cloth on her head and she sighed in relief. I left her to rest.

Antigone sat on the floor of the workroom surrounded by bundles of cloth. She looked up as I came towards her.

"What is all that?" I asked.

We spent most of our days weaving cloth for our household and I recognized everything made by our hands. These were not made by us.

"Pyrrha had these in an old *pyxis*," Antigone said as she rifled through the material. "What?" She raised a brow at the look on my face. "You're not the only one who sneaks around. Here." She pulled out a woollen *chiton*. It was dyed a light blue. Tossing it to me, she ordered, "Put it on."

I unpinned my *peplos* from my shoulders and let the cloth sink to the ground. The *chiton* was unlike the ones that we wore. Our *chitons* were held in place from the neck to the wrists with several pins, the skirt so long that we bundled the fabric above a belt fastened high on our waist. This *chiton* fastened at one shoulder and was short enough to bare my thighs. I put the *chiton* on and turned to my sister.

"I look ridiculous."

"Not ridiculous," she mused as she walked around me. "But not like a boy. Not yet." She went over to the pile of cloth and picked up a length of linen. She unpinned the *chiton* from my shoulder and wrapped the linen around my chest, binding my breasts. After she pinned the *chiton* back in place, she stepped back. "That looks better. Now let's fix your hair."

She plucked the pins from my hair and loosened my braids, letting my hair fall down my back. She sectioned my hair and began to re-braid the small sections, a hairstyle favoured by the aristocratic young men. She placed a band around my forehead as the finishing touch.

"That's better. Just keep to the back of the retinue." She took one look at my face and put her hands on my shoulders. "You can do this. Don't draw attention to yourself and follow the others." She steered me to the exit of the women's quarters.

I whirled towards her. "Come with me."

"I can't. They might not notice one of us gone, but both of us?" She shook her head. "This is your moment, Ismene. Go out into the world. And tell me everything."

She pulled me close and hugged me.

"Go!"

She ushered me into the hall.

I walked down the hall, my head held high. This time, people went to great lengths to stay out of my path, keeping to one side. To them, I looked like an aristocratic boy. If they stumbled into me it could cost them their position in the palace.

The *megaron* was crowded with men young and old. The *Spartoi* were gathered there, bidding their young sons goodbye.

The young men were all but trembling with excitement. They must want to get out of the city as much as I did.

I slipped into the group. When I was a girl, it was only my sister, brothers, cousins and I in the palace. When my brothers came of age years later, the sons of the *Spartoi* showed up. No doubt their mothers and nurses were reluctant to part with them. Antigone and I agreed that I would pose as one of them.

Curious glances cut my way but no one approached me to demand who I was. I was safe. For now, anyway.

I joined a cluster of younger boys lingering at the back of the group. They turned and eyed me.

"Joining the *theoria*?" the eldest of the group asked. He was a head and shoulders taller than I was, with soft down on his cheeks.

"Yes." I could see they were losing interest so I added, "Mother finally allowed me to come."

"It took my mother a long time to let me leave home, too," another boy drawled, this one the same height as me. "Chromis." He gestured towards himself. "That's Theron." He nodded to the tall boy who had spoken to me before. "And that's Dorylas." The third boy ducked his head and smiled at me.

My mind raced as I thought of a name. Something close to my own name that I would still answer to. "Ismenos." Maybe a little too close.

"Named after the river?" Chromis asked.

I nodded.

The Ismenos was the river that flowed to the east of Thebes, named for a son of Apollo by the nymph Melia. Was it fated that the god would come for me, a girl named for his own son? I tried not to think about it too much.

Soon, the crowd surged out of the hall out into the city. I spotted my brother step into a chariot, Haemon at his side. Menoeceus lingered behind them as my uncle spoke softly to them. Grooms led over horses for the older boys. The youngest among us had to walk.

The procession to Delphi had begun.

"What are you most excited to see?" I asked as we moved forward.

"The games, of course," Chromis answered with a grin. "It's probably the most exciting thing to happen for us since the plague. We've never been outside of Thebes. You?"

"I've never been out of Thebes either," I said.

As we left our home behind, I thought of the journey ahead and the mission given to me by the god. I didn't know what he wanted from me. But I was going to find out.

4

THE ROAD TO THE GOD

The journey to Delphi would only take a day on foot. Our group planned to split the trip over two days to allow time to rest.

That first day felt like an eternity to me.

We were outside the city gates, marching across the fertile plains for growing crops and grazing cattle and sheep. The sun bore down on me. I felt sweat drip down my skin, running into my eyes and dampening my hair. My feet ached.

Thank the gods I had Chromis for company. His never-ending chatter was the only thing that could take my mind off my aches and pains.

"What a send-off for the king. Ending his first year of rule with a trip to the Pythian Games!" He looked at the crowd ahead of us, leaned in closer and said, "My father says Eteocles should stay king."

I stiffened.

My brothers made a sacred agreement, in front of the gods and our city, to alternate rule. The crown was Polynices' by right.

It was as if Dorylas read my thoughts.

"But what about Polynices?" he said in his quiet way. "He is the rightful heir."

"Don't start talking like that in front of *them*," Theron muttered, jerking his head towards the head of the group. "I know for a fact the heads of the five families want Eteocles to stay king. He does whatever they say, after all."

I was surprised these boys would echo what my own sister had said at the feast only a few nights before.

"No, he doesn't."

The boys looked at me incredulously.

"The king does everything his uncle says!"

"Well, he is his advisor, isn't he?" I retorted, the heat rising in my face.

"He does a lot more than just advise the king," Theron replied. "The five families tell Creon what to do and he tells the king. That's why everyone wants him to stay. They don't think Polynices will be as obedient."

My uncle could have seized the crown for himself when my parents died of the plague. Instead, he made sure my brothers received their due, protecting the crown until they came of age. I was sure that everything he did was for the good of our family.

The *Spartoi*, on the other hand. The years of the regency gave them a taste for rule and they were not ready to relinquish it yet. Of course, they would want someone in power they thought they could control.

They didn't know my brother if they thought they could control him.

I had not seen much of my brothers since they came of age. When we were all still in the care of our nurse, it was Eteocles that took control, not Polynices. Eteocles must be planning to shake off the *Spartoi* and take charge. I longed to defend my brother to the arrogant boys around me, but I would not tell such things to the sons of the men who wished to control him.

The talk of politics was abandoned for more exciting talk of the games. All I knew of the Pythian games was that they took place every four years at Delphi. The boys told me that, during the first day of the games, there would be a sacrifice and feast. On the second day, the athletic contests were held. The third day marked the most important day of all: the day to visit the oracle.

While the younger boys and I would be observers, it turned out that the older boys would compete. Eteocles himself would compete in the chariot race, with my cousin Haemon as his *parabates*, the one that would stand beside him in his chariot.

Traditionally, the *parabates* was the warrior who stood next to the charioteer and protected him from danger. I doubted there would be much danger in a race, but I was comforted to know Haemon had my brother's back all the same. Haemon would also be competing by himself in the footrace. Even Menoeceus would compete in the boxing contest.

Knowing my family would be competing heightened my own excitement. But I was most excited to simply be there, to have journeyed to a place other than my home, to see new cities and meet new people. I wish Antigone had that chance as well.

Helios drew his fiery chariot across the sky and evening fell. My feet felt heavier and heavier with each step I took. Finally, the *theoria* stopped for the night, setting up camp by the side of the road. I had never been so glad to sit down. I sat with my new friends in companionable silence, watching the embers of the fire crack and spark.

"I am exhausted!" Chromis groaned. "I have never done so much walking in my life."

"Me, too," I said, easing off my shoes. "I've never been outside of Thebes before. I was kept inside because of the plague."

The boys nodded in agreement.

"So were we. For *years*."

"My family was so afraid of the plague they scarcely spoke of it. Can you tell me about it?" I asked, leaning towards my new friends.

The firewood cracked and splintered as it burned, embers flew up, lighting our faces with a crimson glow before they snapped and went out, leaving us in the dark.

Chromis looked into the fire and spoke. "It's thought that the plague was brought through the gates. The first to fall were those living in the outer corners of the city. Physicians did not know how to treat it. Unknowingly, they spread the disease wherever they went, until they succumbed to it themselves. Throngs of citizens swarmed the temples, praying to this god and that, but still, they fell.

Fever, inflamed flesh, bleeding tongues and fetid breath were the first signs. Their skin went red, pustules breaking out across their bodies, and their fevered flesh could not bear to feel the touch of their clothes.

Their greatest desire was to soothe their burning flesh in cool water. Sentries were posted around the wells to prevent the sick from throwing themselves in and contaminating the water. Bodies piled high in the streets, waiting to be taken to the cremation pits outside the city walls. Not even birds and beasts touched the dead, as if they sensed the taint of their flesh.”

His words made a chill spread through me. If that was what Pyrrha was so afraid of, no wonder she kept us locked up in the palace all those years.

“That sounds terrible,” I murmured, remembering that it was the plague that claimed my parents’ lives. “Do they know what caused it?”

Chromis nodded and opened his mouth to speak but timid Dorylas answered before he could.

“It was Apollo.”

Chills ran down my spine.

“What do you mean it was Apollo?” The voice that whispered to me in the night and showed me so many wonderful things was responsible for the deaths of my parents?

“You know how Apollo is called the far-shooter? That name refers to his arrows. Apollo turned his plague arrows on our people when they offended him,” Dorylas replied.

“But how did they offend him? What did they do?” I could not reconcile my god of light and wonder with a god of sickness and death.

Dorylas shook his head. “I don’t know.”

Here Chromis found his chance. The light of fire was reflected in his eyes. “I heard it had to do with the murder of the former king. To lift the plague they had to catch the killer.”

“Did they?” I breathed.

Chromis shrugged. “They must have. The plague’s gone now, isn’t it?”

Theron leaned forward, the light of the fire bathing his face in an orange glow. “The king did catch the killer. That’s how he caught the plague himself. By going out to investigate."

The boys talked animatedly about what it must have been like to walk through the streets where bloated corpses waited to be burned in cremation pits. But I wasn't listening. I was thinking about the king. It was my father who lifted the plague. I was so young when he died that I barely remembered his face. His voice a distant echo. But thinking of him made warmth seep back into my bones, the chill of the plague gone.

As I thought of my father, the flames burned brighter, the embers glowing white hot in the heart of the fire pulsed like blinking eyes struggling to open.

As we drew nearer to Delphi the road grew steeper and more difficult to travel. The crowds of travelers backed up the road and our pace grew painfully slow. The trees were taller in the mountains, affording more shade to weary travelers. The higher we climbed, the cooler it became. Despite the slow pace, it was far more pleasant than walking across the plains of Thebes.

We climbed higher, until I began to wonder if the sanctuary of Delphi was up in the heavens and we were climbing the sky. My breath came short and all talking ceased. Even Chromis kept silent as we struggled to breathe as we hiked. Without his endless chatter, I was alone with my thoughts once more. Something I had been striving to avoid.

Before the god took me outside the confines of the women's quarters, I was content to sit there day after day, listening to stories of the world and weaving those stories onto cloth.

Now, I wanted to be a part of those stories. The god showed

me the world outside and gave me a reason to join it. He wanted me to follow the path to him, but now I was on that path, now that I had almost come to its end the more afraid I became. The god wanted something from me but I didn't know what. What if, after everything, the god decided I wasn't enough? What if he told me to go back to being the girl I was before? I don't think I could go back to who I was content to sit in a prison fed on stories while I starved for a life I never even knew I wanted. I did want it. I wanted to live so fiercely I felt as if my want was a river, swollen from the rains, my waters overflowing to flood everything around me. I had grown too much to be forced back into that small life.

No, I couldn't go back. I knew the moment I went back to my quarters I would long for the sighing of the wind, the warmth of the sun, the sight of my land stretching out as far as my eyes could see. How could I ever go back to those small rooms, to being that small girl?

The clamour of voices shook me from my thoughts.

"What is it?" I asked.

"We're here!" Chromis exclaimed.

Here?

I looked around at the rocky mountains, dotted with green trees.

"I don't see anything."

"Not yet, wait until we get to where the head of the retinue is," Theron told me.

We continued in silence, listening to the exclaims of wonder of those ahead of us. I could see the boys were getting excited, they jostled each other and grinned.

Finally, we passed a large rock face, and I was blinded by the sun. I covered my eyes and listened to the hush that fell upon my group. The trickle of a stream was the only sound. There, guarded by the mountains, was Delphi. One moment, all I could see was the mountain face, the next, the sprawling sanctuary and the city that grew around it lay before me.

The setting sun bathed the sanctuary in a wash of golden light. There, at the heart of the hidden city, I could see the temple of Apollo, where the Pythia, his voice on earth, gave oracles to kings.

Surrounding the temple of Apollo were houses of worship for other divinities, the space glittered with the offerings of bronze, silver and gold. The Sacred Way, the road to the god, was littered with dedications of great statues, exotic plants and other treasures. Just past the temple complex, I could make out a theatre and a stadium, where the games would take place.

The *theoria* set up camp just outside the city, tents sprouted up on the mountainside like poppies in a field. Tall, dark cypress trees stood sentinel over their sacred city, casting long shadows over our camp under the setting sun.

The camp buzzed with excitement about the games. The boys and I unrolled our bedrolls and lay down to gaze at the stars above us.

I thought of the path of light that brought me here. Was the god encouraging me to step outside what was comfortable? Or was there something else? He had said I needed to follow the path of light to find him.

But why did I need to come to him? Why did he choose to be silent now?

I grew up hearing my nurse's stories of mortals involved

with the gods and how it never ended well for them. The god wanted me for some dark purpose. I didn't know what, but I knew deep down that it couldn't be good. But until he chose to show himself to me, I was resolved to enjoy myself.

Years of being trapped inside with nothing but the ghosts of the past for company I felt useless, grey and colourless. I yearned for a full life—a colourful life. With every step outside of my comfort zone, I could feel the colour flood my soul. I went from being a ghost myself to almost as radiant as a god.

The dying fire revived itself, its embers cracking, drawing my attention to its fiery glow. I would not dwell on the darkness of an unhappy past and unknowable future. I would focus on now, on the coming light of day, a day of excitement, a day when all of Hellas came together in this holy place to compete.

I would not dwell on how my life had changed.

I simply had to keep moving and embrace the change while I could.

Dawn was trailing her rosy fingers across the sky when I woke.

And an angry face loomed over me.

Menoeceus.

"What are you doing here?" he hissed, yanking me upright.

The boys stirred around me, protests dying on their lips when they saw one of their princes.

"I wanted to come."

"You snuck out, that's what you did!" Menoeceus glanced at the boys, who averted their eyes, pretending not to hear.

"You're coming with me." He placed a broad palm on the

base of my neck and propelled me forward. I looked back at my new friends who waved goodbye.

My cousin led me through the camp to its centre where my brother and his closest friends were camped. Eteocles' tent was by far the largest and most luxurious. Menoeceus strode to one of the smaller tents and pushed his way inside, beckoning for me to follow.

"Stay here." He pointed to the place where my feet stood and I nodded. He pushed his way out of the tent, leaving me in the dark.

My legs trembled from today's climb and I sat down. I hoped he wouldn't tell my brother who would no doubt send me home. Eteocles would make Menoeceus escort me and then he would forever resent me for making him miss his chance at the Pythian games.

I fought against tears. I refused to cry in front of my cousin. He already thought I was a child for sneaking out. I felt the need to prove him wrong.

Menoeceus came back through the flaps of the tent and Haemon entered behind him. He carried a lamp in his hand, the light casting shadows that danced along the planes of his cheeks. His mouth formed a shocked circle.

"Ismene!" He closed the flap behind him. "What have you done?"

Menoeceus crossed his arms. "I know you wanted to come but you can't just sneak out of the city like that. Does anyone even know you've gone?"

I looked down at my feet. "Antigone does," I mumbled.

"Antigone knows?" Haemon said, surprised. Antigone always did the right thing. I could tell he couldn't believe that my practical sister would allow me to do something so rash.

I had to tell them the truth. "She knows. There's something you should know, too." My cousins looked at me as I tried to find the words to explain my situation. "I was ordered to come here," I began.

"Ordered by who?" Menoeceus interrupted.

"By a god."

Apollo acknowledged me, the dim lamp in Haemon's hand flared so bright my cousins had to cover their eyes with their hands. Lowering their hands they took a step back, staring at me.

"Apollo?" Haemon breathed, his eyes passing from the lamp to me and back. "He ordered you to come to his city. Why?"

"I don't know," I answered. "All he said was to come to Delphi, to come to him."

Haemon shared a glance with his brother. I could tell from the set of his shoulders and the way the corner of his mouth tugged down that he was concerned.

"What else has he said to you?" Menoeceus asked.

"I haven't heard anything else since I left."

"I think he wants us to help you," Haemon said. "Stick close to us Ismene and we will try to keep anyone from guessing who you are. But if Eteocles finds out, you'll have to go home."

"Speaking of Eteocles, you better go to him." Menoeceus began to push his brother out of the tent. "I'll keep my eye on the troublemaker."

Haemon glanced back at me.

"Go on!" Menoeceus shoved him out and turned to me, sweeping a hand through his hair.

"You are in so much trouble," he began. I tensed, waiting for him to reprimand me. Instead, he grinned. "Here I thought the games would be boring." He clapped a hand on my shoulders and led me outside.

I stood beside Menoeceus as the Thebans made their way up to the sanctuary gate.

The Pythian Games were about to begin.

5

THE DEDICATION

It was the first day of the Pythian Games and pilgrims flooded the streets, eager to be part of the festivities.

The *agora* in Thebes was nothing compared to this. People from all over Hellas walked the Sacred Way, priests hurried about with their preparations and small crowds huddled around amateur seers. The would-be seers sat at street corners offering their services, answering simple questions by lot or games of chance like *astragaloi*, the knucklebones.

I joined the small throng and watched as a *mantis*, a seer, cast the knucklebones out in front of herself. The *mantis* played *astragaloi* the way Pyrrha taught my sister and I, casting the pieces to divine an answer.

When the knucklebones were rolled and the bones landed on different sides, the outcome was favourable. When the bones landed the same way, it was an ill omen. I did not arrive in time to hear the question asked but saw the pieces land on different sides, a positive outcome, the man next to me seemed pleased with the answer.

The *mantis* collected her pieces and surveyed the crowd. Her eyes landed on me and said, "You, boy, do you have a question for the god of prophecy?"

The small crowd all turned and looked at me and I felt myself redden from the attention. I was so full of questions I thought I might burst. I struggled to think of something acceptable to say in front of these strangers.

As I wondered something brushed against my arm. Startled, I turned to the person standing close beside me.

It was Chromis. He grinned. Dorylas and Theron waved from behind him.

"Go on, Ismenos, ask something!"

I could see the *mantis* losing her patience, her eyes already scanning the crowd for a more cooperative customer.

"Wait," I said. "I have a question." Seeing a familiar face made me think of my city. I should ask about Thebes.

"Ask, then boy. We don't have all day." She shook the knucklebones within the cage of her enclosed fingers and as she cast them upon the road I asked my question.

"Will Thebes celebrate its new king?" I asked, thinking of the return of my brother Polynices at the end of my brother Eteocles' rule. My fellow Thebans nodded in appreciation of my question.

Time seemed to slow down, the bones suspended in midair. My breath caught in my throat. It was a simple question, and it would have a simple answer. The bones always landed on their sides, the outcome was always favourable—that was the point of the game, to only ask questions one knew the answers to. Time began to move again and the bones scattered among the cobbled path. All the pieces landed upright, the bones quivered on their heads, all pointing upwards. We all went silent.

It was an ill omen.

The *mantis* sensed the change in the crowd and scooped up the pieces in a hurry. Already moving on to the next customer. The crowd moved on as well, eager to leave behind the unfavourable outcome of the bones.

My friends crowded around me, dragging me away from the *mantis* and her ill prophecies.

"It wasn't a real prophecy, Ismenos. It doesn't mean anything," Dorylas assured me as we rejoined our group.

"If anything, it probably means Thebes won't be happy about Polynices. You know how they want to keep control of Eteocles," Theron cut in.

I hoped Dorylas was right, that the amateur seer's prophecies meant nothing. But this was Apollo's city. Prophecies made in this sacred place meant something. And even though the prophecy was made on an inauspicious street corner, I couldn't help but feel it pointed to trouble coming our way.

The hundreds of people who flooded the streets were all headed up the Sacred Way to the altar before the temple of Apollo where the sacrifice would take place. I had found the rest of the Thebans and fell into the back of that group, watching the crowds part before a king.

With the bodies pressing on me from all sides propelling me forward, I looked all around at the statues that dotted the Sacred Way. They were all beautifully crafted, but a few stuck out to me, like faces I recognized in a crowd.

The first that grabbed my attention was a squat bronze cauldron, the rays of the setting sun glinting off its rounded sides nearly blinding me. A tripod, its three feet were carved to look like the paws of a lion. Something about the cauldron unsettled me, its rim gaping like an open mouth.

I tore my attention away. The next statues that caught my attention were *kouroi*, two statues of young men sharing the same pedestal. They were both carved in the same pose, their left foot forward, their hands clenched into fists, the only clothing they wore were sandals. The inscription on their bases labeled them as princes.

Something about these young men arrested in stone reminded me of my brothers. They were so alike, yet they seemed to be competing, one trying to outpace the other yet stuck in the same spot.

We continued forward and I left the princes behind me. My eyes skipped over statues of Apollo and Pallas Athena, water jars crafted of gold and silver, bronze horses and fruits of the harvest cast in gold.

Finally, we approached the temple, the crowd of travelers leaning against the retaining wall. The temple was made in the Doric style, six massive columns barring the entrance to the home of the voice of the god. But I barely noticed the temple, my eyes drawn invariably to the statue high on a column beside it.

Perched atop an ionic column sat a marble sculpture of the Sphinx. I had heard the stories of how the monster killed countless men when they couldn't answer her riddles. The last man who met her at her crossroads to bandy words was my father. He answered her riddle correctly and finally vanquished her, saving Thebes and becoming its king.

What was this reminder of my family, my story, doing here in this holy city?

I pushed through the crowds, trying to get closer. The bodies pressed close, threatening to crush my small frame, but it was nothing compared to the pressing feeling of unease that closed all around me. Dodging around jutting elbows and broad backs, I pushed myself through the crowd and stood beneath the sculpture.

The Sphinx sat on her haunches, her forelegs stretched out so she could sit atop the column beneath her. Her chest was covered with a breastplate of feathers, her wings outstretched behind her. Her leonine body was long and slender, her face carved like the *kore* statues that lined the cemeteries throughout Hellas, with neatly curled hair and an inscrutable smile.

I wondered if the creature had truly looked like this, something beautiful and ordered and still as stone. I knew that it could not be true to life, that the Sphinx was as complex and chaotic as the riddles she told.

I marveled at this piece of my city's history that sat at a prominent place in the god's home. I was turning to push my way back through the crowd to my cousins when I stopped, something pulling me back to the statue, my eyes scanning the column to rest on the inscription at its base.

The word *Promanteia*, privilege, stood out among the words etched in the stone. Another word stood out, the shape of its letters like a familiar face I had long forgotten. I reached forward and trailed my fingers over the inscription, pressing my palm against the last word.

Delphi accorded the Thebans the right of Promanteia, in the time of king Oedipus.

Oedipus. My father.

Bodies jostled me as they rushed around my still form, like the river current around a rock, wearing it down. I was frozen in place staring at the name of my father. Was this what the god wanted me to see? Some connection I had to the Sacred City through him? That couldn't be it, that couldn't be why a god turned my life upside down, to remind me I had a father, a great man who saved a city and then died for his trouble.

I was still standing before the statue when Menoeceus found me. My fingers traced the shape of my father's name, trying to resurrect any memories I had of him through touch. But I remembered nothing.

For once, my cousin didn't have a clever quip or snide comment. An arm wrapped around my shoulder and pulled me close. I let myself be held, briefly, before I stepped out of his embrace, wiping at my eyes.

"Did my father come here?" I asked through my tears.

"He sent my father on his behalf to the oracle to find out how to cure the plague. He gave the sanctuary this statue as a dedication for her help."

"But she didn't help. Her words didn't save him from the plague."

"He didn't ask to save himself. He wanted to save the people of Thebes. And he did."

We stood before the remembrance of our king, the silence between us a comfortable one. The silence did not last long.

A young man pushed his way forward. He stood over the inscription, his eyes scanning the letters while his mouth twisted into a scowl.

It was Polynices.

I was shocked to see the change in my brother. His face had grown hard, his hair long and curling, a beard sprouting from his chin. I almost did not recognize him but for his cloak, his sword with a sphinx carved into the hilt, the brown eyes he shared with the rest of my family.

Menoeceus also recognized him, my brother's name about to fall from his lips, but he remembered me and pushed me behind him. "Don't let him see you," he ordered.

"I don't think he'd recognize me," I said.

Another young man came up beside my brother. He was short but muscled, his thick neck tense and his broad shoulders braced for a fight. A boar hide cloak added to his bulky frame. He clapped a hand on my brother's back. They murmured to each other as they looked down at the inscription.

"King Oedipus," the shorter one drawled as he gazed down at the inscription. He drew back his head and spat, the wad of phlegm sitting directly on my father's name. "What kind of king curses his own sons?"

What curse? What was he talking about? I tried to edge closer but Menoeceus held me back.

"A sad man who lost everything," Polynices answered. "I know how he feels. I've lost my kingdom, my birthright. I'm no one."

"Don't say that," my brother's companion said. "You *are* someone. You are Polynices, son in law of king Adrastos, a prince of Argos." He placed his broad hand on the base of Polynices' neck, drawing him close until their foreheads touched. "We may have both lost our birthrights. But we will get them *back*."

The two men smiled at one another and Menoeceus tried to edge us away. None of us saw who came up behind us.

"There you are, Menoeceus," a familiar voice drawled. Eteocles and Haemon had found us. Polynices whipped around at the sound of our brother's voice and his scowl deepened. "We've been looking all over for you—" Eteocles paused as he recognized Polynices. "I didn't think I'd see you here."

"I didn't think I'd see you," Polynices began, his voice lower, harsher, than I remembered. He circled my brother. Eteocles stood in place, following our brother's movements with his eyes. Haemon's hand fluttered at the pommel of his sword. "I never thought the *Spartoi* would let you leave the city," he continued, his voice taunting. "They have to protect their figurehead, don't they?"

"The *Spartoi* do not control me," Eteocles said through gritted teeth.

My cousins watched my brothers while no one paid attention to the other man. He drew up beside Menoeceus and kicked him in the back. My cousin sprawled forward.

"Get up," Eteocles ordered.

Menoeceus scrambled to his feet, about to draw his sword. Haemon surged forward and batted it away. It clattered to the ground.

"You cannot fight here," Haemon urged, going back to his place between the two brothers. "You know of the Sacred Truce. Athletes are forbidden from fighting outside of the games. It also forbids any harm to the temple or people of Delphi." His eyes skirted to Tydeus who leaned against the retaining wall with a frenzied grin.

"An accident, cousin," Polynices said, going to stand with his comrade. They turned to leave.

"We'll see you at the games," Eteocles called out to them.

Once his brother was out of sight, he whirled on Menoeceus. "You better not let that happen again. If you fight him in the games, *you* win."

Menoeceus gritted his teeth. I could see him force down his retort to his king.

Haemon shot him a sympathetic glance. The three of them headed back to the Thebans but I lingered behind.

Menoeceus must have broken skin when he fell, for a splash of blood stained the white streets. The blood ran through the trace work of cobblestones to pool at the base of the statue. The monument to my father was stained with our family's blood.

The sacrifice was made, the offering went up to the gods and the meat was shared with everyone in attendance.

As I ate, I scanned the faces in the crowd until I found my brother.

I thought back to my childhood, to when Eteocles and Polynices still lived in the women's quarters with us as small boys. The Polynices I knew would not suffer the attention of the *Spartoi*. He resented the way they invaded his home, the way they fought for his attention and approval. He was sullen and brooding. It seemed he *still* was.

I had hoped Polynices would change during his year in exile. I had hoped he would come back and take the throne with grace. But I could see now that there would be nothing graceful in his rule. There would be no forgiveness.

I left my place and pushed my way through the crowd until I found my cousins. Menoeceus was having a drinking contest with one of the *Spartoi*, knocking back a *kylix* of wine. Eteocles laughed as the red wine dribbled down their chins to stain their *chitons*. Haemon watched with a bemused expression on his face. He spotted me as I came up beside him, frowning at the look on my face.

"What's wrong?" His brows furrowed, following my gaze. "Are you worried about what happened earlier between Eteocles and Polynices? Don't be. Everything will work out."

I shook my head.

"That's not all. Do you remember where we were standing this afternoon? Did you see the statue?"

"The statue of the Sphinx?"

I nodded.

"Some thought that it was the Sphinx herself who sent the plague on Thebes and once her riddles were solved the plague would be lifted. I'm not convinced there ever was a Sphinx. Your father knew what would cure the plague on the land—deference to the gods. His triumph simply mythologized into this story."

I mulled over his words. They made sense, the plague on the land was sent from the gods and once they were shown the proper respect it was lifted, my father knew this and implemented it when he was king. It was easy to create monsters in times of death and fear.

But one should not dismiss monsters.

"I can see why you would think that," I replied, turning to face him. "But a land of gods and heroes would not exist without monsters to vanquish. I believe she was real."

I could tell Haemon was humouring me now. He ruffled the hair on my head, ruining the braids Antigone had so carefully done days before.

"Do not dwell on monsters, Ismene." He leaned in close, my name a secret between the two of us. "This is a holy place. Turn your thoughts to the gods. And all will be well."

I smiled. "A very diplomatic answer from a prince."

He threw his head back and laughed, the light of the sacred flames limning his face. I followed the crimson glow to their source, watching the flames dance.

I looked into the flames and lost myself.

In the depths of the flames, I saw a man stumbling up a barren rocky place, his fingertips red from scrabbling against the rock, the seven gates of Thebes ahead in the distance. The walls of that great city were guarded by twin cliffs, like spiteful jaws, looming above him. Human bones littered the road, bleached white by the midday sun. Few had flesh still attached, those that did provided meagre feasts for the birds circling overhead who swooped down and plucked at the sinews.

Just ahead, a jagged slab of stone intruded onto the path. From within a cave atop the rock, shrouded in shadow, came a voice. It was a female voice, muttering and singing to itself. When the man stumbled upon a bone and the birds flew up with a disgruntled shriek, the voice went silent.

"Who approaches?" the voice called. And from the shadows emerged a beautiful face, just as quickly she ducked back into the darkness.

The young man looked up and with a jolt, I realised that he was my father. He could have been my brother—he looked so much like Eteocles and Polynices.

"I am Oedipus, son of Polybus. Tell me, what has happened here? It seems as if this is the lair of some fierce beast."

A laugh carried from within the cave atop the jagged rock. It grated against my ears like the screech of metal upon metal.

"I will tell you. But first you must answer me this: What goes on four feet in the morning, two feet at noon and three feet in the evening?"

My father considered her riddle for a few moments. As he pondered the figure crept out of the shadows. Only then did I realise what I was witnessing.

The figure had the face of a woman, her hair was stiff with filth. The once white column of her neck, her shoulders, her bare breasts, were fouled with dried blood. From her shoulders great wings unfurled, and with her lion's body she prowled towards my father. She poised to pounce at the edge of the rock.

She was nothing like her statue.

"Man. The answer is man. Man is a baby in the morning of his life, crawling on all fours. He is an adult at noon, standing on his own two feet. When he is old, and in the evening of his life, he walks with a cane and has three feet." Finally, my father looked up.

The Sphinx froze before him. Closer now, I could see the blood smeared about her mouth, the yellow shade of her eyes. With a cry, she leapt from the rock, her sharp teeth going for my father's throat.

Realising that she was the beast responsible for the carnage around him, my father darted out of her grasp. She fell upon the jagged rocks below her, tearing open her belly, its contents spilling out onto the rocks, a gory feast for the birds.

6

THE ATHLETIC CONTESTS

I woke on the morning of the second day quivering with excitement. Today was the day of the athletic contests.

I tried to let my excitement for the day ahead distract me from what I had seen in the flames last night. Nothing like that had ever happened to me before. Perhaps that was what the god wanted me to see in his sacred city. But the god had said he would tell me himself. What I saw in the fire couldn't be what he wanted me to know.

I shook my concerns from my mind and tried to focus on the day ahead. My cousins were competing and got up at dawn to stretch and get ready. The first contest of the day was the *pygmachia*, the boxing match.

I watched Menoeceus as he prepared for the match. He wrapped his hands and knuckles several times with bands made of ox hide called *himantes*, the band contained loops to insert four fingers to clench into a fist. *Himantes* protected the knuckles of the boxers, but they did nothing to soften their blows.

The opponents faced one another. On the one side my cousin, on the other, my brother's companion. I did not like him. I wouldn't put it past him to fight dirty.

"Put up your fists!"

Polynices' friend, Tydeus, charged at Menoeceus, jabbing at his face with his right fist. Menoeceus danced out of his way. It went on like this for some time, barrel-chested Tydeus rushing forward and Menoeceus stepping out of the way. The crowd grew restless, calling for blood.

I saw what Menoeceus was doing. He was tiring out his opponent. Sure enough, Tydeus began to waver, his breathing laboured, sweat coursing down his back. Menoeceus took his chance. He lunged and landed the first blow upon the other youth's brow, his head snapping to the side. Menoeceus leapt out of his way but Tydeus did not come after him immediately. He brought his head forward, spitting a wad of bloody phlegm on the ground between them. He cracked his shoulders and charged.

Drunk on his small victory, Menoeceus had dropped his guard and Tydeus smashed him on the chin. Knees buckling, my cousin fought to stand as Tydeus rained blow after blow upon him. Menoeceus couldn't stand any longer, his legs giving out beneath him, he sank to the ground.

I let out a sigh of relief, glad to see the carnage over.

But Tydeus did not stop. He hooked an arm under my cousin, holding him aloft to strike him in the stomach again and again. Polynices had to rush forward and intervene. Tydeus received his laurel crown, leaving my cousin in the dust.

The crowd assembled around the victor and I raced to Menoeceus. Haemon was already there, crouched beside his brother.

Menoeceus had his arms wrapped around his middle, his lip burst and bleeding, livid bruises already flowering on his skin.

"Is he alright?" I asked.

Menoeceus opened a swollen eye. "He can speak for

himself." He let Haemon lift him to his feet, wincing as he raised an arm and placed it around his brother's shoulders. "I'm fine. I wish he looked as bad as I did."

"Look at his face." Haemon nodded towards the crowd around the winner. Tydeus' eye was as swollen as Menoeceus', a cut split his brow in two and blood ran down his face like tears.

"I got one punch in," Menoeceus complained. "That's nothing to be happy about."

"You're lucky to have got one punch in," Haemon continued. Glancing around, he lowered his voice so that only Menoeceus and I could hear. "I have been asking around about Tydeus. He is the son of Oeneus of Calydon. They say he murdered his own brother."

Menoeceus and I flinched, both turning to watch Tydeus embrace Polynices. So my brother's great companion was a kinslayer. I tried to shake off the unease I could feel settling around myself and followed my cousins as we melded into the crowd.

As we joined the crowd of Theban youths, I saw Eteocles watching our brother, his eyes narrowed.

The next event was the footrace. The competitors would run the stadium, a racetrack of packed dirt in an open field. The judges watched the race from a stone platform called the exedra while wooden seats were set up for the spectators. Menoeceus and I found seats near the front, a perk of being a prince. My cousin sat gingerly, nursing his bruised side.

The runners lined up at the stone slab that marked the starting line, fitting their feet in the grove chiseled into the stone. Haemon stood head and shoulders taller than the rest. He stretched his limbs, his eyes looking forward towards the post that stood just beyond the finish line. The muscles of his legs quivered like those of a skittish horse.

The horns sounded and the runners flashed past the starting line, their feet barely skimming the ground. Haemon was in the lead, his long legs propelling him forward. Polynices was close behind, his hair thrown back over his shoulder. But he could not catch up to his cousin who sped by on winged feet. All too soon the race was over, Haemon taking the victory.

The next contest was the *harmatodroia*, the chariot race. This contest made me nervous, for my brothers would be competing against each other.

"Take your places!" The call rang out and the chariots crowded forward. Among them, my brother Eteocles stood tall in his car, my cousin close behind him. Four fine horses drew their chariot, gifts to my brother from our uncle. The stallions stomped and champed at the bit, ready for the race.

A man passed an upturned helmet around the crowd, the others placing their lots in. They were taking bets on who would win.

The drivers waited for the call to start, their whips held high.

They were off, shouting at their teams, whips lashing the horses' backs and disappearing in the rising clouds of dust. I flinched as each lash fell. I tried to focus on how the ground beneath them was churned by sharp hooves. The horses ran at breakneck speed, their manes streaming behind them like ribbons. I had never seen anything move like that, swift as a river.

"They're so fast," I breathed, not taking my eyes off the horses.

"They are fast. But you need a lot more than a fast horse to win the race," Menoeceus replied.

My gaze snapped to his face. "What do you mean? If they didn't need to be so fast why would the charioteers whip them into a frenzy like that?"

"Speed isn't everything." My cousin gestured to a chariot surging before the rest. "See him? Sure, his horses are fast and he is in the lead. But not for long. Look how they are already starting to lag. See how he takes that turn so recklessly? He should have slowed down. He can't control them. Look how they're veering left and right, swerving all over the course." Sure enough, the chariot in the lead lost control, the charioteers fighting to rein in their team of horses. "Your brother now, *he* is in control. Did you notice the way he turns? You have to hug it close, with a tight grip on the reins."

I watched Eteocles and Haemon lean to the left as they turned, their bodies upright despite the rattling of the car, my brother's hand never relaxed the reins. He tugged hard with his right hand, the horse so close to the turning post the wheels of the chariot looked as if they would scrape against it. They made the turn and took off, passing the driver who had lost control of his team.

Close behind Eteocles was Polynices, his grip on the reins so tight I could see his white knuckles. His team hugged the turn, but they were too close. The turning post shattered on the impact. A horse screamed, its leg maimed. The car of the chariot crashed against the post, smashing the back of the car to pieces.

While Polynices fought to bring the horses to a stop, his

parabates tumbled out of the back of the car. The delicate skin of his elbows and knees split as he hit the ground, spots of red blood blossoming on his limbs.

My hand flew to my mouth, stifling a scream. He would be trampled by the next chariot for sure. But I needn't have worried. He rolled to his feet and ran forward towards the horses, yanking harshly at the bridles. The maimed horse let out another pained scream. The man unyoked the injured horse from the team. With one hand he held on to its bridle, and with the other he drew his sword. A flash of bronze as the blade cut across the horse's throat. It fell to the ground in a cloud of dust. Without a glance at the form heaped on the ground, he leapt back into the car, my brother driving the team slowly to the end of the track.

The casual violence I saw before me left a copper taste in my mouth. I stared at the limp body, not registering the cars that swerved to avoid it. The crowd of spectators let out a deafening roar as a winner crossed the threshold. But the sound was muted, dull, as if my head was submerged under water. A dark pool grew around the horse, the wheels of the chariots stained with its blood.

Then, it was as if I had been yanked out of the water by the hair, pain tingled along my scalp as sound raced back into my ears all at once. I clapped my hands over my ears. My cousin paused his cheering and peered down at me.

"Are you alright?" Menoceus placed a hand on my shoulder. He followed my gaze to the horse so cruelly slain. "He had to do it. It was maimed. It will never race again."

I fought against the lump forming at the back of my throat. "Why must it race in the first place? It had a life of its own, it was not meant to be killed in a foolish game for empty glory," I said thickly through the tears that now ran down my face.

"This is one of the reasons why you shouldn't have come. The real world is too much for you." His hand squeezed my shoulder in sympathy.

I shrugged it off. "Maybe the world needs to change," I replied, walking away from the crowds that formed around the winners, Eteocles and Haemon. A crown of laurels sat atop their heads.

If I had gone to join them, maybe I would have seen the look of hatred flash across Polynices' face, his hands stained red with blood.

As the sun set on the Pythian Games, I sat with my cousins and thought of my brothers. In ignorance, I thought Polynices would return and everything would be alright.

Now, after I saw the violence of the games, I could sense that something had fractured between my brothers. I saw from the reactions of the Thebans which brother they preferred. I knew now that Eteocles would find some way to stay king, and that my city would aid him in this, to keep Polynices out of the picture.

And I was ashamed to admit I hoped he would stay out of the picture too. For all our sakes.

7

THE ORACLE OF DELPHI

It was the morning of the third day. The day all of Hellas had been waiting for. We descended to the Castalian Spring to wash and purify ourselves before going to see the oracle. Once we were purified the *querents*, or *theopropoi*, gathered around the temple, waiting to hear whether the oracle could be consulted. The procedure to find out was a rather strange one. The priests sprinkled cold water on a goat at the sacred hearth within the temple. If the goat shuddered from the water, it meant the god could be consulted that day.

"But how will we know what the goat did?" I whispered to Menoeceus.

The Thebans had assembled under the *chresmographeion*, the shaded space for querents to wait to meet the oracle. It wasn't a very large space but since we had come with a king our group had the monopoly on the coveted space. I stood close to the front, flanked on either side by my cousins.

"If the god can be consulted the priests will come out with the goat and they will sacrifice it on that altar there." He nodded to the altar across from the temple. We watched as the priests came out of the temple, leading a white goat to the altar. I did not look when the sacrifice was being made.

I looked back at the temple, a frown on my face. I had been waiting all this time for Apollo to come to me and reveal what he wanted from me. If he were to appear to me anywhere, it would be within his temple. I had to find a way inside.

"Do you think we could go see the oracle?" I asked my cousin.

"One does not simply go to see the Oracle of Delphi," Menoeceus drawled. At my blank look, he continued. "First of all, the oracle can only be consulted one day a month, and she is only available nine months of the year. During the winter months, Apollo is absent from his temple. So, as you can see, a lot of people have come here today to see her."

I looked around at the throngs of people waiting in the shade of the *chresmographeion* for the priests to wave the first querents forward.

"Does she really see all these people in one day?" Some of the people in line had been waiting for days for their chance to consult the oracle.

Menoeceus shook his head. "I'd be surprised if she sees half."

Haemon cut in. "See the dedications all around us?" He gestured to the statues and offerings dotting the Sacred Way. "If you bring an offering, you get to see the Pythia first."

"That hardly seems fair," I argued. "Most of these people can't afford to give an offering like that. Only kings could afford to do that."

The boys gave me a knowing look.

"No, it's not fair to them, but sometimes affairs of state trump the affairs of the individual," Haemon replied.

"People are important, too, not just their cities." I looked back at the temple and watched the priests approach our place in the shade. My brother went out to meet them waving the men behind him forward. They carried a great statue of bronze. Of course, my brother would see himself as too important to wait in line.

"What do you think he's going to ask her?" I nodded to my brother as he presented his dedication to the priests.

"Whatever he asks, he isn't going to get a straight answer. Oracles are obscure. Many men have taken her words to mean one thing when they really pointed to another," Haemon replied.

"Then why isn't she more clear with her answers?" I asked.

"She doesn't have to be." Haemon straightened and ran his fingers through his hair. "The men asking the questions must be clear with themselves, they need to know if they are asking the right questions."

I frowned. "That's confusing."

Menoeceus laughed, clapping me on the shoulder. I buckled beneath the strength of his hand. "Of course it's confusing! This is the will of the gods we're talking about. It isn't for us to know."

We fell silent as the priests waved Eteocles forward. He glanced back at us and my cousins left their place in the shade to follow.

"Where are you going?"

Menoeceus didn't pause as he answered. "We have to accompany your brother."

"Why?" I asked, trotting behind them.

"Because he is a king. He can't go anywhere alone. He needs protection," Haemon replied. Then, he stopped and I bumped into his back. He whipped around. "Where do you think you're going?"

"With you?" I asked, hopping from one foot to the other.

Haemon considered me for a moment. "You can come. But you *have* to do what we say. Stay close to Menoeceus." He chose two other Theban youths to join the king's escort. I tried to suppress my grin as we approached Eteocles. I ducked behind Menoeceus, another aristocrat to escort my king.

Eteocles smiled as the priests escorted us into the temple. As we entered the *pronaos*, the vestibule, we walked beneath the inscription *Know thyself* and I thought of what Haemon had said. The querent had to know themselves, their hopes and fears, needs and desires, to truly understand the question they were asking and the answer they would receive. I only hoped Eteocles was wise enough to know himself and interpret the oracle correctly.

Another sacrifice was performed, this time on the inner sacred hearth. The sacrifice was burned as an offering to the god. The priests waved our small group forward into the *adyton*, the most sacred place in the world.

Within the *adyton* was the *omphalos*, the stone representing the centre of the world. Flanked around that stone were two statues of the god, one of wood and the other of gold. Apollo's lyre was leaning against the wall. The instrument, carved from a tortoise shell, was said to have been made by the god Hermes on the day he was born. In the centre of the room sat a bronze tripod, and perched atop it was the Pythia herself.

I had heard so many stories about the Pythia, how the god Apollo spoke prophecies through her while she was in a dreamlike trance. Maybe getting close to her was what the god wanted, was why he had brought me to his temple.

The Pythia was young, close to my own age. A veil covered her head and obscured most of her face. On the ground in front of her, there was a rift in the temple floor. Wisps of vapours drifted up from the rift to trail across her skirts like grabbing hands.

One of the priests stepped forward to speak to her before he turned to us. Facing my brother, he spoke. "To you, Apollo now speaks. Take heed."

The Pythia raised her bowed head. "Ask your question."

I remembered the whispered conversation between my brother and my uncle in the *megaron*. From what I gathered from their discussion, the real reason for this trip wasn't to participate in the games, but for my brother to consult the oracle.

My uncle's words came back to me now, an echo of the past. *We need to know what the god thinks of your decision.* What decision? What was Eteocles going to do?

Eteocles stepped forward, his face calm, but his jittering fingers betrayed his nerves.

"What path must I take forward?"

The Oracle of Delphi is notorious for her ambiguous answers. I did not expect my brother's question to be just as baffling. What did he mean?

The Pythia lifted her veil from her face. She waved the vapours towards her, breathing them in. Her eyelids fluttered closed and when she opened them again only the whites showed, for she had rolled her eyes back into her head. When she spoke, words spilled from her lips like water being poured from a jar.

"You must make your own nature, not the opinion of others, your guide in life."

A chill ran up my spine. As if one of the Furies had snuck up behind me to run a taloned finger down my flesh. Something about her answer, something about the way my

     ❋ MEAGAN CLEVELAND ❋

brother's eyes gleamed, scared me. I knew my brother to be rash, to be selfish. The god was allowing my brother to be a tyrant. But that would never happen. Would it?

Pleased with his answer, Eteocles turned to leave, the priests and the rest of our group crowding around him to escort him from the temple. I lingered behind. I thought of when I had entered the temple entertaining the notion of asking the Pythia a question of my own. Now was my chance to do just that.

I approached the still figure wreathed in the fumes that wafted up from the fissure in the ground. She did not stir as I drew closer and closer, her head bowed low. "Are you alright?"

Her head snapped up. She looked me directly in the eyes. I had thought her mad when words poured from her mouth like water from a fountain head. But there was nothing mad about her level gaze.

"You think me mad, girl?" She said, her voice husky from the fumes. It was as if she read my mind. "The best things come to us through madness when the gods give it as their gift." She smiled. "But you know that already, girl who hears the voice of the timeless god."

"How do you know that?" I whispered.

"The god we serve knows all things and tells me what I need to know." Her eyes flickered over me as she murmured, "And I see his mark on you as clear as I see it upon myself. Come, ask me your question."

"Apollo has led me to this place, to ask something of me. Do I have to do what he commands?" I asked through trembling lips. I saw the vapours from the ground rise and drift about me, curling around my legs like a cat.

The Pythia's eyes rolled back in her head until only the whites of her eyes showed. Her voice rumbled from deep within her.

"In seeking things apart from those that the god commands, you seek only tears."

Her words made my blood run cold. There was no choice. I had to do what the god commanded. But what did he want? And why didn't he tell me himself?

Again, it was as if she could read my thoughts.

"He cannot, not yet. Tell me, what words did you read as you entered the hall of the god?"

"Know thyself," I answered.

"Look deep within yourself. What do you want to ask me next?"

I thought of my journey here, the conversations I had with the children of the *Spartoi*. I thought of the animosity I saw between my brothers during the athletic contests, a dislike that had grown into hatred. I thought of the dedications I saw along the Sacred Way, my own father's name inscribed upon them beneath the claws of a monster.

I thought I had grown so much since I left the threshold of the women's quarters, my eyes finally open to what was going on around me. But I was still learning to see, still learning to distrust the safe world I thought I knew. A seed of doubt had been sown within me, and with everything I had learned since I left the city it had grown and flourished. I let that doubt blossom, its petals falling from my lips the questions I needed to ask. The questions I needed answered.

"Why did the god bring me here? What do I need to find out about my family, my kingdom?"

 ❋ MEAGAN CLEVELAND ❋

The Pythia closed her eyes, her jaw tight. I could see she did not wish to tell me.

"You will tend the holy house of Lord Apollo the far-shooter when all is ruined by the God of War. War and destruction will find you when all your father's shadows come to light." Her eyes flickered open.

Her words had stopped my heart, had stolen the breath from me. I had to remind myself to breathe, I had to remind my heart to beat, if only so I could understand what she meant.

Though I did not want to hear it, I knew the truth hidden behind her words. My city was fated to fall, my family fated to die. But why?

"The curse on your house."

My thoughts raced through my mind. "Curse? What curse?" I thought of Polynices and his friend, the words they had uttered at the feast now making sense. "The curse of my father? That's it, isn't it? My father's shadows… I need to learn about my father. Creon will know, he will tell me what to d—"

"It depends on you alone whether Thebes lives or dies."

I stumbled back. Her words were a blow I could not recover from. Alone? Everything I cared about was destined to be destroyed and I had to carry this fate alone?

"*I* am the only one who can stop my city from being destroyed, my family from falling apart. But how can I do that if it is fated to fall?"

The Pythia hopped down from her perch on the tripod and walked towards me. Her footsteps resounded throughout the empty chamber, an echo to my pounding heartbeat.

"Zeus knows all things and he tells his son what the Fates have in store for us. Apollo tells me these things, not so we can change our fate, but so we can come to grips with them. It isn't fair, but that is how it is."

"So what do I do?" I whispered, the weight of my fate and the fate of my family crushing the breath from my lungs.

"You must embrace your fate, Ismene. You are destined to be the last survivor of a great house. The sole survivor of a city in ruins."

I thought of my city, of the palace teeming with people, of the crowds that milled around the marketplace, the farmers that worked the fields outside the city's walls. I could not sit back and watch those lives snuffed out like the flame of a candle. I would not see fields lie fallow, the marketplace empty.

"No," My voice rumbled from deep within me, my answer echoing throughout the dark hall. "My fate is my own. I will save my city. I will keep my family together."

The Pythia looked at me sadly. "Then, you will fail."

"I will fail if I do not try."

I turned and raced out of the *adyton*, that sacred chamber where hopes so often died. I raced past a group of startled priests leading in the next querent. I ran past the line of people waiting to hear how their lives will be ruined, past the reminder of my father, past the temple complex.

When the cobbled path turned to grass, I slowed my pace. I drifted through the grass until I came to the Castalian Spring. Pilgrims who had traveled to Delphi to consult the oracle or compete in the games purified themselves in the sparkling waters. I turned from them and followed the spring up towards the mountains.

As I walked, the setting sun painted the sky crimson and gold. Here, with only the gurgle of the stream for company,

     ✳ MEAGAN CLEVELAND ✳

I sank to the ground and began to weep.

"How can I keep my family together when it is destined to fall apart?" I sobbed.

"You can't," a voice responded from behind me.

Not just any voice.

The voice.

But it wasn't coming from inside my own head. He was here with me now.

"You cannot change destiny. No one can. You must learn to bear it."

I dug my fingertips into the dirt at my feet, anchoring myself in my surroundings.

Slowly, I stood and turned to face him, clumps of earth falling from my fingers.

"Hello, Apollo."

8

ᴛHE ᴃARGAIN

He was the most beautiful person I had ever seen. He was not much older than my brothers, his youthful face clean-shaven, his bronze skin shimmered faintly with an otherworldly inner light. His blond hair was thick and curly but not unruly. Everything about him exuded order. And it was his eyes that frightened me the most. Large and framed by thick dark lashes, his eyes shone like the sun in the sky.

"Hello, Ismene."

The god responsible for the plague and my family's curse finally stood before me.

I tried not to tremble in his presence. I could feel my terror grip at my throat like a pair of gnarled hands.

Gods only appeared to those they favoured, those they took a special interest in. I did not want the god to focus any more of his attention on me.

"What do you want?" I managed to push the words through the lump of fear in my chest, the words slipping around the lump like water slips around ice in a stream.

"I want to talk to you, that's all." He smiled at me, moving closer like a cat advances on a mouse. "To tell you that I am pleased to see you have already started to make use of my gift."

"What gift?" I whispered.

"The gift of prophecy I bestowed on you."

"What do you mean? I don't have any gifts—" I started to protest.

Though he had been across the clearing moments before, he had moved right in front of me. He leaned towards me, his face inches from my own. He narrowed his shining eyes.

"Careful, Ismene. You sound ungrateful. You should thank me for my gift." He straightened, the setting sun passing behind a cloud and casting his face in shadow.

I took a step back from him. "What are you talking about? Gift? So far, you've cursed me with the knowledge that my family will fall and that I can do nothing to change it." Furious, I turned my back on the god and attempted to flee from him.

"There is *something* you can do," his voice called after me.

I paused at his words. I glanced back at him.

"You can use your gift to understand your family."

Irritation rose within me. "What gift—"

But then it came to me. The images in the flames.

"The flames showed me my father."

Apollo nodded.

I thought of my vision in the flames. Though they had shown me the monstrous Sphinx and the carnage she wrought, they had also shown me the face of my long forgotten father which *was* a gift to me, if not the one the god intended.

"Thank you for your gift," I said. It was best to be courteous to a god, no matter how infuriating he was. "Thank you," I repeated, moving closer to him. "But why would you give me the power to understand but not allow me to do anything with that knowledge? What kind of a gift is that?"

Apollo's eyes narrowed again at my impudence, the clouds overhead darkening. Just as suddenly, the clouds passed and sunlight glanced off his golden hair.

Then, he began to laugh. He laughed as if I had said something amusing. "You are not like the others."

"What others?" I whispered, afraid to misspeak again in his presence. I was afraid to do anything else that might offend him.

"The other seers, of course. I always find them. They always agree to come into my service in some way or another. And they are grateful. I can tell that it will not be so easy with you. You know that Father Zeus knows all things, and he shares his knowledge with me alone of the immortal gods. There are mortal men and women that are privy to this knowledge but only if it is favourable to me." He leaned towards me again, his lips brushing my cheeks. "Will you accept my favour?"

I shrank back from him. He smiled, as if my fear was a game. Fury melted the fear within me.

"Why would you favour me?" I drew up, anger making me bold.

"A mortal princess, gifted with prophecy, the flame of her life burning so brightly among the flickers of the lives around her. You blaze with purpose. I want to see what you will do."

My eyes narrowed. "I thought you were privy to the thoughts of all-knowing Zeus? You know what I will do."

His mouth hardened into a thin line. "Yes, I do. I know that you plan to use my gift to thwart fate. This is not possible."

"Everyone keeps saying that!" I interrupted. I flinched when I realised my impudence, but he took some strange pleasure in my defiance.

"That's because it is true. If you were anyone else, Ismene, I would strike you down for trying to defy the gods. Your efforts amuse me."

He took a step forward, the grass below his feet undisturbed. He stood before me, so close we shared breath.

My heart began to pound a primal beat within me. I did not know if it was from fear or something else.

He leaned closer, his lips brushing my cheek as he said into my ear. "I will give you a chance to change your fate, to save your kingdom and your brothers. I will give you three months to find the source of your family curse. You must discover the curse and break it, and then your fate will change."

He placed a kiss upon my cheeks. His lips burned hot, like the heat of the sun on my skin at midday. He stepped back and grinned at me. Then, he was gone. As he left the sun set behind the mountains and darkness descended.

My knees gave out and I sank to the ground. Laying back, hidden to all by the tall and waving grass, I thought over what just happened.

A god was giving me a chance to change my fate. If I was wise like my sister, I would think it a cruel trick, that he only wished to watch, amused as I scrambled to save my family only to watch it fall.

But.

My hand fluttered to my burning cheek, pressing the kiss to my palm and bringing it to my lips.

The god favoured me, there was no doubt about that. I believed he would keep his word. He would let me use those three months to save my family. And I would save them.

I had to.

I trudged my way back to the Theban camp, my cousins furious at my absence. I walked past them and collapsed on the ground. Later, I went to sit by the fire and look into the flames. The fire had shown me glimpses of the past, glimpses of the future. My eyes burned from the smoke, tears brimming on my lashes and streaking down my cheeks.

But I did not look away. The flames shied from my glance, licking timidly at the air. Soon, sparks flew up to hang suspended in the night air like a handful of stars. The embers cracked and an image formed in the heart of the fire. I could see the Sacred Way.

The dedications that dotted that holy road had come alive, a procession of gold and bronze statues followed the path to the god's temple. I darted around the statue of Pallas Athena, waded through the sacrificial animals cast in bronze.

And I pulled up short. That first day three of the dedications had stood out to me like familiar faces in a crowd. The cauldron that made me uneasy hopped over on its three lion's paws. A grating sound echoed throughout the sanctuary as the bronze legs dragged across the stone. The two princes walked off their pedestal and joined me, each one striving to outpace the other. They flanked me on either side, their marble arms brushing against my own. The ground heaved beneath my feet, undulating like a serpent, and I fell to the ground. And from her pedestal, the Sphinx unfurled her great wings and soared overhead, landing lightly before me, blocking my path. Smiling her inscrutable smile, she looked me over, her head cocked to one side. Prowling forward on her lion's legs she circled me.

She drew closer, her face inches from my own. She shook herself and the marble melted from her form like fat on a spit. Beneath the marble lay the Sphinx I had seen in the flames days before, her feathers ruffled and stiff with filth, her pale skin marred with flakes of dried blood. I could smell her breath, like death and decay.

The statues of the two princes seized me by either arm and lifted me into the air. The cauldron hopped closer, closer. It tipped itself until I found myself staring into its gaping maw. It seemed to be fathomless, a hole into the centre of the earth. I kicked at the statues but they did not ease their grip. The statues lowered me into the cauldron, the bronze devouring me. I screamed.

I was still screaming when my cousins shook me at my place by the fire.

The journey back to Thebes was a silent one. I did not speak to my cousins or the friends I had made.

I was too busy trying to figure out how to save my family and my city from destruction.

I had made a foolish bargain with the god. There was nothing I could do, no way I could fulfill the bargain I made. I should have accepted my fate and the fate of my family.

But the Pythia said it was *up to me* whether my city lives or dies.

If only I had some idea of what would cause the destruction. If I could find out what it was, would I be able to stop it?

I thought back to the Games to the growing animosity between my brothers. I feared what would happen once Polynices came back to Thebes. I feared that my own brother might bring about the destruction the Pythia warned of.

From what I had heard, Polynices had made a new home in Argos, had found a new brother in his friend Tydeus, and they had married to the king of Argos' daughters. I prayed to the gods that Polynices would find joy in his new home, his new family. I prayed he would not try to reclaim what was no longer his. He had a kingdom—why did he need to come back to ours?

What kind of sister was I, wishing for my brother to stay away?

9

HOME AGAIN

I felt empty after returning home.

There was no fear. No hope. All the joy and wonder of new adventures gone, replaced by the drudgery of the familiar, with a new accompanying feeling of unease and the growing distrust of those who were once dear to me.

Everything had changed, yet remained the same. I had changed but my life in the palace had not changed with me. I could feel myself shrinking to fit back into my old life. Perhaps it was my way of trying to make life go back to the way it was before I knew Thebes was destined to fall. Perhaps if I acted like nothing had changed, nothing *would* change.

I parted ways from the others without a word, trudging back to the women's quarters and the stifling life it represented.

People darted out of my path as I walked by. I savoured the last advantages of my disguise. Soon, I would be just a girl again. Soon, I would fade into the background, as ineffectual as a shadow as my world fell apart around me.

As I crossed the threshold into the women's quarters, a pale hand darted out and pulled me within. A pair of arms clasped around me.

Antigone.

"You're back!" she cried, drawing back from me to look me over. "You look dreadful. What's the matter? Didn't you have a good time?"

I raised my eyes from the ground and met her curious stare.

She looked at me warily. "Say something, Ismene. You're scaring me."

"I spoke to the god."

She took a step back. "What did he say?"

I hesitated. I longed to share the burden of the fate of my family with someone. All my life, I had looked to Antigone for comfort. I longed to lay together in our narrow bed, her hand wrapped around mine, her voice whispering assurances that everything would be alright, that I had her and we'd be together no matter what. I had always found myself reaching towards my sister the way green things grew, reaching for the sun. She gave me warmth, she helped me grow. Our roots tangled together.

But I had to face this alone. I must uproot myself from her and find my own way. This was no one's burden but my own.

"Say something," Antigone urged, gripping my arm so hard it hurt.

Then, a voice called out from within our chambers.

"Did you call for me, love?"

Pyrrha.

Antigone and I shared a quick glance. Pyrrha couldn't see me like this. Antigone's fingers flew to my hair, unpinning the boyish braids, while I yanked the pins from my shoulders and tossed my short *chiton* to the ground. Antigone pushed me into a corner of the room where she had secreted one of our longer, feminine *chitons*. Hurriedly, she placed the cloth over my head and began to fasten the pins from my shoulder down to my elbows, her white hands fluttering like birds.

"Antigone?" With a huff, Pyrrha came out from where she had been sitting.

Guilt struck me like a stone.

I barely recognized the woman who raised me. It was as if she had aged a decade in the short time I had been away. She was pale and thin, her bright hair dulled by the threads of silver that crept up her temples like frost. She took small, tottering steps towards us. Her body quivered like a leaf in the wind.

When I first snuck out, my nurse had been ill. I had been glad to find her ill so I could go about the palace as I wished. Only now did I wonder at the timing of that sudden sickness.

The gods go by many names, names that reveal their powers over mankind. Apollo also went by the name *Smintheus*. The Mouse god. When I was a child, I thought it funny that he was associated with such small creatures when really, he was associated with the sickness the creatures carry. The god of healing, of light and of civilization, was also a god of sickness.

How did I not put it together? My nurse had fallen sick just as the god's voice began to resonate with me. How could I not realise that he was the cause of her sickness?

Pyrrha's eyes widened when she saw me. She rushed forward to wrap her arms around me. I was surprised by the strength of her embrace.

As swiftly as she had pulled me to her, she drew back and shook my shoulders.

"Where have you been?"

My guilt and shame deepened.

"I'm sorry." Tears welled in my eyes and I rested my forehead on her thin shoulder and wept.

"There, there," Pyrrha murmured, patting my back in soothing circles. "Tell old Pyrrha what's wrong."

"I can't," I cried.

"Well, then." Pyrrha stooped to look me in the face. "It can't be all that bad. Can it?"

She was wrong. It was very, very bad.

Pyrrha drew me to my bed, urging me to lay down while she went to get me something to drink. While she was gone, Antigone continued to plague me with questions about my journey to Delphi but I would not respond. I could not. It pained me to keep the truth from her, but I had to do as the Pythia said.

It was up to me alone to save my family. I could not tell Antigone about the destruction of our city, our family. I could not tell her of my bargain with the god. I wasn't sure I *wanted* to tell her that part. I knew she would call me a fool for trying to divert fate, for making deals with gods. Maybe I was an even bigger fool for not trying to do something, anything, to protect those I loved. For if I refused to face the fate that loomed over me, threatening to destroy my family, then maybe it wouldn't happen.

The end of my brother's year of rule was fast approaching. Preparations for a great feast to mark that end were underway. Tucked away in the depths of the women's quarters, I hoped I would be oblivious to the flurry of activity going on in the palace but Pyrrha talked of it non-stop. According to her, the *Spartoi* had sent for Tiresias, the greatest seer in all Hellas. The name of the seer roused me from the stupor that had gripped me ever since I had come back from Delphi. Tiresias was the one people appealed to in times of crisis. Maybe he could help me discover the origins of the destruction of my family.

I stepped back from my place at the loom and forced myself to leave the women's quarters. As I crossed the threshold, I felt a spark of hope flicker within me. Hope that the old seer could help me save my family. I tucked that hope deep inside me, and prayed that its flame would not go out.

Lingering in the courtyard with a crowd of curious servants, I waited for the seer to arrive. Whispers passed through the group like the wind through a field as grass, as every woman turned to her neighbour to remark on the old prophet. Standing at the back of the group I couldn't catch sight of him. The women around me would not budge as I tried to slip around them, they barred my way with their bodies, checking me with cocked elbows and jutted hips and snapping at me to wait my turn. I scanned the courtyard for somewhere to go to get a better look. I clambered to the upper level of the palace so I could peer down at the arrival from around the large tapered columns that held the roof aloft.

I could see why the women were so eager to get the first look.

Tiresias was an old man. His face was gaunt, his hair white and listless. His pale eyes stared blankly ahead as he felt his way towards the *Spartoi* who stood assembled in the courtyard to greet him.

It was a brisk day and the wind teased at my hair and cloak, tugging every which way. Unfortunately, the wind made it hard to pick up what was being said down below. As I craned to get a better look at one of the most famous men in Hellas, the seer himself turned his unseeing eyes towards me.

I had to get closer.

I descended from my hiding spot and pushed my way

through the crowd of servant women, receiving elbows to the ribs for my audacity.

Peering between the shoulders and over the heads of the women in my path, I could scarcely make out the *Spartoi* as they addressed the seer. The old man leaned heavily on his walking stick as he listened to the younger men before him. Just as I made it through the throngs of bodies I saw the *Spartoi* turn to leave, Tiresias following them inside the courtyard.

My heart was racing in my chest as I tore across the courtyard. His bones old and weary, Tiresias could not manage more than a slow shuffle and had not made it very far. Before I even spoke the seer was turning towards me, his unseeing eyes fixed on my face.

"Wait," I panted, trying to catch my breath. "Do you need some help?" Forgetting he couldn't see me, I offered the crook of my arm to the old man. A beat of silence passed between us before I realised my mistake. Silently cursing my stupidity, I went to withdraw my arm.

To my surprise, he settled his hand on my forearm. He knew exactly where I stood.

"I would be glad of the help," he croaked, his voice as coarse and deep as a raven's throaty cry.

"Then, please, lean on me. You must be tired after your journey here." I spoke to the seer but my eyes kept flickering ahead to the retreating figures of the *Spartoi*. None of them had offered to help the old man.

"I am tired. But not from the journey." The seer sighed. "Take me inside."

As I led the seer into the palace, I prayed he had the answers I needed.

One of the servants was waiting for the seer inside the hall, and without a word, she beckoned for me to follow. We wove through the palace until we came to a small room by the kitchens. She explained to the seer that someone would come to fetch him when it was time for him to be presented to the king at dinner.

Tiresias relinquished his hold on my arm and took a step into the room, feeling around for the cot he would sleep on. He sank gratefully into the bed with a sigh, closing his eyes. Then, he turned his head towards me.

"Thank you, boy."

I opened my mouth to correct him but thought better of it. No need to explain why a princess was acting as a servant. I left the seer's rooms to find a familiar figure waiting in the hallway. Antigone stood behind me.

"What are you doing here?" I asked, surprised that my sister would flout the rules and leave on her own.

"Looking for you," Antigone retorted. She reached for my arm and clasped it. "Come with me. Pyrrha sent me for you."

With an insistent tug on my arm, Antigone led me back to the women's quarters.

Pyrrha sat on her stool in the corner, but she was not carding wool. She was resting. I looked on at her in concern. The illness she was recovering from must be grave indeed to keep my industrious nurse from her work.

A smile split her face as she spotted us. "There you are. Come! You must dress for tonight."

The *Spartoi* would consult the old seer at the feast tonight and the king's decorative sisters must be in attendance. I tried to stand patiently while Pyrrha dressed Antigone and I, but her illness slowed her once quick movements and I itched to help her. Impatience winning out, I went to grab my veil and place it on my head myself but Pyrrha slapped my hands away.

"That is for me to do," she chided, placing the veil atop my perfumed hair.

Pyrrha dressed Antigone and I in a *peplos* each of royal purple, to match our brother, and placed golden diadems atop our heads. Finally finished with her ministrations, we made our way to the central hall for the feast.

As I sat beside my sister, she leaned over to murmur in my ear.

"Look at him. Does he look like a man about to lose a kingdom to you?"

I followed her gaze to the dais where Eteocles sat. He seemed happy tonight, happier than I expected him to be at the end of his reign, right before he relinquished power to our brother.

The dancing flames of the *megaron* cast long shadows on the painted walls. I stared at the flames until my eyelids grew heavy and in their depths, I could see an image.

My brother.

Instead of robes of purple and gold he wore drab grey cloth, stiff with filth. His hair was matted with ash and earth. Atop his filthy hair sat a crown of twisting serpents. Poison dripped from their mouths and onto my brother's face. He turned to me and bat-like wings unfurled from his back. He had become a Fury, like Tisiphone and her sister Megaera. He had become a creature of hatred and vengeance.

I blinked and the image was gone.

The feast began. We dined on sacrificial meat, we drank mixed wine. But everything tasted of ashes in my mouth.

Silence fell as Tiriesias was ushered into the hall. I glanced over at Eteocles and saw him straighten in his seat, his eyes fixed on the seer.

The oldest of the *Spartoi* stood and approached the seer.

"Tiresias, you know the will of the gods. Tell us, is it the gods' will that Polynices return to rule Thebes?"

The crowd's murmurs echoed throughout the hall. Every person here had thought the same but dared not speak it aloud.

I looked on in horror, fearing what Tiresias would say next.

"I have seen the will of Zeus," Tiresias' voice rang out. All else was silent. My hands clenched into fists, fingernails cutting into the soft flesh of my palms. "It is Zeus' will that Polynices does not rule Thebes."

The hall erupted with cheers for the words of the seer.

Antigone seized my hand, I turned to her and saw her face blanch beneath her veil.

Eteocles rose from his throne to stand before the *Spartoi* and their sons.

"Citizens of Thebes, do you share the will of Zeus? Do you wish for me to remain your king?" The room stilled for a moment.

Phlegyas, one of Eteocles' friends, stood. "I would."

Labdacus stood. He said the same. So did Dorylas and Theron, Halys and Phaedimus, Deilochus, Phegeus, Gyas and Chromis. Soon all the *Spartoi* and their sons stood behind their king. Creon stood and so did my cousins beside him, Haemon following his father without a thought, Menoeceus more hesitantly.

"I would, my king," Creon said solemnly.

Eteocles beamed.

As bodies sprang from their seats to proclaim fealty to their king, I alone remained seated. I was watching the curse unfold before my eyes.

10

Broken Vow

The feast went on late into the night, until even the fire of the *megaron* was reduced to glowing embers. Finally, the feast came to an end and the jovial crowd withdrew to their rooms, stopping to congratulate my brother on their way out.

Antigone rose to leave with Pyrrha, her eyes searching mine. I shook my head and she nodded. She knew I wanted a moment with our brother.

Soon, Eteocles was alone. I rose from my seat to follow him as he swept out of the hall. Gaining on him, I reached out and pushed him.

He stumbled but regained his composure, glaring over his shoulder. When he saw who it was his face slackened with surprise.

"What do you think you are doing?" Eteocles said, bemused.

"What do *you* think you are doing?" I hissed, pushing him again. He caught my wrists in his hands and held me away from him. "You gave your word. One year of rule and then he would have his turn. You would go into exile."

He dropped my hands. "Oh, but I don't think exile would agree with me, do you?"

"You can't do this," I pleaded with him, knowing the damage

was already done. "It will destroy him. It will destroy *everything*."

Eteocles paused. He fiddled with his purple *chiton*. "I think you are overreacting. Polynices is a grown man. He can take care of himself."

"Do you think he will just let you take his birthright? For a second time? You know what a temper he has, you know how long he will bear a grudge. Don't do this, Eteocles, please." I bent on my knees before him, a suppliant before her king. A sister begging her brother.

But brothers were often selfish creatures.

He shook his head. "It's already done." He looked at me, crumpled on the floor in front of him. "Go back to the women's quarters. There is no place for you here."

Eteocles left me in the dark hall. Stunned, I remained on the ground, unable to find the strength to rise.

The Pythia had said it was fated that the curse would destroy my family. She told me again and again that there was no way to change my fate. But sitting back and watching that fate unfold would destroy *me*. I couldn't sit back and watch any longer.

Eteocles said there was no place for me here. He was right. There was no longer a place for me as a passive princess any longer. I needed to discover the source of the curse and break it.

I knew what I needed to do.

Creon and the *Spartoi* crowned Eteocles king of Thebes, as if this was what they had planned all along. They were visibly relieved that my estranged brother would not come back to rule.

Creon smiled, one arm around Eteocles, the other reaching for Haemon and Menoeceus, but no one's smile outshone Eteocles, who beamed at the crowd of his friends, his subjects.

Antigone and I sat off to the side, clad in matching *peploi* of royal purple. A thin diadem perched in our hair, twins to the one that sat atop our brother's head. He turned to smile at us, letting us share in his joy. Antigone managed a weak one in return but I did not smile. He did not know that his actions of the day before had been the catalyst of the war that was yet to come.

I spent days trying to think of how to find the source of the curse, how to break it. Should I go back to Delphi, to the Pythia and demand that she help me? Should I go to my uncle Creon and tell him the truth so that he can give me guidance? None of these seemed like the right option. I knew I needed to find the right course soon, but how?

Antigone sensed something was wrong. She did not push me for answers, though. Instead, she sought to distract me from myself.

Our nurse's illness had left her frail and weak, and she no longer had the strength to watch over us at all times. My sister and I snuck from the women's quarters to make our way to the ramparts of the seven gates, where I had shown her the path to the god weeks ago. There, on top of the world, we sat in silence, watching the world unfurl around us.

I was weary of my troubling thoughts, and I almost wished the voice would return and tell me what to do. The absence of the shining god now seemed a punishment—I must watch the effects of my family's curse occur but be unable to do anything about it. Is that how the god rewards those he favours? Why would he favour me anyway, after I had defied him?

I looked over the wall and was startled to see a figure approach the gate. I recognized that imperious walk, the set of those broad shoulders, the rage packed into that small but bulky frame. It was Polynices' friend Tydeus.

I raced down the steps, darting around the sentries, my veil flying behind me. I ran into the hall where my brother and the *Spartoi* stood. Creon was there, too, and my cousins. They all looked up as I tore into the room.

"What are you doing here?" Eteocles demanded.

"Someone is approaching the gates." I panted. "I think it is a messenger from Polynices."

Eteocles sat on his stone throne and bid the guards to allow the messenger in. Tydeus stalked inside, an olive branch clutched in his large hand. A symbol of peace, but in his hands it was brandished like a weapon.

He stood before the king and spoke. "It is you who should have sent a messenger to your brother to yield the throne to him. But there you sit on your brother's throne, while he is forced to roam the unfriendly earth in exile."

Eteocles smirked at him and I could see Tydeus' temper ignite. "Not so unfriendly it would seem, if the first door he stopped at offered him a kingdom and a wife."

"Your brother wandered for months, sleeping on the roadside until he came to Adrastos' hearth. Now, it is your turn for exile."

"And if I'm lucky, find a rich wife on the way," Eteocles joked. Everyone in the hall laughed except for Tydeus, Antigone and me.

I could see Tydeus trying to restrain himself from going for

Eteocles' throat. He closed his eyes a moment, breathing deep, before he spoke again. "You mock your brother's year of exile."

Eteocles rose from his throne, his purple robes swirling about him. "We made a fair bargain. I would be first to rule. I have earned this throne and I will bear this sceptre for years to come. In Argos, Polynices has a wife, a new father, a new mother." He waved at Tydeus. "A new brother. What is left for him in Thebes? He has no father here, no mother. Just a brother he despises. Sisters he has long forgotten. Would he force his wife to leave her home and her family? The citizens of Thebes have grown accustomed to me—would you and my brother force uncertain leadership on them? Who knows how my brother would punish my people. No, no, for their sake, I cannot leave the throne."

Tydeus threw the branch on the ground. It splintered.

"Then we shall take what is rightfully ours." He glared at all assembled in the hall, turned and left.

The hall was silent in his wake.

Creon approached my brother. "My king, what would you have us do?"

"Do?" Eteocles repeated, puzzled.

"We cannot let him walk away after the grave insults he hurled at your person," insisted Labdacus, one of the sons of the *Spartoi*. "Let us punish him."

The assembled men cheered. Labdacus took in their attention and began to speak again. He let his words hang in the air before him like laurel crowns held before the victor of a chariot race. "Tonight, we will ambush him at the Sphinx's pass. Show him what Thebes is made of."

Labdacus chose forty nine youths to accompany him on his mission, among them my friends Chromis, Dorylas and Theron.

He had reached forty eight when Creon stepped forward.

"Sire," he spoke to Eteocles, "what will you have us do? Shall I stop this madness before it begins?"

I could hear the plea in his words. Eteocles did as well, I could see it in the way his eyes shuttered, the way he avoided Creon's gaze.

"I would have your support," he ordered.

Our uncle obeyed. He ushered the youths from the hall, leading them to the armoury to arm them for their mission.

After the crowds had trickled from the hall, when only Eteocles remained, still seated on his stone throne, his head in his hands, did I approach him. My anger rose up inside of me.

"You should have listened to Creon," I said.

He started. He did not hear me approach as he was so fixated on his own troubles. "He should not have questioned me in front of everyone."

"Stop this. There is still time, send someone to them before they commit this crime. You know as well as I that it is a sacred crime to kill a messenger—"

The words died in my throat. My brother's hand would not let them emerge. He had leapt from his seat to wrap his hands around my neck, to throw me against one of the four pillars.

"I am the head of this family. It is not for you to question me. My word is law," he hissed, his face held close to my own. He saw the alarm in my eyes and dropped me.

I caressed the bruise at my throat glaring at him all the while. "It is not for men to flout the laws of the gods."

He sneered. "It is not for girls to question men."

We stood there in stony silence, glaring at each other. Finally, Eteocles stormed out of the hall, leaving me alone.

His words sparked an idea.

"If it is not for girls to question men," I said to the empty hall, "then, I must no longer be a girl."

I raced to the women's quarters, calling out to Antigone. She appeared before me with a frown.

"Be quiet, you'll wake Pyrrha," she whispered. Then she looked at me and sighed. "Out with it. What is the plan?"

"I need you to help me dress. Do you still have my clothes from Delphi?"

Antigone looked startled. "Ismene, what are you going to do?"

"I have to join the other youths before they get to Tydeus. I have to convince them not to ambush him. I have to *stop* this war before it starts."

Antigone went still, all colour leaving her face. "War? Is that what you found out at Delphi? Will our brothers go to war?"

"Not if I stop it from happening."

"Let's get you dressed."

Antigone bound my chest and dressed me in a boy's *chiton*. We did not have much time for her to style my hair like she did before. She turned and fumbled around the room until she found what she was looking for, a band to tie around my forehead. She fastened it in place and stood back and looked into my face.

We stood in silence for a moment. Then, Antigone took me by the shoulders and held me close. Too soon, she let me go.

"You better go. You don't want to miss them."

"Thank you."

"Don't thank me. Just come back."

I nodded and made my way out of the women's quarters to the armoury.

It was empty.

I rushed from the armoury to and out the Cadmeia, down to the gates. I could see the group of young men. I raced towards them, melting into the throng just as they passed through the Neis Gate.

I pushed through the group until I spotted some familiar faces.

"Chromis, Theron, Dorylas!" I hissed.

They turned.

"Ismenos!" Theron took hold of my upper arm and drew me closer to their small group.

"We haven't seen you since Delphi! Where have you been?"

"There is something you need to tell us, isn't there?" asked Dorylas.

"You aren't who you say you are, are you, Ismenos?" Chromis chimed in.

I faltered. Had they seen through my disguise? Did they know I was a girl?

"You are part of the royal house, aren't you?" Chromis went on.

I stiffened. They knew. They knew I was a princess—

"We saw how Prince Haemon and Prince Menoeceus were with you, and saw the similarities between you. You're their brother, aren't you?"

I suppressed the urge to sigh with relief. They hadn't seen through my disguise.

"I didn't know lord Creon had a third son," Theron said, suspicious.

"Creon has always been a father to me," I answered. It was true. I had lost my own father when I was so young, Creon was the only father I ever knew.

"That's it then! We know your secret," Chromis said with a grin, draping his arm around my shoulders. "Don't worry, we'll keep it."

"Actually," I began, an idea taking hold of me. "That's why I am here. Lord Creon sent me. To stop the ambush."

My friends stopped in their tracks. The youths behind us bumped into us with angry words.

"Why?" Dorylas asked.

My mind raced.

"You heard him in the hall earlier, he urged the king to be cautious. He wants to stop this ambush before it begins. Help me find Labdacus, please. You know it is a sacred crime to kill a messenger. We *have* to stop this."

Dorylas considered my words and nodded.

"You're right, Ismenos. We need to stop this."

Theron held out a hand. "You can't just stop everyone. Look at them, they need to do this, to prove their worth to their king."

"They do not need to sin against the gods to prove themselves to their king," I snapped. "There is another way, a *better* way. Instead of harming the messenger, we give him a message of our own. A message of peace. We need to stop the rift between the brothers."

Chromis nodded. "We will. Come on, Ismenos. Let's see if we can find Labdacus—" He paused as he noticed all the still bodies around us. Everyone had fallen silent. They stood watching and waiting in the shadows.

A chill ran down my spine. We had stopped in a rocky clearing I recognized from my vision of the Sphinx. We were at the site of the Sphinx's lair.

And there, a figure lurked on the Sphinx's rocky perch. It was Tydeus.

He crouched in the darkness, a spear in each hand, ready for battle. He called out into the night, "Who's hiding out there?"

I looked around me, seeing hands clench around spears and knew I needed to act now. I stepped forward to answer him, to attempt to parlay with him, when a spear soared beside me. I whipped around to see one of the sons of the *Spartoi* had made the throw. He looked around the group, a crease between his brows, as if he expected his comrades to cheer for his daring. But the clearing was silent, all eyes followed the course of his weapon with bated breath.

The spear arched through the night sky, the light of the moon limning its blade with silver, time seemed to slow in that moment, the spear suspended in the air until swiftly it fell and pierced the boar hide Tydeus wore, its point embedded in his shoulder. With a hoarse cry, he pulled the spear from his flesh and hurled it to the ground.

"Come out and fight me face to face!"

As one, the young men let out their breath, as if the night itself sighed at what was about to come.

All around him, my brother's men stepped out of the shadows and into the rocky clearing. They waved their spears and cried out as one, their single voice making the mountain tremble.

I was too late.

Dorylas turned and pushed me into the shadows. "Quick,

Ismenos, go! If you are who you say you are, we cannot let any harm come to you.”

“Go, Ismenos, go!” Theron urged.

Terror seized me and I couldn't move. I couldn't leave them. I reached for the dagger Antigone had given me and clenched it in my hand.

Tydeus scrambled back on the rocks' edge. I thought he was drawing back from the group of men advancing on him. I was wrong. He reached behind him and pried the rocks loose from the Sphinx's lair. They rumbled to the ground. He hurled the remaining rocks against the Thebans. Six men were buried alive under the cascade of stones, left to suffocate beneath their weight, their limbs broken.

With a fierce cry, the Thebans approached, throwing their spears towards their target. Tydeus' small stature was to his advantage here—he ducked out of range, catching their spears and hurling them back at them. I watched in horror as my brother's friends and the few friends I had made fall around me. Dorylas lay at my feet, the bronze tip of a spear embedded in the socket of his eye. There was Theron, the shaft of a spear poking out from his abdomen.

Chromis alone lingered, one eye on his fallen friends and the other on me, frozen with fear. He opened his mouth to rally me onward. “Go on, Ismenos! Go! You need to get out of here—” His words ended in a wet gurgle. Tydeus' spear had gone through his throat, pinning him to the trees behind him.

I screamed. Bile rose in my throat and I retched on the ground. But nothing came up. In just a few moments, all those young men had fallen.

All of the fifty men my brother had sent to ambush the

Argive prince, his friends, were dead.

I was the only one left.

Realising I was the last target, I scrambled over the fallen men and rocks to flee. But my ankle caught on a fallen Theban and I went down. The rocks shifted around me and rained down, my arm caught under the rockfall. I fought to pry myself loose as Tydeus approached.

I felt my heart rise in my throat, my stomach roiling, I readied myself to join the others in death, my eyes squeezing shut.

The death blow never came.

I opened my eyes.

Tydeus stood over me. He threw his spear to the ground and kicked at the rocks. The stones shifted and I was free. I scrambled backwards, clutching at my numb arm.

"Tell your king war is coming for his city." He spat on the ground at my feet.

Wasting no time lest he change his mind, I stumbled to my feet and ran. I glanced over my shoulder and saw with disgust that Tydeus stripped the weapons from the fallen men. I paused to watch him strip them of their shining armour and erect a trophy to the virgin goddess.

"Fierce goddess, maiden of war, accept my offering. I will wage war on Thebes for you, and my brother in marriage, Polynices. Favour us and we will bring you glory!" He took a knee in front of his trophy and bowed his head.

I froze in terror as I saw the air shimmer around him. I saw a beautiful young woman appear, clad in shining armour of gleaming gold, her fair hair curling over the metal. Her grey eyes roamed lovingly over the battlefield.

When her eyes rested on me, I gasped. She saw me. Her

eyes narrowed. I turned to run but stumbled and crashed to the earth, smashing my head against the rocks.

Everything went dark.

I woke to murmured voices, muttering the same phrases over and over.

They were offering prayers to the fallen.

My eyes fluttered open and I almost cried with relief when I recognized Thebans milling around the carnage.

I tried to get up but slumped over. I felt a pair of hands brace me under my arms and pull me into a sitting position.

"You're alive! We thought there were no survivors," a familiar voice said.

My eyes flew open.

Haemon.

This time I did cry, the tears flowing in a steady stream as I clutched my cousin and wept.

I felt him stiffen in surprise.

"Ismene? What are you doing here?" he whispered.

"I tried to stop the ambush, to convince the others to reason with Tydeus. But he killed them *all*." I gripped his arm. "He spoke to me, Haemon. He told me to tell Eteocles to prepare for war."

Haemon held me closer, so close my words were muffled against his cheek. "Ismene, be silent." The urgency in his voice stilled my sobs. "Lie down, play dead. No one can know that you were here. I will relay your message to the king. I'll tell him there was one survivor who succumbed to his wounds shortly after giving me Tydeus' message."

Gently, he laid me down upon the ground, passing his hand over my eyes. I closed them and remained perfectly still. "Be still. I will be back in a moment. I am going to direct the others to go back and bring biers for the dead. Do not move, do not speak, until you hear my voice again." He squeezed my arm in reassurance then he was gone.

I laid there among the dead for what seemed like an eternity. Not daring to move, scarcely daring to breathe while I waited for Haemon to return.

Muffled footsteps and murmured voices died away until there was nothing but silence. I was alone. But not for long.

I gave you the chance to change your fate and this is what you do? Delay for weeks and play dead?

The voice had returned.

I had promised Haemon I would not speak until he returned. I did not answer the god.

Now, do you understand, Ismene? Your efforts are futile. You tried to stop the carnage last night and here you lay among your fallen comrades. I know you plan to find the source of the curse and break it. This is not possible. War is coming to Thebes, a war ordained by Zeus himself. You cannot stop it. Do you really wish to suffer like this for three months? Pledge your service to me now, and I will protect you from this bloodshed. Stop this foolishness now.

Haemon bade me to stay silent until he returned but I could not ignore the god any longer. Barely moving my lips, I whispered my reply.

"I will not stop. Not until I have tried to save them."
You will fail.

I felt a tear roll down my cheek. "I still have to try."

 ❈ MEAGAN CLEVELAND ❈

The voice was silent then. But I could sense the god's presence in the still air, the warmth of the sun that trailed down my face, as if the rays were tracing the tears that spilled down my cheeks. His presence kept me sane. Instead of thinking of the bodies of my friends, I focused on the warmth of the sun, the sound of the wind.

Soon, I heard footsteps. The men had returned. I could hear them grunt as they heaved the bodies of the fallen onto biers. They would return the fallen to their families. I felt the earth around me shudder as footsteps came closer and closer. I willed myself to stay still but every nerve was on edge.

Someone knelt beside me. One hand cupping the back of my head, the other sweeping under my knees. I was lifted into the air. I silently wished they wouldn't throw me onto the bier with the others.

"It's me."

Haemon had returned.

I relaxed in his arms. He carried me for some time and then I felt him lay me down.

"You can open your eyes."

I blinked and looked up at the face looming over me. Haemon looked pale and tired, but a small smile tugged at his lips. He had carried me to a different spot, hidden amongst the rocks.

"Here." He placed a mantle in my hands. "Put this on and stay here. I will come back for you in a moment. Then, we will join the others."

"Thank you."

He smiled in reply, rising to leave. "I'll be back."

I swung the mantle around my shoulders and waited for him to return.

The sun had rode his chariot across the sky when Haemon

had returned. He pulled me to my feet. I did not wish to get up at all but I followed along as Haemon led me back to the city and the central hall.

The *megaron* was blazing and I watched the smoke rise into the opening in the ceiling, the grey smoke drifting like the souls of the men who died late last night.

Crowds filled the hall but were eerily quiet.

Eteocles stood to fill the silence. "So many lives were lost. Lives that could have been spared if I had the foresight to kill the man as he stood in my hall."

Murmurs of agreement echoed in the hall. Perhaps it would be better for everyone if Tydeus was dead. I thought of the apparition of the goddess beside him after the bloodshed. I shuddered. Tydeus would not fall easily with a goddess on his side.

Eteocles looked solemnly at the faces in the crowd. "Last night, I sent fifty men to their deaths. I should have listened to you." Eteocles nodded to Creon. "Now, your friends, your sons, are dead. I am sorry."

Haemon stepped forward, looking around at the broken, confused faces in the hall. "Tydeus killed our men. But one lived long enough to deliver a message." He turned to Eteocles then. "He declared war on you."

Shouts rang throughout the hall. Calls for blood. My heart sank. War had truly come to Thebes.

Eteocles stepped forward, taking his cousin's hand. He turned to the crowd. "We will fight him. We will take vengeance for what the savage Tydeus has done. We will show him what Thebans are made of."

The cheers of support turned my blood to ice. The hall began to empty. The families of the fallen had gone out to the gates, where they would find the bodies of their sons, their brothers laid out on biers.

I could not bear to remain and witness my city's terrible grief. I slipped away.

There was someone I needed to see.

I raced down the halls to Tiresias' quarters, my mind flooded with questions to ask the old seer. Not even bothering to knock, I flew into the room. Tiresias was packing his things.

"You're leaving?" I gasped, all my questions trickling from my mind like water from cupped hands.

"Yes, I am leaving. I have been called to another city."

"And what city will you go to next?"

The old man smiled. "Argos."

Argos, that was the city where Polynices was living. He had become son-in-law to its king.

I grasped the old man's arm. "Take me with you."

He tilted his head, considering. "Alright then," he murmured. "You can come. I need someone to guide me through the hills. We leave at daybreak. Make your preparations and say your goodbyes. Meet me in the *megaron* at dawn."

I agreed and made my way to the women's quarters to say my goodbyes. When I entered, Antigone flew to me, her arms holding me tight.

"Oh, thank the gods!" she cried, pressing her face into my shoulder. "When I heard that all the youths sent to ambush Tydeus were killed, I thought—"

"I'm sorry. I would have come sooner but Haemon advised

me to be cautious."

She withdrew and wiped tears from her eyes with the back of her hand. She saw the look on my face. "What now? Where are you going this time?"

"I'm going with Tiresias to Argos. To see if I can talk sense into Polynices."

Antigone nodded. "You'll need supplies." She turned and together we found the *pyxis* of old clothes.

While Antigone dug through its contents, I went to wash the grime of the battlefield from myself. Who knew when I would next have the chance?

I was brushing my hands through my tangled curls when I noticed Antigone watching me. Wordlessly, she disappeared for a moment. When she returned, she held a dagger in shaking hands.

"It would be best if we cut it."

She was right, of course. Only aristocrats had long hair while servants were marked by their shorn locks. No one would believe I was a servant looking like this.

My hand went to my hair, unbound it flowed down my back. I saw the way my sister's hand shook as she approached, the dagger quivering in her fingers. I gathered my hair just below my shoulders and held it in place with one hand, while the other I reached towards my sister.

"Here." I held out a steady hand. "Give it to me."

She placed the dagger in my palm. I grasped my hair and brought the dagger close and began to shear. Dark curls fell to the floor.

Antigone laid out a fresh *chiton* for me, as well as a woolen mantle and a broad brimmed hat called a *petasos*. She bound fresh linen around my chest and helped me dress.

"Be careful, Ismene. Tread cautiously."

"I will."

We stared at each other, neither knowing what to say next.

"Say goodbye to Pyrrha for me?"

Antigone nodded.

Equipped for my journey, I sat and waited for Dawn to arrive.

As I stood in the courtyard outside the *megaron* to meet Tiresias, I marveled at the changes made overnight. Mounds were dug around the gates, pits dug around the walls, the shafts of spears sticking outwards from their depths to dissuade anyone from approaching. The smiths' hammers echoed throughout the city, forging weapons for the men, young and old, volunteering to fight. The *Spartoi* had made camp in the *megaron*, drawing up battle lines, counting men and sending messengers to collect allies to fight for our cause.

Everywhere I looked, men and women, young and old, I could see hatred on their faces. Hatred for Argos had united everyone, stirring them to war. It was like Apollo rained plague on the city again. This time, there were no fevers, no coughs or boils, no bleeding mouths. This time, there were hard faces, tears falling from the corners of eyes, weapons were everywhere, being counted, collected, forged. There was no time to mourn the dead. Their families were not confined to their homes in mourning—they swarmed the palace, their grief casting a shadow on the bright halls.

Tiresias arrived and together we set out through the gates for Argos.

11

THE JOURNEY BEGINS

iresias and I traversed over the plains of Thebes. The roads were packed with farmers and their families who had abandoned their homes for the safety of the city's walls. I tried not to look back at everything I was leaving behind.

Curiosity won out and I glanced back as the city walls shrank out of sight, the cypress trees along the road waving in farewell. I stumbled but kept marching onwards. I squeezed my eyes shut and repeated the same words over and over to myself like a prayer.

I will save them. I will save them. I will save them.

I walked in front of Tiresias, his hand braced on my shoulder. We walked in silence. I found myself missing the excited chatter of Chromis, Dorylas and Theron that had made my first journey outside the city so exciting. Such a recent trip. It was hard to believe all three boys were being mourned by their families within the city walls.

The journey to Argos would take two days by foot. The plains of Thebes were flat, meant for farming, and offered little shade to rest. I was glad of the *petasos* hat Antigone had found for me, its wide brim acting as protection from the sun.

I wished the *petasos* could act like Hades' helm of invisibility and hide me from the sun and its god altogether.

A breeze knocked the *petasos* from my head and felt the sun blaze down, its heat settling on my shoulders like phantom hands.

You know you can never hide from me, Ismene. I see all things.

I scowled up at the sun, holding my hand over my eyes to block its rays.

"You said you would give me a chance to change my fate. Tell me, will my trip to Argos help my cause?"

Are you asking for a prophecy? The voice sounded amused as it usually did.

"I suppose I am," I muttered, reaching for my hat and placing it back over my head.

The voice was quiet for so long I didn't think he would answer. When he began to whisper in my mind once more, I jolted with surprise.

Your journey to Argos will aid you, but not in the way you expect. Remember what I told you that day at Delphi, Ismene. The key to breaking your family's curse is to find its source.

"Thank you," I murmured.

"Are you talking to me?" Tiresias called out behind me.

I raised my voice and replied, "No, just talking to myself."

We continued on our path until dusk painted the sky the colour of flames. We found a small clearing ringed by short trees and made our camp for the night. I shook out bedrolls for us to sleep on and looked around for kindling for a fire.

Soon a small flame blazed between us, casting shadows across the seer's wrinkled face. Tiresias lay down and fell asleep, his soft snores and the crack and hiss of the fire the only sounds.

I was fortunate that the god gave me some insight on what I should be looking for in Argos. Although I had his favour, I must not rely on him to give me all the answers I needed. I must find them myself. But how?

I thought back to Delphi and how I had looked into the flames and saw my father and the Sphinx. Maybe if I looked into the flames I would learn more about the curse on my family.

I shifted in my seat so that I faced the fire. I peered into the red dancing plumes and an image began to take shape.

It was the cauldron I had seen on the Sacred Way at Delphi. Its feet carved to resemble a lion's paws flexed and pierced the ground. A hollow ringing came from its centre. And then, a voice began to speak from its depths.

"Tantalus, a son of Zeus himself, was welcomed on Olympus. As a man, he walked among the gods. But in his age, he became jealous of his divine family. Tantalus wished to prove that the gods were not all knowing. To repay them for their hospitality he invited them to a well-ordered feast in his own home. Tantalus took great care preparing this feast. He took his young son, Pelops, and he cut up his limbs, taking his white arms, legs and shoulder, and cast them into the cauldron so that his guests would divide and eat his flesh. Son of Tantalus, I speak of you."

A pale hand reached out from the depths of the cauldron.

I blinked and the image was gone.

The cauldron looked like one of the dedications I had seen on the Sacred Way. The voice from within the cauldron made me uneasy.

Tantalus. I had heard that name before from one of

Pyrrha's stories. Tantalus was favoured by the gods but he lost their favour when he boiled his own son to a fine stew to serve to them. But, Zeus *alastor*, the avenger of evil deeds, the all-knowing, knew what Tantalus served before him and punished him. Tantalus was thrown into Tartarus, condemned to everlasting hunger and thirst.

His son Pelops did not die that day for all of the gods but one knew the feast for what it was. They arranged the pieces together and breathed life back into the boy. There was one piece missing, a shoulder, for Demeter, sick with anguish over her missing daughter, was not paying attention and had a bite. The gods replaced that missing piece with a shoulder of ivory. Pelops went on and lived a full life.

The story used to scare me as a child. I had not thought of it for some time. Why did the flames mention Tantalus? What did the ancient kings have to do with Argos? How can that vision help me?

The answer came to me. I went cold with dread, no longer feeling the fire's warmth.

Tantalus is an ancestor of Adrastos. The king of Argos and Polynices' new father-in law. Adrastos was descended from a kinslayer. That did not bode well.

I looked into the flames once more, silently willing them to reveal more to me, hoping that they would tell what this meant for my own family. The flames revealed nothing. I would have to rely on my own mind, as much as the visions that Apollo bestowed on me.

Those who had committed blood crimes were punished by the gods, them and their descendants. Somehow, this crime must have some connection to my family.

I had to learn to master my newfound skill of looking into the flames. There, I could glimpse the past and learn how it affected the present.

That night, I taught myself to look into the heart of the fire and to let my mind wander so that I opened myself to the vision waiting for me. I spent hours staring into the glowing embers until a dreamlike calm fell over me.

Embers danced above the flames and snapped in the cold night air.

I saw the Sphinx atop her marble perch at the Sacred Way. She unfurled her wings and swept down towards me. As she landed the landscape changed, to the rocky clearing in Thebes where she had bandied words with my father. She cocked her head to the side, a predator's stance, assessing her prey.

"A raven perches atop four skulls. What will hatch?" she asked. Her eyes flickered towards the skulls at the base of her rocky perch. White maggots tumbled from the eye sockets.

"Death," I whispered.

The Sphinx smiled and lunged towards me. I stumbled backwards, tripping over something directly behind me. Instinctively, I put my hands out to brace my fall, my fingertips met with rough cloth.

I looked down. There were corpses littering the ground around me. Dorylas, the bronze tip of a spear embedded in the socket of his eye. Theron, the shaft of a spear in his abdomen. Chromis, a spear through his throat, pinning him to the ground. Their unseeing eyes fixed behind me, towards the Sphinx. I looked towards her once more.

The skulls were no longer white bone, bleached by the sun, but covered with flesh, the faces recognizable.

The first was my brother, Eteocles. A golden diadem perched atop his dark curls.

The face turned towards the head beside him, Polynices, his face obscured by the horsehair helmet atop his head.

The third head belonged to my beloved sister, Antigone, a noose hung from her severed neck.

The fourth head was my own. My eyes were closed, dark lashes fanned across my cheeks. I crawled forwards, my hand reaching towards my own face.

My eyes snapped open.

And the Sphinx, forgotten atop the rocks above me, pounced.

12

ᴀRGOS

It was nearly evening when we reached the end of our path and saw the city laid out before us. I stood atop the hill Argos overlooking the Argolid plains, its twin hill Larissa in the distance. Nestled between these hills was the great city of Argos, its monumental walls looming large before me.

We made our way towards those monumental walls until we came to a gate. When I told the sentries posted there that the seer Tiresias had come to counsel King Adrastos, they opened the gates at once to let us into the city.

The city was sacred to Hera, the queen of the gods, and I found her likeness smiling benevolently down on me wherever I looked. Her great temple, the *Heraion*, sat nearby. But I did not come to Argos to visit with the goddess.

A guard met with us and escorted us to the citadel where we could find the king. Soon, we found who we were looking for. King Adrastos stood in his courtyard, laughing, his hand clasped on the shoulder of a younger man.

My brother.

I looked at him, willing him to recognize me. He didn't even look my way. His eyes followed the figure approaching behind me, a smile brightening his face.

I craned my head to see who he was looking at so fondly. A fair-haired girl approached. My brother's wife, Argia. I was shocked to see the baby she held close to her chest—the child had my brother's dark curls. Adrastos left his son-in-law to see his daughter and grandson.

"Argia, Thessander! What are you doing out here?" he asked, his hands reaching for the child. Argia handed him over and watched silently as her father cooed over the baby. "Why so quiet? What's wrong?"

Argia sighed. "It's my husband. See how his brother's betrayal weighs on him? I give him my heart, give him a son, but nothing is good enough, nothing will make him happy. Not until he has defeated his brother and taken back his homeland. Please, Father, if you love me, you will do this for him. For me. His happiness is my happiness."

"Oh, Argia," Adrastos said, cupping her face with his free hand. "You know it is not for me to declare war. It is for the gods to decide." He kissed her cheek and handed his grandchild back to her and turned towards us.

"You have come to us just as we need your counsel, Tiresias. No doubt you've heard of the Theban prince's betrayal. Tell us, is it fated that we go to war?"

My shoulders tensed. I knew what the seer would say, yet my heart could not bear to hear it.

Tiresias swept me to the side and faced the king. "It is fated for the princes of Thebes to wage war."

Argia cried out and embraced her husband, the two of them smiling, happy that the gods seemed to be on their side.

If only they knew how wrong they were.

Adrastos, to his credit, did not smile nor did he look

pleased at this outcome. The seer's words weighed heavily on him, his shoulders stooped. He faced the seer once more.

"Is there anything else you can tell us, Tiresias? Can you tell us the outcome of this war?"

Tiresias shook his head. "I cannot."

Adrastos shrugged. "I thought as much." He stepped towards us and I flinched back, worried what he might do. He laid a hand on Tiresias' shoulder and drew him alongside him. "I thank you for your service here today. You and your boy there are welcome in my house. You must share bread with us, as Zeus *xenios* commands."

"Thank you, sire," Tiresias replied. His hand reached out and grasped my *chiton*, pulling me close to him.

Adrastos waved a few of his guards over. "Show Tiresias his room for the night. I will send someone to you when it is time to eat."

The guards jerked their heads, indicating that I should follow. I placed Tiresias' hand on my shoulder once more and we made our way inside the citadel.

We wandered through the halls of Adrastos. Dotting the wide halls were statues of Zeus and the Olympian gods and one mortal man. I paused before the statue of the mortal. Something about it caused my guts to clench with unease. The guard escorting us realised we had paused and stomped over to us.

"You aren't here to laze about," he snapped, his eyes following mine to settle on the statue.

"Who is this man?" I asked, knowing in my bones that his identity would have something to do with my search.

"That's Tantalus, son of Zeus, and ancestor to our king Adrastos. Now come on, there is someone that wants to speak to your master." He took hold of my arm and pulled me along.

Tantalus, the figure the cauldron had spoken of in my vision. The kinslayer. It was a great shame to be related to a kinslayer, one tainted by a blood crime. And here Adrastos was showing off that lineage proudly in a hall dedicated to the gods.

Either the king was very brave or very foolish.

We continued throughout the citadel, exiting to enter a small temple. Inside, a tall man stood over an altar. He rubbed a hand at his temple, disturbing the wool fillet across his brow that marked him as a priest.

The guard leaned closer to me and murmured, "That is Amphiaraus. He is a seer, too. The king has also ordered him to divine the gods' will with sacred rites."

Behind me, Tiresias chuckled. "It seems as if the king is not content with my word alone."

"Well, it doesn't hurt to get a second opinion," the guard huffed. "Amphiaraus isn't like you—he does not hear the voice of god, he consults his auguries."

We stood by and watched the seer have a sacrificial animal brought to the altar. He took a knife and opened its abdominal cavity to search the organs of the animal, examining a liver here, a heart there. I knew that their mottled hearts foretold trouble, the thick veins promised adversity. These omens were unfavourable.

Amphiaraus looked down at the organs with a frown. He raised his head and noticed his audience.

The guard cleared his throat. "The seer Tiresias." He stood aside and made his way outside the temple, leaving the seers alone.

Amphiaraus approached. "I cannot lie and say I am pleased to see you here. I know what you have told the king, and I fear what will come to pass."

"You know as well as I what is to come," Tiresias replied.

Unease settled on my shoulders like a heavy cloak. It was bad enough for the Pythia to speak of the war between my brothers, it was entirely worse to see other seers proclaim their fate as well.

Perhaps this would change once I find the source of the curse.

"I have seen what is to come. But I will continue to look for signs that point to a brighter future." Amphiaraus brushed past us and exited the temple. I grabbed Tiresias' arm and pulled him along to follow.

We wandered outside the temple and stopped beside the Argive seer.

Amphiaraus stood out into the open air and looked to the sky. I wondered what he was looking at when I remembered that Zeus' will can be divined through swift birds. I watched how the birds flew unsteadily, how they dipped and fell, unable to soar or glide upon the wind. Not a single raven dotted the sky, a bird of prophecy. Nor Athena's owls, birds of war victorious.

I could see scores of swans drift down from the sky and settle in the fields below swollen from the rain, their masses a white army. From above, seven eagles descended upon them, their flashing talons and hooked beaks promising blood.

Soon, the white circle was red with bloodshed, the swans falling to the eagles. But then, the eagles fell one by one, until all seven were dead as well.

The field had become a massacre.

I was not sure what it meant but I was uncomfortable all the same and I turned to Amphiaraus to discern his reaction. He squinted into the sky, a trembling hand reaching up to shield his eyes. He was crying. He knew what the omens meant, he knew they boded ill. He would make sure Argos did not go to war, I was sure of it.

Tiresias and I retired to our room to rest and wash away the grime of the road. Soon, an attendant arrived to convey us to the central hall for a feast.

Hundreds of men bustled about me, all smiling, all in good spirits. They were celebrating that they were about to go to war.

I saw Adrastos in their midst, a *kylix* of wine in his hands, the only figure in the hall to wear a frown. My brother and Tydeus standing at his side, grinning. I saw the seer Amphiaraus with them. His long face was mournful, his dark eyes sad. How could he allow them to go to war? How could he let them do this when the omens spelled disaster?

There was another man with them. He was broader even than Tydeus and as tall as Haemon. His fair hair was slicked back, his face half-hidden behind a bristling beard. He clapped the seer on the shoulder and the smaller man buckled from the force of that hand.

"Why must we wait for more omens from this one? The gods do not control what we do. We as men make our own decisions! We fight our own battles, we win our own wars without their help."

Amphiaraus skirted away from him. "Keep that blasphemous tongue away from me," he muttered.

Adrastos set down his drink with a sigh. "Capaneus, we all know you scorn the gods. Just do it away from us. I am a pious man and I look to the gods for their approval."

"I already told you," Amphiaraus said, looking mournfully at his companions. "The Fates and the Gods oppose this war. No matter what I say we will go, we will fight, and we will all die."

Capaneus laughed. "You learned this from a bunch of birds? I do not believe it. I have already outshone the deeds of my father and his father before him. No man can compete with me. We have Tydeus, who is a match for fifty men. Polynices is skilled in combat and has justice on his side. We will be victorious no matter how the birds fly." He spat at the seer's feet. "I spit on your prophecies."

Amphiaraus' eyes narrowed. "No man can escape death. Not even you, Capaneus, son of Hipponous."

The five men were soon blocked from my sight as a figure stepped in front of me. "Hey!" I began to protest, pushing at the shoulders that blocked my view. I needed to get closer and hear what they were saying. I went to stride past the man but another blocked my way. The press of bodies propelled me to the outskirts of the room. I was about to dive into the crowds once more when I paused.

Tiresias was busy dining with the king. The hall was so busy no one would miss me.

Now was my chance. While everyone was assembled in the hall, I had to go looking for clues of the curse.

I slipped through the crowds until I came to the long hall the guard had led us through earlier, dotted with statues, their features cast with flickering firelight from the braziers standing alongside them. I walked among each figure, Zeus, Poseidon, Hades, Hera, Demeter and on and on until at last I came to Tantalus. The bronze figure bore a striking resemblance to Adrastos.

I gazed at the figure, hoping it would reveal the clues I was searching for. It stared blankly back at me, half its face cast in shadows. I looked around and noticed another figure, one I had not seen when we first arrived.

Facing the statue of Tantalus was another statue of a youth, unsmiling, looking ahead at the figure across from him. At the statue's feet sat a small, bronze cauldron.

Heat raced through my veins. I rushed across the hall. The cauldron was a miniature version of the one I had seen at Delphi, the one I had seen when I had looked into the flames. It was a statue of Pelops. I stood there for some time, waiting for some clue to reveal itself. But nothing happened.

Look into the fire.

I took a breath and closed my eyes before turning to the brazier that stood beside the statue. I gazed into the small flame, counting each intake and release of breath. Soon, I lost myself.

I was in a darkened chamber, the cauldron I had seen at Delphi sat within the centre of the room, a fire lit underneath it. I drew closer and that hollow voice began to speak.

"The gods, disgusted by Tantalus' act, had brought Pelops back to life. Pelops won the hand of Hippodamia from her father Oenomaus, the fearsome king of Pisa, who challenged all his daughter's suitors to a deadly chariot race. Pelops won through deception. He had the king's servant Myrtilus replace the pins of his master's chariot with ones made of wax and watched with delight when the chariot fell apart and the king was dragged to death by his own horses. The price for Myrtilus' betrayal was one night with Hippodamia, but Pelops killed him before he could take his reward. With his dying breath, Myrtilus cursed Pelops and all of his line."

A pair of hands reached out from within the cauldron and I stumbled back, falling onto the ground. When I looked up, I was back in the hall of statues, the statue of Pelops looming over me.

Pelops was cursed as well, his father's impious acts affecting his own future. But what did his curse have to do with the curse of my family?

I did not sleep well that night, the words from within the cauldron playing in my mind again and again. Pelops, the son of a man who offended the gods by committing a blood crime, had been cursed for breaking a vow. I knew that Eteocles had broken a vow, but what else was the vision in the flames trying to tell me? That a blood crime would be committed?

The worst blood crimes were committed against kin—fathers killing sons, sons killing fathers, brothers killing brothers. Was my vision trying to tell me that if I could prevent my brothers from committing the crime of fratricide, I could then stop the war?

I lay in bed thinking over my vision until the pale light of morning reached through the window. I rose with a yawn and went to wake the old seer.

Tiresias and I sat in the courtyard that morning and watched the Argive men prepare for war. Hundreds of men bustled about me, all clad in armour, all armed.

I saw Adrastos in their midst, a horse tail plumed helmet held under the crook of his arm. My brother at his side, his arms around a broad figure. Tydeus. The sight of him made my skin crawl and visions of my friend's bodies dance before my eyes. From the looks on their faces, it seemed as if the three figures were arguing. I left Tiresias' side to get closer.

Polynices let go of Tydeus and gripped his father-in-law's

forearm. "You know what I have lost, what my brother denies me still. I must do this."

"Your brother will pay for his crimes against you. We do not need to wage war to do it," Adrastos said.

"I need to wage war on my brother and take back what is rightfully mine, to prove what kind of man I am."

Adrastos sighed. "We *know* what kind of man you are. You don't need to prove it to the world."

I bore no love for the family Polynices had found to replace our own, but listening to Adrastos, I could tell he was a wise man. I only wished he could make Polynices see how pointless his war really was.

"I do," Polynices urged.

Tydeus nodded. "The Thebans have no piety. No sense of right or wrong. They attacked me, a messenger, sacred to Zeus himself! If we do not wage war on them, they will wage war on us." A speech on piety from a kinslayer. I was not impressed.

"We do not have the men," Adrastos insisted.

"It took fifty of their men to face me, and I killed every one of them. One Argive is worth fifty of them."

Adrastos did not look convinced by Tydeus' argument.

"We do have the men. I have called for allies." Polynices began to list men. He gestured towards another man who stood off by himself, tending to his horses, the armed men who milled about giving him a wide berth.

The man was taller even than Capaneus and just as broad. His horses foamed at the mouth, the white flecked with red. The man reached into his saddlebags and handed red meat to them. He fed them carefully, those dreadful mares were just as likely to start feasting on his own flesh as the meat he fed to them. I recognized them from stories that Pyrrha had told me—they were Getic steeds bred by Diomedes the fearsome king of Thrace.

"Be still, Podargos. You too Lampon. Here now, that was for Xanthos, not for you, Deinos," the giant man murmured to his horses.

The others kept their distance from his monstrous steeds, even Tydeus. He drew as close as he dared and said, "Leave off, Hippomedon. He should be here soon."

"Alright, one moment," Hippomedon replied as he wiped his bloody hands on his *chiton* and joined the others. The person they seemed to be waiting for rode into the courtyard.

The boy seated atop the wild horse was younger than the others, his face bare, no beard on his smooth cheeks. His fair hair fell down his back to where a bow and quiver rested. He was as beautiful as a girl but he had a fierce expression on his face, daring anyone to mention his looks. He swiftly dismounted and approached the king and princes of Argos.

"You have Arcadia." He grinned as the others clapped him on the back.

"He is too young to go to war," I murmured to myself. I jumped when a voice beside me answered.

"That boy is among the greatest warriors of his age," Tiresias said. "That is the son of Atalanta, who sailed with Jason and the Argonauts and felled the Calydonian boar that ravaged the woods. His name is Parthenopaeus."

It was difficult to reconcile Tiresias' words with the boy who stood before me. Small and slight and pretty as a girl, Parthenopaeus didn't look like he could hurt anyone.

It was as if Tiresias read my thoughts. "He may not look like much but that boy and the men he stands with are the

Seven against Thebes. Men will sing of their deeds, their fearsome siege of the city. Argos has three thousand men."

I remembered Amphiaraus' words, that all the seven would die. Even though my greatest wish was for this war to end, I hoped his omens were wrong.

As we spent our last night dining in the halls of King Adrastos, I took this opportunity to watch my brother.

Polynices seemed happy here, among his new family. But try as I might to be happy for him, I found his smiles making me angrier and angrier. Instead of reconciling and taking his place among his new family, my brother chose to use the resources of that new family to wage war on his old one. Like a spoiled child, he wanted what he cannot have, what he thought belonged to him.

The king of Argos seemed like a good man, a pious man. But his efforts to change his family history by embracing his lineage seemed to be a grotesque display of his inherited guilt. How could anyone live with a family like that, how could they stand to be descended from such violence? I thought back to the voice from the cauldron and resolved to learn more before we left Argos.

I slipped from the hall to view the rows of statues, stopping before the statue of Pelops, hidden at the end of the corridor.

I breathed in and out and looked into the small tongues of flames licking at the edges of the braziers and willed myself into that ghostly chamber with the cursed cauldron.

And there I was.

A fire was lit beneath the cauldron, casting eerie shadows along the walls of the chamber, smoke billowed out from the gaping maw and a voice spoke from within.

"I speak to you now, of the sons of Pelops. When an oracle declared that the kingdom of Mycenae would be ruled by a son of Pelops, an intense rivalry sprang up between Atreus and Thyestes. Atreus won the throne with the golden fleece. But Thyestes seduced Atreus' wife Aerope, who stole the fleece and delivered it to her lover. Thyestes took his brother's throne, his wife, and cast him into exile. When his exile was finished, Atreus returned to Mycenae to claim his throne and to deal with his brother."

The smoke cleared and a figure emerged from the cauldron. No, two figures. The statues of the two princes I had seen at Delphi. The figures stood together, each with a foot forward, trying to outpace the other. These were the sons of Pelops, Atreus and Thyestes.

"What did Atreus do?" I asked, looking from one figure to the next. The figure on the right opened its marble mouth to continue.

"You must journey to Mycenae to find out how the curse of the house of Tantalus will affect the brothers."

Brother fighting brother. The similarity to my own family's situation was not lost on me. Two princes warring over succession. I *needed* to get to Mycenae and learn how to stop the two brothers. If the crimes of their father and grandfather were any indication, the outcome of the two brothers coming to a head could be disastrous.

I closed my eyes and steadied myself. When I opened my eyes, I was back in the corridor. I looked into the face of Pelops. I watched the light of the braziers flicker across his bronze face, the shadows made it look as if Pelops was also watching me.

Without glancing back, I returned to the hall to find Tiresias and ask him how to find the sons of Pelops, Atreus and Thyestes.

13

MYCENAE

I must understand the curse on my family to break it, only then can I save them.

To learn more about the curse, I must heed my visions and come to know more about the cursed families who also left dedications for the god, hoping to change their fate. In Mycenae, I would learn more about the twin statues and the warring princes they represented.

We headed across the Argive Plain to the city of Mycenae.

One of the greatest cities in Hellas, the citadel was guarded by the hills themselves, the city protected by the crook of rock around it. Fortification walls added to the protection of the landscape, the stones of the walls so large they could only have been moved by the Cyclopes themselves.

Mycenae was quiet. Unlike Argos, there were no crowds of soldiers preparing for war. In comparison, Mycenae seemed like a ghost city. Though it was eerie, it was also peaceful.

The Mycenaean fortifications sat atop a hilltop, a defensive position. Up there, I felt as if I could touch the heavens themselves, the blue sky stretched out above me, like a bolt of cloth dyed with crushed lapis lazuli. White clouds hung low like balls of unspun wool scattered across the sky, waiting to be spun by the winds.

It was a beautiful place, but I couldn't help but feel uneasy.

To gain entrance to the citadel, we had to pass through The Lion Gate, so called for the stone lions that sat atop the lintel of the gate. The lions stand opposite one another, their forepaws resting on the twin altars supporting the column between them. Their faces looked forward to those approaching the city, their mouths twisted as if they would let out a great roar.

There was a word in our language for these beasts of stone. Each lion was *apotropaic*. It meant to turn away, to banish. They acted as symbols to turn away evil, to banish danger from that city.

As I crossed beneath the threshold, gazing up at the lions standing guard above me, I couldn't help but think they were failing at their job. For something evil lurked in that city, some danger I had seen in the flames. A threat that would help me discover the truth about the evil that threatened my own family.

The palace at Mycenae was much like the Cadmeia. The central hall was arranged around a *megaron*, the walls surrounding it painted with brightly-coloured animals, guardians meant to protect the space from harm. Or, they were once brightly-coloured. The billowing smoke from the fire had stained the walls with black, the darkness creeping down from the ceiling, obscuring the guardians meant to protect the hall.

The tables dotting the hall showed evidence that a feast was underway. Wine flowed from *kylikes*, their rims adorned with painted eyes that watched as Tiresias and I approached the throne.

Sitting on a chair amidst the preparations was a young man, a sheepskin of glittering gold was draped across his shoulders. He watched our approach from underneath lowered brows, a scowl twisted his features.

Tiresias placed a gnarled hand on my shoulder and I made my way towards the man. He did not rise to greet us.

"These halls are not as welcome as they once were, Thyestes, son of Pelops," Tiresias said, his voice echoing throughout the empty hall.

Thyestes stood, kicking his chair out of his way as he approached.

"Last time you were here, seer, I ruled these halls. They are my brother's now. Expect no welcome from me old man. You and your gods have taken my kingdom from me." He spat.

"Your kingdom was taken from you due to your own folly," Tiresias quipped in response. "You were advised by the gods themselves to vacate the throne for your brother, yet you refused. Saying you would relinquish power only if the sun would rise from the west and set in the east. Lord Zeus punished you for this folly by making it so."

Thyestes strode towards us and stood facing the seer. His face darkened with anger. "Yes, Zeus has punished me. Now, I must be a guest in my own hall while my brother prepares a feast in honour of my departure."

As he spoke, I saw a flicker of movement out of the corner of my eye. A man strode by the four pillars around the *megaron* to approach us. He bore a striking resemblance to Thyestes, but while Thyestes' face was darkened with anger, Atreus' was bright and cheerful.

"Greetings, Tiresias! To what do we owe this honour?"

"I have been sent by the gods to watch over your reconciliation with your brother," Tiresias replied, his lips pursing slightly.

Atreus' smile sharpened and he cast his eyes on the servants that bustled about the hall preparing for the feast.

"By all means, join us. You can see how I forgive my brother for his deeds." Though Atreus smiled as he spoke, his words were hardened with ill feeling. He gestured to one of the servants who appeared dutifully at his side. "Take Tiresias and his attendant and prepare them for the feast."

The servant nodded and made her way out of the central hall. I followed, lifting a hand to my shoulder to make sure Tiresias' hand was still there.

As we walked through the grand halls of the citadel, I felt the unease rise within me.

I thought of my purpose here in Mycenae. Was I here to watch the brother's reconcile? Would this give me a clue on how to reconcile my own brothers?

After what seemed like an age, a familiar voice began to whisper in my mind.

Remember what I told you. You must come to understand the curse on your house. You cannot reconcile your brothers.

"How can you say that?" I muttered, hoping no one could hear me. "Look at Atreus and Thyestes. Thyestes stole Atreus' throne and his wife and here, Atreus is holding a feast of reconciliation before his brother leaves. Despite their violent family history, the brothers are attempting to end the feud between them. Is it so crazy to think I could end the feud between my brother?"

You continue to willfully ignore me. You cannot change your fate. The best you can do is come to understand it.

"You're wrong. I can change the fate of my family."

You will fail.

"You're wrong," I repeated.

The servant leading us to our chamber paused in her journey and came scurrying back to us.

"Come along, I am instructed to show you to your room," she huffed.

I hurried after her, hoping to leave the voice of the god behind me.

The harried servant showed us to a small room with two small beds. Tiresias sank into the nearest one. I stood in the doorway while I decided what to do. I was surprised when the woman spoke behind me.

"You look like you've had a hard journey. If you aren't going to rest, the least you can do is clean up before the feast. I will bring the oils." She nodded her head at me and left.

The woman returned bearing a *lekythos* of oil and a *strigil*, a blunt blade. She handed the items to me without a word and departed.

I cast a quick glance at Tiresias and then chided myself. The man was blind. But I had to make sure no one else came into our quarters to discover that I was not a boy.

I went to the doorway and looked down the hall and waited to see if anyone would approach. It seemed as if everyone was preparing for tonight's feast. Even then, I undressed as quickly as I could, keeping the strip of linen bound about my chest even though I ached to take it off.

I poured the oil onto my body and used the *strigil* to scrape all the grit from the road from my skin. When I was finished, I hurriedly got dressed, wishing I could have washed my clothes as well.

Though there was a feast to look forward to, I found I wasn't hungry. The sense of unease gnawing at my insides made me feel queasy and unwell. I waited anxiously for the woman to return to take us to the feast so I could watch the reconciliation between the brothers.

After Tiresias was well-rested, the servant woman returned to take us to eat. We entered the central hall for the feast. Tables were laden with sacrificial meat and wine, the splendour of the tables at odds with the darkness that prevailed over the halls.

Thyestes appeared in good spirits, gorging himself on the food laid out before him.

I sat and reached for food but Tiresias slapped my hand away. I glared at him and was surprised to see the horror etched on his face.

Atreus, seated on his throne, looked over at the aghast seer and smiled.

Thyestes followed his brother's gaze and looked towards us, his face darkening. His hand dripped with grease, morsels of meat slipping from between his slick fingertips.

"Why aren't you eating? You disrespect my brother and the gods by not partaking in his welcome."

Tiresias' next words came out in a horse croak. "This is no feast of welcome, Thyestes. This is a cursed feast."

Thyestes laughed, half chewed morsels flying from his lips to litter the table before him. "Don't be ridiculous, old man. This is the finest meat I have ever tasted! Tell me, brother, what beast did you sacrifice for such a feast?"

And though he was blind Tiresias closed his eyes, as if willing himself not to witness what happened next.

I looked on in fascination as Atreus waved a servant over.

The servant approached her former master with a basket covered with a white cloth. As she passed, the shadows of the *megaron* flickered over her, casting her in shadow, yet its light seemed to illuminate the hidden contents. Red firelight outlined two faces beneath the cloth. As soon as the light appeared it disappeared, casting the hall in shadow once more.

My stomach plummeted. I gazed at the basket in horror as the servant came to a halt before Thyestes.

"Go on, show my brother what he has dined on tonight," Atreus called out jovially to the servant woman.

With a grimace, the woman drew back the cloth and turned her head away.

Thyestes looked eagerly into its depths and immediately recoiled.

Inside the basket sat the severed heads and hands of two boys.

Thyestes looked once more and let out a wail. He grabbed the basket from the woman and she fled the hall.

Thyestes cradled the basket in his arms, gazing down in anguish as he recognized the faces of the boys in the basket.

Atreus had served Thyestes his own sons.

I stood, my chair crashing to the floor behind me. I raced out of the halls into the open night air. I rushed out onto the ramparts and wrapped my head in my hands.

Just as his father before him, Thyestes had broken a vow.

Just as his grandfather before him, Atreus had held a cursed feast.

Now their family lay in ruins. And for what? A throne?

I beat my hands against my head and tried to shut out the image of the boys in the basket, to shut out the look of terror and betrayal frozen on their faces.

I felt a hand on my shoulder.

"Go away, Tiresias!" I sobbed, shaking the hand from me.

"It's not Tiresias," a familiar voice answered.

I looked up in alarm.

Apollo loomed over me. In the dim light of the evening, he shone like a star.

"What do you *want* from me?" I shrieked, launching myself towards him. Apollo kept his ground. I wanted to pummel him with my fists but dared not to. "Why are you doing this? You say I have the chance to save my family if I discover the source of the curse, yet all you've really done is sent me on a wild goose chase around Hellas, watching these families do the most horrible things to each other! Why won't you let me save my family?"

"Do you remember what your cousin told you the day you went to see the Pythia?" Apollo replied.

I stared at him, not comprehending. "What does that have to do with anything?"

"Think, Ismene. What did your cousin tell you?"

I thought back to that morning at the Pythian games, while we waited outside the Temple of Apollo. "Oracles are obscure. Many men have taken her words to mean one thing when they really pointed to another. They aren't clear with their answers because those asking the questions must be clear with themselves. They need to know if they are asking the right questions."

"Are you asking the right questions, Ismene?"

I stared at him as I tried to think. Of course, he wouldn't tell me outright. To save my family, I had to earn it. I had shouted my frustrations at the god, but I hadn't thought my questions through. I had to understand the curse on my family to try to break it. But how was the curse on my family related to that of the curse of the house of Tantalus?

"Please." The word was stuck in my throat as I addressed the god intent on destroying my family. "Please, tell me. How does the curse of Tantalus relate to my own family curse?"

Apollo smiled. "Better. Think, Ismene. What have you learned on your travels?"

"I have learned how Tantalus and his line have been cursed for his crime against the gods."

"And what crime was that?"

"He is a kinslayer. He killed his son. And though his son was revived by the gods, the taint of that crime clung to him. He broke an oath. And now his sons have broken oaths and killed their kin in turn," I answered. Silently, I wondered what all that had to do with my own family.

Apollo smirked. *I heard that.*

I glared at him in response, cleared my throat and repeated

the question aloud. "What does that have to do with my family?"

Apollo leaned in close. Heat emanated off his body. "What was our bargain?"

I shuddered at the flood of warmth his presence brought. "I vowed to go into your service if I could not find the source of my family curse and try to break it."

He stared at me, not responding.

"My visions pointed me towards Tantalus and his descendants. I have witnessed firsthand how Tantalus' crime has contributed to the violence between two brothers. So…" I floundered, looking up into the god's eyes. They blazed like the sun. I looked away. "So…there must be some crime that was committed by one of my own ancestors. A blood crime that has tainted our line and is responsible for the violence."

Apollo smiled again. "You've got it."

"So what do I do next? Wait for another vision in the flames? You are here now. Can't you just tell me?" I knew I was being bold, too bold, with the god, but he seemed to like that.

"I suppose. But I won't tell you outright. Like Atreus and Thyestes, the crime tainting your family goes back to your father and grandfather. You must come to know your father to know the curse."

"Come to know my father," I mused. I stared off into the night. "Oh! I must go to Corinth. The city that raised my father, I must meet my grandparents, the king and queen."

Apollo nodded.

We stood in silence for some time, watching the stars shine in the night sky. But even their light did not compare to the light emanating from the god standing beside me.

I cast him a suspicious glance.

"Why are you even helping me? I thought you wanted me to fail?"

"I want you to understand," he corrected me.

"I think you need to understand where I am coming from. People don't want to believe that the Fates control their lives. Is it so bad to want to be in control? Is it so bad to believe that things will turn out well despite the odds against them?" I was thinking of my own family and the curses that foretold our doom.

"That's the problem," Apollo answered. "You think you are acting against fate when all you are doing is playing into it."

I shook my head. "Enough. Are you starting an argument to try to distract me?"

He grinned. "Is it working?"

I smiled back at him despite myself. I should hate this god that cursed my family and city to be destroyed. And yet...

He tilted his head, as if he was listening to my thoughts. He probably was, I realised, a blush creeping up my neck and into my cheeks.

"You should go in. Rest. The journey to Corinth will be a tiring one for you."

One moment he was there, the next he had disappeared.

I glanced around the empty hilltop, his absence leaving me in the dark.

The next morning when I woke, Tiresias and I prepared to leave. On our way out, we stopped in the central hall to say our farewells.

The food from last night's feast was strewn across the table, quickly going dark with rot, a musty stench wafting about the room. The halls of Mycenae were truly a place of darkness and decay.

Still on the same chair amidst the rotting feast sat Thyestes. He stared at the table before him, his jaw slack, his hands clenching and unclenching. He was in shock.

Tiresias patted his hand on my shoulder, consoling me. I steeled myself against Thyestes' grief, his guilt.

As we came to a stop before him, Thyestes remained seated, tearing his gaze from the table before him to glare up at us.

"What do you want?" he growled, glaring up at the blind old man. His eyes skirted towards me and I averted my gaze and turned my attention to my surroundings. Maggots spilled from the rotting food atop the table.

"I have come to give you guidance," Tiresias replied, unfazed by the angry man before him.

"Where was your guidance when I welcomed my brother home? Where was your guidance yesterday when I let him hold his little feast?" Thyestes snarled.

I gazed around in mute horror, staring at the aftermath of the cursed feast. This wasn't a dining hall anymore, it was a tomb.

"Atreus will pay for his impiety," Tiresias said, his voice resounding throughout the dark halls.

Thyestes froze, hearing the authority in his voice. For all his anger, he knew that Tiresias spoke the future. "You swear it?" he whispered, the anger in his face replaced by eagerness.

"It is ordained by the gods. Atreus and his sons will suffer for their impiety."

Thyestes smiled so broadly his lip split and blood trickled down his chin. "Come." He stood and waved a hand to usher us forwards. "Tell me, what other guidance do you have to offer me?"

"You have suffered greatly at the hands of your brother. But you must move forward. You have lost your sons, yes, but you will have another. Your son Aegisthus will avenge you."

Thyestes' eyes narrowed. "How?"

"He will kill Atreus." Thyestes brightened at this news. "You must leave these halls, know that you will be avenged by your son."

I turned away as Thyestes eagerly listened to how he would be avenged.

I wished we had never come to Mycenae.

14

CORINTH

It was half a day's journey from the citadel of Mycenae to Corinth. Tiresias and I took our time on the road, walking in uncomfortable silence.

Though the god insisted that I had needed to witness the impiety of Atreus to better understand the curse on my own house, I wished I had never seen it. How could someone hate their own brother so much they would do something like that to him? Thinking of my own brothers, I thought of all the jealousy between them and how it had festered into hatred. Just what might they do to each other? And would I be able to stop them before they could do it?

When the midday sun blazed overhead, Tiresias and I searched for some shade to eat. We reached a grove of short trees and settled beneath its cool canopy. I withdrew the bread the servant woman had thrust at me before we left, a wordless apology for last night's events written on her face.

I handed some to Tiresias and we ate in silence. Through the gaps in the canopy of leaves overhead, I watched the flight of birds, thinking of Amphiaraus and the way he divined his own doom by watching bird flight. I glanced up and saw Tiresias' face turned towards mine.

"Considering the signs are you?" Tiresias smiled without humour. "While I cannot see the birds that fly overhead, I know that as we speak your brother's ally Hippomedon now leads the Argives across the Asopos River. Intent on war, the men march night and day, barely pausing to eat or rest. They ignore the signs that point to death."

"What signs?" I leaned forward.

"Oh, you know, the usual. The entrails are bad, birds flying the wrong way, rivers running backward, stars refusing to shine. Disembodied voices, rains of blood. That sort of thing. The signs, those *augurs*"—he sneered as he spoke the word—"use to divine the will of the gods. As if the gods speak to them." He scoffed.

I never knew how he felt about other seers. Being the greatest seer in all Hellas and being able to commune with the gods himself, it was no wonder he scorned the lengths other seers went to trying to divine the future.

"Even though the signs are bad, they ignore them." He drew his knees up, his bones creaked with age. "If a seer only looks for signs that point to victory, then they are responsible for their own downfall."

We sat in silence for a few minutes until my curiosity drove me to speak.

"If the gods don't speak to the seers through signs, then what is the point?"

"That's not what I meant." Tiresias sighed. "The gods do not always speak to us through signs, but signs do carry importance. When signs convey importance to an individual, that importance, that sense of meaning it conveys, can become fuel for the gods."

"I don't understand." I shifted, drawing my legs out from under me and repositioning them.

"What is placed upon an altar as an offering to a god?" Tiresias asked.

"Part of the feast," I replied.

"Which part? The meat?"

"No, bones wrapped in fat."

"And do the gods eat that?"

"No, the gods only eat ambrosia."

"So why do we offer it?"

I sat in thought. "We offer it because of what it represents. We give the gods a place at our tables, we offer them what they believe is the choicest part of the feast."

He nods. "It is what it represents that is important, not the object itself."

"I still don't understand," I admitted.

He smiled. "You will, little princess. "

I froze.

"How do you know who I am?" I asked.

A smile spread across his face.

"How do I know? Really, girl. I thought another seer would have more sense. You are like me, little princess. We both hear the voice of the god whisper in our minds. While I cannot see what is in front of me with my eyes, I can see all that is happening, before, after, even now."

"What do you see now?"

He tilted his head to the side, as if looking past me.

"Wait a moment." He sat like this for what seemed for some time before he came back to himself. "Your brother's men. They've crossed the river into Boeotia and they've made camp. The sentries atop the seven gates have seen them, and they are afraid. The gods' ears are plagued with prayers, and families hold each other close."

"It took all that time just to learn that?" I asked, impressed and slightly jealous that my visions came to me in riddles while his visions came as they happened.

"Not just that. There's something else."

"Well?" I prompted when he did not continue.

"Your sister has gone to the Argive camp to meet with your brother."

I bolted upright. "Did he meet with her? What did she say?"

"She is trying to persuade him to come with her, to speak to Eteocles. She promised to mediate the meeting so that they can come to some sort of bargain."

"What did he say?" My hands twisted in my filthy *chiton*. "Did he say he would go?"

"Before your brother could answer her, Tydeus spoke for him."

My heart sank.

"He reminded your brother of the attack on him when he went to meet your brother months ago. Polynices will not meet with the king." Tiresias cocked his head to the side again. When he came back to himself once more, he rose to his feet. "We should leave now if we want to arrive in Corinth before nightfall."

I nodded and stood, allowing him to rest his frail hand on my shoulder. A nervous flutter in the depths of my stomach. So far, I had learned of how a curse had made monsters of the men of a single family, and now I was on my way to learn how my own family's curse might make monsters of my brothers.

I hoped Corinth would give me the answers I sought.

On our way to the city, we watched an ambling cart of traders approach. Tiresias grabbed my arm and urged me to go over to them.

"What for?" I asked.

"You need to change."

"What?"

"Your clothes. You need to change your clothes," Tiresias snapped.

"Why?" I looked down at myself. My short *chiton* had gone grey with dust and was splattered with dried mud.

"You can't approach your grandparents like that. You need new clothes."

"Alright, I will get a new *chiton*." I started towards the traders but Tiresias held me back.

"Get a long *chiton*."

"But then, I would enter the city as a girl," I protested.

"That is the point. You need to meet your grandparents as their granddaughter, not as a boy, not as my servant."

"But that changes everything! It isn't proper for an unwed girl to travel with a man she isn't related to, people will talk."

"Then we'll tell them we are related," he snapped. "I'll say you are my daughter."

I raised an eyebrow. "Oh? And what is the daughter of the great Tiresias called?"

He thought for a moment. "Manto."

I laughed. Manto meant seer in our language. "A little on the nose, don't you think?"

"It is a good name, you'll see," he huffed. He pressed on

my arm and urged me forward. "Now go, get something fitting for the daughter of the greatest seer in Hellas."

Still laughing, I waved at the traders and they halted their cart and watched eagerly as I approached. Luckily, they were cloth merchants and carried *chitons* of soft wool to trade. I asked their price but the traders recognized my companion and asked for a prophecy as their payment.

The traders headed over to Tiresias to ask their questions and the remaining man handed me a girl's *chiton* dyed with onion skins to a deep orange. The weaver in me, recognizing the fine work, complimented their skill. The traders returned, pleased with their prophecy, they handed me some ribbons as well as a new mantle for the old man.

We waved our farewells and once the traders' cart had rolled out of sight, I headed over to the stream that flowed nearby and stripped out of my filthy *chiton* to wash. I splashed the cool water onto my limbs to wash the dust from my skin. I ducked my head into the stream and combed through my hair with my fingers and used the ribbons the traders had given to me to pull my shoulder length hair into a knot at the base of my neck.

I fastened the long *chiton* at my shoulders, luxuriating in the feel of clean clothes. I gazed down into the stream and stared at the stranger reflected there.

She was not a princess of Thebes, a son of the *Spartoi*, or a servant to a seer. She was just a girl. She could be anyone. *I* could be anyone.

Staring at the stranger I had become, I toyed with the idea of becoming someone else. Someone free from the expectations of being an aristocratic woman. I would no longer be urged to stay indoors, as a girl should, hidden from the men around her until she was ready for marriage. Instead, I could forgo social norms and live on the outskirts of society, to do as I pleased, to answer to no one.

I could do anything, I could be anyone.

I raised my eyes from the stream to look at the gentle rise of mountains in the distance, the fertile plains for growing crops and grazing cattle and sheep, and down again at the spring, its waters clear and cool in the rising heat of the afternoon. I imagined what it would be like to be a farmer's daughter or a shepherd who leads her flock to graze at the foot of the mountain. I imagined being anyone but a girl whose city, whose family was destined to be destroyed. It would be so easy to walk away and become someone else.

But to do that I would have to forsake my family.

I turned from that fantasy I had created for myself and went to join the seer so that we could continue on our journey to the city.

The city of Corinth sat atop a hill whose height rivaled that of Mycenae, the hill overlooking a rocky plain. Corinth was a powerful city in their own right. While Mycenae gained its power from its defensive location amidst the hills, Corinth was a powerhouse of trade, its city situated closely to the *isthmus*, a narrow land bridge connecting the Peloponnese to the rest of the mainland.

The sight of the city stirred a strange emotion in me. I was afraid but eager, glad but sad. It was in this place, the home of my father, that I would learn how to save my family. But I would also learn how my father had cursed that family in the first place.

We made the climb to the city and were admitted at once, the name of famous seer Tiresias a curiosity for the aristocratic elite. Men at arms escorted us to the palace and into the ceremonial hall.

Two stone thrones sat on a dais, but only one was occupied. A frail older woman perched on the edge of the throne, her eyes hungrily watching the seer's approach. This woman was my paternal grandmother, Merope, the queen of Corinth. I searched her face for some echo of my own but found none.

"Greetings, Queen Merope! My daughter and I thank you for your welcome in your halls," Tiresias called to the woman who sat before us.

Merope smiled. It was not a friendly smile. She flicked a hand at her guards and they departed so that we were the only three figures in the hall.

"I have waited long to speak to you, seer. Doubtless you know that when my son was a young man a rumour spread like wildfire through these halls. A rumour that he was not the true prince of Corinth. A drunk guest of our hall, cast aspersions on my son, saying he was not the true born son of King Polybus and Queen Merope. Now, my son did not like that and he went off to Delphi to ask the god about his parents himself. It was in Delphi that my son heard of the prophecy. A false prophecy.

The *Pythia* told him that it was his fate to kill his father. Instead of returning home to Corinth, to my husband and to me, my poor son fled trying to turn the course of his fate and to save his father from death. If he didn't go home, the prophecy would not be fulfilled. He journeyed to Thebes, and there saved its city from the Sphinx and married its queen. The prophecy was wrong. If you are here to tell me of any more prophecies, you are wasting your time.”

I trembled beneath the old seer’s hand. The prophecy about my father sounded more like a curse. I shook myself from Tiresias’ hold and approached the queen.

“We have not come to tell you prophecies. We came so that I might meet you.”

I readied myself for ridicule, for the queen to laugh in my face outright, saying she had no interest in meeting the daughter of a blind old man. But she did not laugh. She gazed at me in silence, her eyes skimming me up and down, resting at last on my face. While I could find no echo of myself in her face, she found an echo in mine.

The queen stared down at me, eyes wide with surprise. “And who are you?”

“I am Ismene, princess of Thebes. I am the daughter of Oedipus and Jocasta.”

Merope rose from her seat and approached me warily. “I should have you beaten for lying to a queen. The seer just introduced you to me as his daughter, and now you are claiming to be my granddaughter? And yet—” She reached out a quivering hand to rest on my chin, tilting my face one way and then the other. “Yet, I see him in you. In the colour of your eyes, the shape of your nose. Why have you come to me?”

I grasped my grandmother’s hand.

“I have come for your help. There is a curse on our house, a curse on my father. If I cannot break it, my brothers, your grandsons, are doomed to die at each other’s hands.”

I told her everything, about Apollo, Delphi, Eteocles' broken vow and Polynices' war. As I spoke, I did not notice Tiresias depart from the hall so that my grandmother and I were alone.

When I had come to the end of my tale she gazed at me with sadness, her eyes welling with tears.

"You poor child, burdened with such a fate," she murmured, cupping my cheek in her frail hand.

"But don't you see, I can change my fate, I will change it," I vowed.

"You sound just like him. Your father. He believed he had the power to change his fate as well. He heard the prophecy he was destined to kill his father and fled from it. To stop himself from hurting my husband, you see?" She smiled, her eyes unfocused, as if she were watching her distant memories. Then, her face changed. Her eyes focused, darting around the room. Her hand gripped mine hard. "But he didn't know, you see, we never told him. Never said a word." She went on, eyes searching the dark corners. Her tongue darted out to wet her lips, the image bringing snakes to my mind.

"What didn't he know?" I asked her warily.

Her eyes passed over the shadows to fix on my face. "I was, I *am*, his mother. Always have been, always will be. But I never gave *birth* to him." She settled one of her hands over her womb.

Unease gnawed at me. "You didn't give birth to him?"

"No, no... A shepherd found him exposed on a mountainside."

"Exposed?" I repeated, puzzled.

"Yes, exposed. Exposed to the elements. They pierced his feet with a nail, bound them together and took him to Mount Cithaeron to die. Like they do with all the unwanted children."

I did not know people disposed of their children, let alone *how* they did it. I drew back in horror. How could someone have done that to a baby?

"The shepherd found him and knew that Polybus and I longed for a son of our own and brought him to us. We raised him as our own. He is our son."

"But the prophecy, that he would kill his father, never meant Polybus. So he *could* have killed his own father but never knew it." The flames in their braziers blazed, and I knew the god was signalling his agreement. I had to find out who my father's true father was. And whether my father became his murderer.

I left my grandmother and sought out the seer.

Tiresias sat in the corridor waiting for me. I sat down next to him.

"So, what did your grandmother tell you?"

I glanced at him. "I think you already know, don't you?"

He smiled. "Clever girl. Yes, I know the truth about your grandparents. I know they could not have any children of their own and were brought a child that was found on the mountainside to raise as their prince."

"So Polybus is not my father's father. Merope is not my father's mother."

"No."

"Does that mean that the prophecy came true? Did he meet his true father and kill him?"

Tiresias seemed to stare at me from his sightless eyes for some time before responding. "This you must discover for yourself."

"Right," I said, getting to my feet and smoothing out the creases in my *chiton*. "I guess we must return to Thebes?"

Tiresias shook his head.

"No. You must return."

I froze.

"Alone?"

He nodded. "Yes, you must return to Thebes alone. You must solve the riddles of the Sphinx to discover the truth of your father's curse so that you can understand the curse on your brothers."

"How can I do this on my own?"

Tiresias rose to his feet, his joints creaking as he moved.

"You can do this, Ismene. *You* taught *yourself* to look into the fire. If you do not know where to turn, look to the flames and they will show you what to do." He reached out and grasped my arm in silent farewell. I would miss the familiar weight of his hand on my shoulder.

I would no longer have Tiresias as my guide. I must return to Thebes alone. I must solve the riddles of the Sphinx and save my family. Before it was too late.

15

Riddles of the Sphinx

I left Corinth and headed back to Thebes in the early hours of the morning, taking the same road my father once took. It was a day's journey between the two cities and I could not afford to waste any more time.

I hurried as I could along roads dotted with olive trees. It was now so late into the year that farmers were beginning to harvest, laying out blankets beneath the twisting trunks to catch their bounty as they struck the branches above with thick rope, the olives falling to the ground like rain.

If I was still travelling with Tiresias, we would have stopped for the night. But the urgency to save my family spurred my feet onwards. I carried on late into the night, a torch held aloft in my hands until at last I arrived at that same barren, rocky landscape that I had visited in my vision of my father and the Sphinx. It looked the same—the twin cliffs loomed overhead, the path clear of the splintered bones that had littered it once before.

Two ravens soared overhead, diving at each other, their sharp beaks clashing, their talons entangling. One carried a golden sceptre in its talons. They fought over it. One landed upon the jagged rock that marked the entrance to the Sphinx's cave, the sceptre tumbling to the ground in a cloud of dust.

The other raven landed beside it, hopping towards it, jabbing it with its beak. Cawing raucously, they did not hear what crept up behind them. The Sphinx, alive once more. She caught one raven in her paw, drawing it towards her. She bit it in two. The other rose in the air with a hoarse cry. The Sphinx tossed her meal aside, began to beat her great wings to pursue the other. She batted the raven to ground, dashing its head upon the rocks and dove to finish her meal. The sceptre lay forgotten.

I screamed.

The Sphinx looked over at me and smiled, blood dribbling down her chin.

"You've come!"

She abandoned her meal and took to the air, flapping her wings once, twice and then landing at my feet in a cloud of dust.

"I have waited long for this, daughter of Oedipus." She smiled again, cocking her head to the side to assess me. *"You will tend the holy house of Lord Apollo the far-shooter when all is ruined by fire and the God of War. War and destruction will find you when all your father's shadows come to light."*

"That's not a riddle. That is what the Pythia said to me when I went to Delphi." I squared my shoulders to face her. "I am here about my father."

The Sphinx did not reply for some time. Instead, she stalked around me, eyes never leaving my face. "I know. I will tell you about your father. But first, you must answer me this: What goes on four feet in the morning, two feet at noon and three feet in the evening?"

I stared at her incredulously. That was the same riddle she had given to my father all those years ago. The answer my father gave was man. Man was a baby in the morning of his life, crawling on all fours. He was an adult at noon, standing on his own two feet. When he grew old, and was in the evening of his life, he walked with a cane and had three feet.

I opened my mouth to echo the answer of my father but hesitated. It couldn't be so easy.

I thought of her previous words, the way she had echoed the prophecy of the Pythia. I thought back to my meeting with her at the temple of Apollo where the words *Know thyself* were written in stone. The use of the Pythia's words must be a clue. I could not simply echo the words of my father, but I must also know myself to learn all my father's secrets. I thought that on my travels with Tiresias I was learning clues to my family's curse but it was more than that. I was beginning to know myself. To know my deepest fears and wishes and how they influenced my actions, the advice I listened to.

The Sphinx continued to circle me as I thought, coming so close to me I felt the edge of her wings, stiff with blood, trail across my shoulders. I suppressed a shudder.

Know thyself.

I knew the answer.

"My father answered the same riddle once. He told you the answer was man. But my answer is this. A life. Your riddle follows a man through all the stages of his life. And you will show me my father's life, from when he crawled in the morning on four legs, stood on his own two feet and noon and died before he could reach the evening of his life. You will show me my father's life from the beginning, the crime he committed that cursed him and how I can lift that curse to save my family."

The Sphinx stilled.

"Very well." She lowered herself onto her front paws and pounced.

I reeled back, stumbling to the ground.

I threw out my hands to brace my fall and was startled when my fingers brushed grass and not the hard, packed earth of the Sphinx's pass. I looked up. I was on a mountainside.

The Sphinx was gone.

I heard a strange sound coming from behind me. I looked over my shoulder to see a man approach, a bundle in his arms. The man wore a mantle dyed in rich colours, a sign of his wealth. His face was devoid of all emotion, and though it was dark night, a fierce light gleamed in his grey eyes. He walked towards me, but did not seem to see me. He took the bundle from his arms and tossed it upon the ground and turned on his feet, leaving the bundle behind him. Once that bundle hit the ground, a peculiar sound emitted from its depths.

After making sure the man was long gone, I drew closer, peering at what lay in its centre. I crawled over and let out a gasp. It was a baby. It wailed piteously. I went to touch it and drew back at the bronze spike that had been embedded in its tiny feet.

"Who did this to you?" I cried out in horror.

I reached for the baby but my arms passed through him as though he were a ghost. Or maybe I was the ghost.

I sat with the baby until another man approached, a man with a shepherd's crook. He pulled off his tattered and worn mantle and stooped to wrap the shivering baby. He cradled it in his arms and set off down the mountainside. I stumbled to my feet to follow alongside him.

As our feet fell, our next steps took us from the mountainside to the halls of Corinth. My grandmother sat perched on her throne, her face unlined with age. At her side sat a man, my grandfather, Polybus. The shepherd paused before them, offering up the child. I realised then that the baby was my father.

My grandmother stood from her stone throne to take the baby from the shepherd's arms. She stared into the little face and smiled. As she walked beside me, her form dissipated, as if turned to smoke.

I turned to follow her. I was still in my grandparent's halls but a boy raced before me, his face so like my own. As he passed me, he aged into a young man and the hall filled with ornate couches and tables, a banquet was taking place. The young man, my father, stood beside me, moving to take his place at a couch with others in his age group. One of the youths, his cheeks red from too much wine, leaned towards my father and told him a tale. My father listened intently, his expression changing from amusement to confusion, confusion to alarm, alarm to anger. He leapt from his couch and struck the other youth. I realised this was the moment Merope told me about, the moment one of her court cast aspersions on my father's parentage. My father stormed angrily past me and the hall turned to smoke around us, and instead of crossing the stone tiles, he crossed the Sacred Way to the Temple of Apollo.

Priests escorted my father inside that same dark room I myself had been in a few months before. Grey tendrils of smoke and incense trailed the air, swirling around the downturned face of the Pythia. She looked up and spoke.

"You will kill your father."

My father took a set back and stumbled. He rose to his full height shaking with anger. *"I will not! I will change my fate."* His voice echoed my own words that I had spoken to his adoptive mother in the halls he had grown up in. Watching the scene unfold before me, the gnawing sensation in my stomach told me that he would not change his fate.

I trailed behind my father like a shadow as he stormed out of the temple. He marched down the Sacred Way and stepped out onto a rocky path, the landscape around us changing just as swiftly as his footsteps. My father wore a travelling cloak, covered in a fine coating of dust from his travels. He stood at a crossroads. The ground beneath us shook and I turned over my shoulder to see a chariot approach. My father did not step aside.

Pebbles at my feet skittered this way and that as the chariot gained on us. Still my father did not move. The driver raised an arm and cast it down, the whip in his hands striking out at my father as he grew closer. My father stilled and then turned around.

The driver raised his arm again, casting his whip at my father, who let the whip curl around his raised forearm and then grasped it with his other hand and pulled. The driver lurched from his chariot and landed on the road in a cloud of dust. My father fell upon him and the two men grappled wordlessly until at last one of the two figures lay still. The attendant stepped down from the chariot, fumbling at the sword at his waist. My father rose and struck him down.

I looked at the bodies in the road, the attendant lying face down in the dirt, the driver facing upwards. I approached the bodies and was struck with fear when I recognized the upturned face of the driver. It felt like I had seen him moments ago on the mountainside, laying down a squirming bundle upon the grass. His face was no longer devoid of emotion but twisted with rage, all light was dimmed in his unseeing grey eyes. The same eyes as my father's. The same eyes as my own.

Had the Pythia's prophecy come true? Had Oedipus killed his father?

The dust at my feet picked up and swirled around me until I was engulfed in a cyclone, dirt and grit scratched against my face, my arms, my legs. I covered my eyes and the wind died. I hesitantly moved my arm and found myself in a familiar place.

The Sphinx's pass.

I watched the same scene I had seen in my first vision weeks before. My father answering the Sphinx's riddle and ending her reign of terror. He strode out of the pass and was met with welcoming arms and carried off to the palace.

My father was brought to the Cadmeia and was met by my uncle Creon who, in his youth, looked so much like Menoeceus that I felt my heart ache with homesickness.

Another figure stood beside my uncle, a woman. She was the spitting image of Antigone. This must be my mother.

Oedipus stepped towards her, caked in the dust and filth of his travels and stained with the Sphinx's blood. As he stepped up onto the dais he changed, bathed and perfumed, he wore royal robes. He stood beside my mother, a united front.

I looked around me and found myself in the midst of a delegation. The delegation prostrated themselves before Oedipus and held out branches wrapped in wool, a symbol of their supplication. Oedipus ordered them to rise.

"Apollo, the far-shooter, has turned his plague arrows on our people. But why? How have we offended the shining one? What message from the god do you bring?"

The head of the delegation rose and embraced our father. It was my uncle Creon.

"Apollo Epikourios, the helper, spoke of a curse. A

corruption in our city that threatens to spread to our people, enflaming their flesh, rotting their insides. He bids us to drive the corruption out from our seven gated city. Only then will the curse be lifted and the land healed." Creon spoke to Papa, but his eyes roamed over the *Spartoi* assembled in the hall, men from aristocratic families that had almost as much power as their king.

"What corruption does the god speak of?" My mother leaned forward and I found myself leaning towards her, savouring the sound of her voice, a sound I had long forgotten.

"Murder," Creon replied.

The hall erupted with noise.

"Murder? Whose murder?" My father's sure, strong voice rang out in the hall, but confusion clouded his grey eyes.

Mother's face paled. *"Do you mean the murder of my first husband?"* she asked, her knuckles white as she grasped the fabric of her peplos in her hands. The former king had died long before we were born, before even my father had come to Thebes.

"Laius. We must find his murderer, bring him to justice and drive him from the land."

The hunt for Laius' killer began. I stood by and watched as time rushed by, moments turned to days, men rushed in and out of the Cadmeia, bearing messages to and fro, my father the permanent figure amidst the chaos.

Time began to slow and the rushing figures disappeared from the hall. Now, there was only Oedipus and one other familiar figure. It seems that to aid him in finding the killer of the former king, Oedipus had sent for Tiresias. The old seer looked the same, even all those years ago.

Tiresias began to shuffle towards my father and time sped up once more. I stood by and watched as my father received the old seer with a smile. I watched as that smile froze on his face and curled into a grimace and then a sneer. I could tell that the seer's words displeased him. He grew angrier and angrier, his posture became threatening as he loomed over the frail old man and shouted in his face. He turned and stormed inside the Cadmeia, leaving Tiresias standing alone in the central hall.

The central hall dissolved around me and I found myself standing in my parent's private chambers.

My father stood beside my mother, his head bent in resignation. My mother stroked his face with her hand.

"What is it, my love? What did the seer say?"

"It's what he wouldn't say that's the problem. I asked him what he knew of the old king's murder and he refused to help. I was so angry I said some things I shouldn't have."

"What did you say?" my mother asked, her hand pausing at his cheek.

"I taunted him and insulted him and even accused him of committing the murder himself." He raked his hands down his own face and spoke softly to his wife through his fingers. *"He did answer me then. He said I was the murderer."* He lifted his hands from his face. *"Which is nonsense. I spoke harshly to him and he replied that the murderer of Laius will turn out to be father and brother to his own children, the son of his own wife. What do you think he meant?"* He reached for his wife but she stepped away. Their rooms faded around us, and I found myself following my mother Jocasta as she met with a man in the courtyard.

The man bowed as my mother approached. I watched as the two figures spoke, my mother's mood improving the longer she spoke to the man. She turned from him with a smile and as she stepped forward the scenery around us shifted once more.

We were back in my parent's private chamber.

"I have news, my love!" I watched as my mother embraced my father. *"News that will ease your troubled mind. A messenger arrived from Corinth today, announcing that your father, King Polybus is dead and asked that you go to Corinth to rule in his stead."*

"And that news is supposed to ease my mind? My father is dead."

"Yes, but not by your hand! I know that the prophecy you were told as a young man has been troubling you more than you admit. That false prophecy that you would kill your own father. You have escaped your fate! I always knew you would. I have escaped fate myself. I have never told you this, but Laius and I had a child, a son. A prophecy was made about the child. It was foretold by the Oracle that any son the king would have would kill his father. But my son died when he was a little baby. He never grew up to kill his father. No, Laius was killed by bandits at a crossroads. So you see? We are both blessed to escape such dark fates."

I watched as my mother rejoiced at their good luck, but a shadow of unease crossed my father's face. I too, felt the shadow of unease fall upon me, a sinking feeling in the pit of my stomach. The chamber around us shifted to the courtyard and I watched my parents go out to meet with the messenger.

The man was stooped with age. I recognized his features but couldn't place where I knew him from. The man bowed as my mother and father approached and repeated his news.

Oedipus thanked the man but declined the offer to return to Corinth with him.

"Forgive my impudence, but why would you not come to comfort the woman you call mother?"

Oedipus looked around. *"A prophecy was told to me long ago, one so terrible I fled from my home. The oracle told me I was doomed to kill my father. But there was a second part of the prophecy I have not spoken aloud to another soul, something so terrible I could not put it into words. The oracle told me I was doomed to kill my father and marry my mother. I can't return to Corinth, for I still fear that fate."*

My mother's face paled at this news, but the messenger laughed, his reaction surprising my father.

"Forgive me, your majesty. But you have no need to worry about that! Queen Merope is not your mother. You were brought to the king and queen as a baby. I know this, because I was the one who found you." I then recognized him as the shepherd on the mountain side. *"I took you to the king and queen of Corinth, because I knew they had no child, and they raised you as their own."*

Oedipus leaned towards the shepherd to hear more but my mother stepped back, her face white as marble. She turned from the courtyard and began to run.

My surroundings faded in and out, the only thing I could make out was the figure clad in white, my mother, her dark hair streaming behind her, unbound. Strands of it were clenched in her fists, trailing from her fingers like black ribbons. She let them fall to the floor as she reached up to twist the delicate fabric of her *chiton*, and then to rend the soft skin of her face so that beads of blood left crimson trails down her smooth cheeks. Her frenzied eyes were fixed on the empty air before her. She paused.

"Monsters. All of them. Monsters," she gasped.

Although I was as insubstantial as a ghost I took a step forward, reaching for my mother's hand.

She flinched, as if she could sense my touch.

"No. No," she sobbed, rushing through the halls.

My eyes blurred with tears. I longed to follow her but my feet were frozen in place. Terrified at what would happen next, I remained still, listening to her agonised cries ring throughout the empty corridor, my heart rising in my throat. Even as her shrieks became more and more frenzied, I dared not follow her. I heard her crash about the room, her wails becoming louder and louder all the while.

And then, they stopped.

Quaking now, I shuffled forward, moving so slowly towards her. I paused outside her rooms, not daring to enter but terrified not to see, not to know. I wished for my father to appear, to save the day.

As I stood, as still as a statue outside my mother's chambers, another figure entered the hall. I was not surprised to see my father approach, as if I had summoned him with my own thoughts. He ran past me, as he bellowed mother's name and entered where I dared not.

His screams echoed throughout the palace, throughout my very soul.

I began to move, an unseen force tugging me into my mother's rooms, drawn by my father's distress.

At first I didn't register the scene before me. Something was swinging from the timber that held up the roof.

It was my mother. She had hanged herself.

I longed to cover my eyes, to will the scene away but I shrugged off the urge, knowing that I had to see what my father would do. He would fix this. *He had to.*

Oedipus untied her makeshift noose. Gathering her in his arms he stood for a few moments, clutching mother to his chest, his face buried in her dark curls. She was limp in his arms. Gently, ever so gently, he sank to the floor, cradling her to him. He drew away from her and we could see her face, mottled and purple, her dark eyes unseeing. With shaking hands, he traced the lines of her hair, her face, trailing down her neck where a noose still hung. His hands paused at the bronze pins at her shoulders. He plucked them from the cloth and with a cry, he dug them into his own eyes.

I covered my eyes, as if I could also cover the sight from my mind.

But I saw. I saw it all.

I finally understood. It was my father who had killed Laius all those years ago. They *had* met at a crossroads, just as I feared. Laius was the old man in the chariot who struck at my father, the one my father had killed in retaliation. He did not know who he was.

The prophecy had come true, after all. Not just the prophecy that Oedipus would kill his father. He married his mother, too.

The son of Laius and Jocasta had not died in childbirth as my mother was led to believe. He was exposed on Mount Cithaeron to die by Laius.

It was my mother who learned the truth first. When she realised that her husband was the baby that she had long thought to be dead, that she had married her own son, she went mad. She killed herself to escape the shame of her incestuous marriage, the shame of mothering monstrous children.

The weight of the truth crushed me to the ground. I wrapped my arms around my shoulders, trying to console myself. "Because of my father, they found the killer of Laius. Because of my father the plague was cured. Because of my father the curse on Thebes was lifted."

But my words did not console me. Though the city was no longer cursed, *I* was.

16

All Your Father's Shadows

At last, I had found out the truth about my father, who he really was, what he had done and how it had ruined our family forever. How my brothers and sister and I were monsters, products of an ungodly union.

At the thought of my brothers and my sister, the landscape around me blurred and changed once more.

I groaned and held my hands around my head, not wanting to move, not wanting to see anymore. I wanted to sit with my grief, to work through the truth of my mother's death.

But the visions wouldn't let me, already another memory swirled around me like smoke. I watched the form of my uncle appear out of the smoke and swallowed my tears. If anyone knew what to do, it would be my uncle, the man who had raised us and acted as our father in Oedipus' stead. Hesitantly, I rose to my feet.

I found myself standing beside my uncle Creon and watched as he entered my parent's chambers and took in the carnage before him. Without a word, he turned and barred the doors behind him. He strode over to my father, his face pale, his lips white. But his eyes burned with intensity. At first, I thought he was overcome with emotion and the strange sheen was because tears were filling his eyes at the sight of his sister. But I had seen that look on Menoeceus' face when he was thinking of a way to get out of trouble.

"Get up." He grasped my father's arm and brought him to his feet.

"Creon, is that you?" My father, newly blinded, fumbled at Creon's *chiton*. He did not see the look of disgust flicker across his brother in law's features.

"Yes, it's me. You must come with me now." Creon reached for a mantle and draped it over my father as he ushered him out through one of the servant's corridors, leaving behind the corpse of his sister.

"Creon, it was me, it was me. I killed Laius. I am to blame for the plague on Thebes," Oedipus cried as he grasped Creon's arm.

"I know," Creon replied shortly, hurrying Oedipus through the empty corridors and outside of the palace. *"And you know what you must do. You said it yourself. The killer of Laius must be driven from the land for Thebes to heal. Will you do this?"*

Oedipus turned to Creon and laid a hand on his shoulder. *"Of course. I would do anything to save my kingdom."*

That same flicker of disgust crossed Creon's face, this time it lingered to curl his lip with distaste. *"It is your kingdom no longer."* His cool voice held no trace of the disgust on his face.

"You're right. But Creon—" Oedipus grasped at Creon's *chiton* again, bunching the rich fabric in his bloodstained hands. *"What of the children? How will you tell them the truth about their parents?"* Tears streamed down his face.

Creon laid a hand over my father's, his voice reassuring. *"I won't tell them. They never have to know."*

Oedipus stilled. *"But how will you explain the death of Jocasta? My own absence?"*

"It's simple. I will tell them that through your investigations into Laius' death, you and my sister contracted the plague yourselves, but did not succumb to it until you had driven the murderer from our land."

Oedipus' body sagged with relief. If not for his hold on Creon, he would have slid to the ground.

"Thank you." He sobbed. Creon pried Oedipus' hands from his *chiton* and watched the other man crumple to the ground.

I stood, frozen in place. I had never seen my uncle's face twisted with disgust like that before, never seen the truth behind his warm voice. I shook my head, as if I could shake the memory of the encounter between my father and uncle from my mind.

The forms of the two men dissipated and I found myself in the Cadmeia once more. My brothers stood in the central hall, their small bodies almost swallowed in the crowd of older men gathered around them.

Creon stepped out onto the dais, clad in rich clothes. He called out for silence and the crowd obeyed.

"I come to you today with bittersweet news. Apollo has been appeased! Our king has found the murderer and driven him from Thebes." A cheer erupted in the hall but Creon waved them down. *"However,"* he continued in a sombre voice and the hall went still. *"The investigation into the murder of Laius took its toll. The king and his wife became sick with the plague. They died last night."*

Voices cried out all around me but I did not hear them as I was too focused on the faces of my brothers. They gazed solemnly at our uncle. They did not cry out.

My heart broke for them. By rights, Polynices should have been made king then and there. But he was too young. Creon and the *Spartoi* installed a regency; they would rule until my brothers would come of age.

I thought back to the twisted frown on Creon's face as he spoke to my father and wondered if there was something more to the regency than just my brother's age.

The crowds around them darkened and the faces of my brothers disappeared. I was in the courtyard watching as a much older Polynices trained in the yard. A flicker of movement caught my eye and I saw my uncle standing in the shadows beneath the rows of columns that held the roof aloft. Soon, he stepped out of the shadows and approached my brother, his robes of purple stirring up clouds of dust at his feet.

Polynices rose from his stretches to greet our uncle, who motioned for him to join him by the shade of the columns.

"You know the crown is yours by right."

Polynices nodded eagerly. From his unshaven cheeks, I could tell I was witnessing a conversation from before his year of exile. Before he had come to hate the rest of our family.

"But, you see, it is no longer so simple. It is the Spartoi that decides. And let's face it, if they had their way, this regency would go on forever. You and I both know they have no claim over the throne. What power do they have to decide your fate? I say you decide for yourself."

Polynices' face slackened with relief. *"You're right. I will decide when I take the throne."*

"That's the spirit!" Creon smiled, clapping his nephew on the shoulder. The smile disappeared, a frown tugging at the corners of his mouth. *"But I fear it may not be so easy. We both know that the crown is yours by birth. But. We also know that you make no secret of your disdain for the*

Spartoi. *While your brother has always appeased them. I fear, if we don't move quickly, the* Spartoi *will give rule to your brother. We need to make our move."*

Polynices' brow furrowed. "But how?"

"I have an idea," Creon began, his voice promising some trouble that Polynices just did not hear. *"To determine rule we will use the same precedent set down by the gods."*

The figures in the courtyard turned to smoke and I found myself in the central hall of the palace once more. Creon stood atop the dais, my brothers standing to either side. Smiling what I now recognized to be a false smile, Creon stepped forward to address the crowd. *"Our young princes are now of age to rule! In the spirit of fairness, the* Spartoi *have decided that the princes will rule in turns so that Thebes can decide their own king. To decide who would rule first—"* He drew a hand inside his robes and produced two pebbles, one black, the other white. *"They shall draw lots, like the gods themselves. Zeus became the lord of heaven by lot and we shall decide the king of Thebes in the same fashion."* He held aloft a white pebble and showed it to the crowd. *"This pebble will determine our next king!"*

Eteocles and Polynices turned to face my uncle to draw their lots. The pebbles were cast into an upturned helmet and held aloft to the two princes. Each boy reached an arm inside and held their pebble in a clenched hand. Although the throne belonged to our elder brother Polynices by right of birth, he drew the black pebble. Polynices was ordered to leave the city and come back in one year's time to assume his place as king. Eteocles' first year of rule began to thunderous applause from the *Spartoi*. He stared down in amazement at the glistening white pebble in his palm.

I stood still as time rushed by around me. I watched Eteocles assume his place on the throne, our uncle a permanent fixture at his side, whispering falsehoods into his ear, his lies creating a rift between my brothers that I knew now would never heal. His betrayal felt like a kick in the stomach. I watched a familiar scene pan out before me, of Creon urging my brother to Delphi knowing that the words of the Pythia would stir Eteocles to keep an unlawful hold on the throne.

I saw Creon rule the Cadmeia in my brother's absence while he made the journey to Delphi. I saw how he sent messengers to Argos, urging Polynices to meet Eteocles at the games and prove his worth to the Thebans through the competition. Polynices' actions at the games only proved how his anger made him unfit to rule.

I watched how Creon egged on Eteocles to take the throne for good on the one hand, and on the other sent messages to Polynices urging him to send Tydeus, the kinslayer and lover of wanton violence, to issue his ultimatum.

I watched how my uncle's actions drove my brothers to war.

Time sped on around me and I found myself in the Cadmeia, in the central hall, the *megaron* blazing. The *Spartoi* and their remaining sons turned to my brother, demanding he refer to a seer on how to proceed. Eteocles called out and Tiresias hobbled before him. It seemed the old man made his way to Thebes without me, after all.

"Tiresias, please, tell us how to save our city," Eteocles asked the old man.

Tiresias knew that Thebes was doomed. Tiresias hobbled towards the *megaron*, that large hearth in the centre of the room. *"Let us divine the will of the gods."* The old seer turned his back on the flames, his face cast in shadow. He pointed at my brother and said, *"Listen, son of Oedipus. There is a way to save your city but it will come at a great cost. The gods demand the greatest sacrifice. The serpent of Ares that Cadmus slayed all those years ago demands blood. The youngest man born from those sown of the serpent's teeth must fall to win Thebes' victory."*

A great cry of alarm went up in the hall. All the men gathered there were *Spartoi*, somehow descended from the five men who had risen from the earth when Cadmus sowed the serpent's teeth. They clutched at their remaining sons and shook their heads.

Creon, my uncle, stood beside the king. When he heard Tiresias' prophecy, he went pale and clapped a hand over his mouth and left the king's side to go to his own sons. Haemon and Menoeceus stood beside the seer, their faces set with determination. They would do what they had to and save their city.

Creon grasped them by the arms and dragged them from the hall. I followed.

"Father, stop," Menoeceus said as Creon dragged his two grown sons with

surprising strength.

"I will not stop until the two of you are safe," he answered. He dragged them into his rooms and slammed the door, barring it with his own body.

Haemon took a step towards him. *"Father, we need to go back out there, to find the youngest of the* Spartoi, *to get him to give himself up to save the city."*

"No! You will stay here!" Creon shouted.

Menoeceus stared at his father, amazed to see the proud man crumble. *"What is the matter with you?"* He moved forward, standing in front of his father and looking at him with distaste. *"What are you so afraid of?"*

Creon ignored him, instead staring imploringly at his son. *"Please, do not believe Tiresias. The king, yes, the king put him up to this. He is jealous of my boys, he wants the throne all to himself. This is all Eteocles' idea. He's always been jealous of you."* Creon's arms darted out to grab ahold of Menoeceus. He grasped his son's face in his hands, pressing his forehead against his son's.

"Father?" Haemon stood still. Realisation dawned on his face. *"Menoeceus!"* he gasped, looking at his beloved brother with horror.

Menoeceus looked back at him, puzzled. *"What?"*

"It's you," Creon gasped, pulling Menoeceus' face towards him. *"It's you. You are the youngest. My son, my youngest son."* He sobbed, pressing his face into his son's chest.

Menoeceus looked stunned. He stared at his father weeping against him. He looked up at his brother. *"I don't have much choice, do I?"*

Haemon's face was wet with tears. *"You always have a choice."*

"What, save my own skin and let the city fall?" He shook his head, his dark hair flapping. He pried his father from his chest, looking into his face. *"Or sacrifice myself and save everyone? I think we all know what the right choice is."* He smiled sadly.

"Right choice for who?" Creon wailed. *"I will not give up my son,"* he cried, grabbing ahold of Menoeceus once more.

Menoeceus shrugged him off. *"It's not your choice to make."* He started to fade from view.

"No, no!" I shrieked, rushing forward to grab ahold of my beloved cousin, closer to me than my brothers ever were. But he turned to smoke between my fingers.

I was in Thebes once more, on the ramparts, the spot I had snuck out to at the god's insistence, flouting the palace rules and starting me on this doomed journey. Menoeceus stood at the edge of the wall, peering down at the Argives swarming at its base. The Argives produced a ladder and leaned it against the walls. The Theban men around us threw spears, rocks, anything to deter the Argives from scaling the wall. One brave man darted around the shafts of spears and made it to the top.

Menoeceus met him there, and with his bronze sword gleaming in the setting sun, he slashed the man across the throat, kicking at the ladder. The man and the ladder fell, taking several other Argives down with them. Menoeceus stood there, his chest heaving, looking at the chaos all around him. He looked towards his brother, fighting a little way down the ramparts.

Haemon looked up and met his brother's gaze. He did not see the Argive scaling the wall. Menoeceus shouted for him to move but Haemon did not have time to dodge from the bronze that sunk into the flesh of his shoulder. Menoeceus ran to his brother's side, striking the Argive down. He dragged his brother over to safety. He called for men to take his brother to the physicians, Haemon had passed out from the pain.

I stood there amongst the blood and chaos, a shade, warriors passing through me to defend my city. They all had their eyes on the enemy. I had my eyes on my cousins. One sorely wounded, the other contemplating something dreadful.

"No, Menoeceus, no," I breathed, trailing his every step, repeating myself as if he might hear me if I said it enough. "No, no, no. Don't do this."

Menoeceus stood there, staring at the men taking his brother away. He turned and approached the ramparts, scaling the turrets. He shook his head free from his helmet, his dark hair plastered against his skin. He tossed the helmet over the wall. Men paused as they fought, turning to him, remembering Tiresias' words. He drew his sword, the bronze dulled with blood.

"Apollo! I will do as you ask. Take me as payment for the city's crimes!"

"No!" I screamed, lurching forward, my hands going for his sword. It passed through my hands. Menoeceus held the sword aloft and gave a great cry. My ghostly hands grabbed at him, trying to usher him away to safety. My cousin—my brusque, strong, impulsive, good cousin—saluted the crowd of Thebans around him and leapt from the turrets to the Argives scaling the ramparts below.

I screamed as he fell, reaching over the ramparts as if I could stop his fall.

He landed upon the Argive siege towers, cutting down their men in droves, the element of surprise in his favour. But soon, other Argives began to swarm around him, a wave of bodies all reaching towards him with their swords. Menoeceus stood in their midst, laughing as he waited for death to arrive.

The last sight of my cousin was his bright smile soon smothered by the scores of Argives falling upon him, his warm laugh cut short.

I was now standing in the temple where everyone was gathered for an offering to Zeus. Eteocles himself attended the altar. Somehow, I knew that as I stood there I was no longer watching the past, but watching present events as they occurred.

"Zeus, we owe our city to you. You led noble Cadmus to our own land and I know that you look on our walls with love. You used your lightning to defend us from the impious Capaneus, you opened the earth underneath the false prophet Amphiaraus. Please, oh Zeus, continue to defend our city from those that would defile it. Continue to defend us, your children."

A huge bull was brought to the altar. It is the custom to bring the sacrificial animal to the altar content and unharmed, to sprinkle water and barley before it, so when it bends its neck to eat the barley it gives its consent to sacrifice. But this bull was wild, its flanks heaving and bleeding, it fought against the attendants. The sacrificial knife, supposed to be hidden, flashed before its eyes and it broke loose.

"Somebody seize that animal now!" Eteocles bellowed, the men in the temple scrambling to do his bidding.

A man burst into the building, running to his king. *"Stop, stop the sacrifice my lord! Your brother stands outside the city's walls!"*

Everyone in the temple began to speak at once, some calling for the king to meet his brother on the field, others lamenting that he should not go, the soldiers beating their weapons on the floor, the sound echoing my own heartbeat.

Creon pushed his way through the crowd until he stood nose-to-nose with my brother.

"Do you not have the nerve to fight your own war? Menoeceus is dead because of you. I will not stand by and let Haemon die for you, too."

Eteocles pulled Creon's face close to his and whispered hotly in his ear. *"Don't hide behind your false tears. I know what you want. I know you long for my death so that you can take my throne."* He pushed his uncle away. *"I'll deal with you later."* He looked at the crowds. *"To arms! Time for the brothers to compete over the throne for the last time."*

The men cheered. Antigone and Haemon remained silent, staring incredulously at my brother.

The temple blurred and shuddered and I found myself looking over turrets, watching Eteocles leave the city through the Dircaean gate. His stallion danced as the horns blared, eager for battle. Eteocles' glorious golden helmet gleamed in the setting sun. I stepped closer to the wall and found myself beneath it, standing beside my sister and she pleaded with Polynices.

"We are not your enemy," Antigone called out to Polynices as he rode around the walls. *"Do you think you will be granted your year of rule after this? The* Spartoi *hate you, the Thebans fear you. Go home to your wife, your son. We do not want you here."* I could hear her voice break and my heart broke with it.

"Thebes is mine," Polynices' voice answered, dismissing Antigone.

The moment I had fought so hard to prevent was happening before my eyes and I was powerless to stop it.

I looked down on the field again. There was Polynices, riding into view, Eteocles spurred his horse forward to meet him. My breath caught. I did not want to see the Pythia's prophecy fulfilled but I could not look away.

The brothers charged at one another through the clouds of dust. The war horns were silent now, even those charged with playing them paused to watch. A third horse had ridden into the fray. The swift Arion, the steed of Adrastos.

Adrastos reigned in Arion and called out to the brothers, his voice echoing through my friend at my side.

"Stop this! Polynices, please, if your year of rule is so important to you, I can give it to you. If you come with me now, I will step down. Argos will be yours and you will have years to rule with my daughter and your son by your side. Come home."

But no reply came from Polynices. He spurred his horse towards his brother, Eteocles mirroring him, their horses rode straining forward. I watched Adrastos pull at Arion's reins, saw him flee from the field, from Thebes, from war, from Polynices.

The brothers were alone. Eteocles raised his arm high and let loose his spear. Polynices caught the tip on the edge of his shield, the deadly blow averted.

Polynices hurled his own spear, its circling shaft speeding towards Eteocles' leg. He yanked on the reins, turning slightly so that he was spared, the spear instead slicing at the flank of his horse. It reared, knocking the king off its back. It sped away from the fight, leaving a trail of bright blood across the killing field. Polynices charged at his fallen brother, his sword raised high.

Eteocles seized Polynices' fallen spear and hurled it at him, his horse stumbling and falling to the ground in a cloud of dust. Polynices strode out of the dust and advanced on his brother. Their swords met with a great clash that echoed up to the tops of the gates. They struck madly at each other, red blossoming on their limbs, they ignored their own blood, hungry for the other's.

With a roar that rumbled through my very soul, Polynices struck at Eteocles, his rage at his stolen birthright, his year in exile, propelling him forward. His sword struck deep, passing by the bronze plates of his armour to sink into the soft flesh of Eteocles' abdomen. Eteocles raised his shield, knocking Polynices back, he huddled behind the protective circle.

Polynices laughed. *"Hiding? You won't hide for long."* He wrenched the shield from Eteocles' grasp and tossed it aside, lunging to finish him off. Eteocles raised his own sword to meet the blow before it fell, using the motion to lurch upright and match his brother's blows.

They grappled like that for a while but I could see Eteocles weaken, his strength waning as the blood poured from his wound. He stumbled, falling down on one knee.

Polynices, thinking him defeated, raised his arms and cried out, *"Thebes is mine!"*

As he gloated, leaving his middle unprotected, Eteocles struck and drove his sword through his opponent.

Polynices, reacting to the blow, drove his own sword through Eteocles' shoulder. He fell atop his brother, his heavy armour crushing him. Just as the Pythia had foreseen, they died in each other's arms, by the other's hand.

I gasped. I couldn't breathe. My chest rose and fell in quick succession, my body panicking at the sight of my brothers' bodies.

My brothers were dead.

I felt as if I had died, too.

17

ᴛHREADS OF FATE

When I awoke, I was no longer on the killing fields of Thebes, but in the barren landscape of the Sphinx's pass. I stared blankly ahead at the grey sky, words tumbling from my numb lips.

"The prophecy, it came true."

I looked up and met the burning bright gaze of the god.

"Prophecies always come true," Apollo answered, settling down beside me on the ground. "Laius thought he couldn't be killed by his son if he killed the baby first. But you saw for yourself that the baby survived and found a kingdom of his own. He too tried to escape the prophecy about himself, just as his father before him. But instead of escaping the prophecy he fulfilled it." He gazed at me in pity. "And just as your father before you, you tried to change your own fate and failed."

"Why did you let me do it?" I asked him, staring at the ground beneath us. "Why did you let me try to escape fate?"

"I told you it was impossible to escape fate," Apollo replied. "But you persisted. You had to discover it for yourself." He rose to his feet and stood over me, his hand outstretched. "Come. I want to show you something."

I raised my head from the ground to look at his proffered

hand, my hand tucked in his. He pulled me to my feet and ushered me across the barren plain. As we stepped, the landscape blurred and changed around us until I recognized the pale hills that surrounded our city. A trio of caves carved into the hill-face. I froze. These were no mere caves, but the burial places of Theban royalty.

Apollo wrapped an arm about my waist and leaned in close to whisper in my ear, his breath stirring the curls around my face. "Come."

We stepped forward and found ourselves within the cave, a *larnax* bearing the remains of my mother sat in the centre. I looked away, not ready to face what it contained, the image of a noose trailing from her neck flooding my mind.

Apollo took us past the *larnax*, towards the shadows at the back of the cave. I thought we would walk into the wall and so I braced myself for the impact, but we passed through and made our descent into the darkness.

The darkness was absolute, black nothing weighed on me, making my breath come faster. I squeezed my eyes shut in fear and heard a soft laugh beside me. I opened my eyes to find the god beside me glowing with golden light in the dim. I was glad to have him at my side at that moment.

"Where are we going?" I whispered to the god at my side. For some reason, I was afraid to raise my voice in the darkness. I didn't know what was watching us from within the shadows. I glanced up at Apollo to see him smile.

"I told you. I want to show you something."

"Show me what? Where are you taking me?" I demanded.

Apollo's glowing eyes flicked down towards me. "I am taking you to the *Moirai*."

My feet faltered beneath me.

The *Moirai*. The Fates themselves. I looked around me in newfound horror as the oppressive darkness swallowed us alive.

He was taking me to the Underworld.

We journeyed through the darkness in silence for some time until I could make out a faint light in the distance, torches blazed along the wall and lit up three figures. We drew closer and I could see that the three figures were women, each one occupied with their task. One sat spinning wool into thread, another measured out their lengths with an ancient distaff and the last figure cut the threads with gleaming shears.

I gasped. It was them. The *Moirai*.

Apollo began to speak softly. "The *Moirai* choose our fate by spinning threads of destiny at our birth, measuring out mortal lives and cutting them short when it is their time. Even though Laius thought to change his fate by killing his son, the *Moirai* made sure he got what they thought he deserved, an early, violent death. And your father was doomed to follow him."

We stood and watched the *Moirai* at work.

Apollo gestured to the figure measuring a series of threads. "As we speak, she measures the fate of your family. Would you like to see what is fated to happen next?"

Before I could shake my head in refusal, the dark rocks of the Fates' chamber dissolved and I found myself in the Cadmeia.

My uncle stood atop the dais in my brother's stead.

An arm brushed my own and I was not surprised to see that Apollo had followed me on my journey. He nodded to the figure on the dais.

"Your uncle Creon took the throne your brothers fought and died for. His first duty as king was to make a decree that would shake the heavens and earth with its impiety. While he sent out men to take Eteocles' body to the family tomb, Polynices was denied burial, the people were forbidden to give him his final rites, even to mourn him. He promised death to anyone who went against his orders."

I stared at my uncle in horror. The gods themselves demanded proper burial for all the dead. By ordering that Polynices and the fallen Argives remain unburied, Creon went against the gods themselves.

My uncle faded to nothing and I found myself standing on the plain outside the city's walls. Cold rain splattered on the loose earth, upturned by the hooves of horses and the marching of soldier's heels.

A figure crept across the field. It was Antigone. She ducked behind the shield of some fallen Argive while the sentries Creon posted to guard the body drifted off to drink some celebratory wine. She approached the body. She cupped the earth in her hands, sprinkling it upon our brother's corpse, his skin mottled with decay. She burst into a long, heartbreaking wail, lamenting his death, she tore at her hair, her cheeks. She smeared the damp earth across her face. She took the *lekythos* she carried with her and poured libations upon him, wailing all the while.

"*Stop!*" one of the sentries ordered.

Antigone stood by the body, acknowledging what she had done, her chin held high. She did not flinch when they seized her arms and carried her back to the city walls. Triumph blazed in her dark eyes.

I ran after them, the grey fields replaced by shining stones and I found myself stumbling down the hall to the *megaron*, knowing in my bones that Creon would be waiting there, that Antigone would be brought before him.

It was already day and people were gathered in the central hall, gazing at Antigone disapprovingly as she stood between the sentries. Haemon stood beside his father, he gazed at his cousin with a mixture of awe and disbelief. But my cousin knew as well as I that Antigone would fight to the death for her family, she would do her duty to them no matter what the cost. We loved her for it, and we would lose her because of it.

"We caught her giving the body of Polynices its last rites, just as you forbid," the sentry reported.

Creon stared at her from his seat on my father's throne, my brother's throne. *"You know the law. No traitor is to be honoured with burial. Your actions last night have proven you to be a traitor just like your brother. You know the punishment for the crime you have committed."*

She stared haughtily back at our uncle. *"Is it a crime to lay my brother to rest?"*

"Of course, it is a crime! I decreed it so!" he bellowed at her.

"Your decrees mean nothing. Who are you, a mere mortal, to override the decrees of the gods? I would break your laws a thousand times to uphold the laws of Zeus." She spat at her uncle.

The hall was silent. I could see the fury boiling in my uncle's heart.

"Take her." He nodded at the guards. They seized her arms. *"Did you think because you are my niece you would*

be safe? I am the king now. You will all obey me. Look at this girl,"* he raised his voice, all eyes on him. *"She flouted my laws and she will die for it."*

I lurched forward. "Stop!"

Apollo chuckled beside me. I glared at him as he shook his head in disbelief.

"Do you never learn? They cannot hear you. We are not here. These events have not yet come to pass. But they will soon."

I gritted my teeth and resolved myself to watch the scene unfold before me.

Creon rose to his feet, stepping off the dais, his audience was not over. *"Take her."*

Haemon, who had up till now been frozen with horror, began to move. He fell to his knees before his father and clutched at his arm.

"Father, no," he pleaded. *"Don't do this. She is the only family we have left."*

"Her?" Creon looked at Antigone with disgust. *"I will not let our noble family be sullied by criminals like her."*

"She's not a criminal!" Haemon bellowed, rising to his feet.

"Do you deny my laws as well?" Creon hissed.

Haemon stood between him and Antigone defiantly. *"You offend the gods by denying their laws!"* He went to grab Antigone from the guards but Creon struck him with his fist. Haemon turned to him. His eyes widened as he stared at the man his father had become, broken by war, death and hatred.

"Get out of my sight," Creon said through gritted teeth.

Haemon took a step away from him. *"If you go through with this, you'll never see me again."*

Creon turned his head away, covering his eyes with a shaking hand. *"Take him."*

More guards approached, attempting to drag Haemon from the hall. But he was a warrior, and he had spent weeks on the field killing men and he would not be parted from what remained of his family.

When a guard drew his sword to threaten him into submissiveness, Haemon jabbed his elbow into the man's face, his nose crunching, blood pouring from his nostrils.

Haemon seized the sword and the other guards made no move to approach him as they knew of his reputation on the field. He stepped towards the guards who held Antigone and they dropped her arms and stepped back from their prince.

Creon snatched a sword from one of the guards, went up to his son and struck the back of his head.

Antigone screamed.

"Get him out of here," Creon snarled.

Now that Haemon was incapacitated, the guards rushed forward and seized him, dragging him from the hall.

I turned to the god beside me, fell to my feet and grasped at him, a suppliant on my knees. "Please, don't do this. Don't let this happen."

He looked down at me, a sad smile on his face. He pulled me to my feet. He stooped low, his head level with mine. He grasped my face in his golden hands and turned my head towards the future that was fated to happen. "Watch."

They dragged Antigone from the hall. The last thing I saw was my sister's defiant face.

I reached for her with a strangled sob but the Cadmeia disappeared and was replaced with the Fates' dark chamber once more.

I turned to Apollo. "Where are they taking her?" I whispered to him, my voice hoarse from screaming, from sobbing.

"Creon will order the guards to take her to some desolate place, where his men will wall her up alive in a living tomb. They will leave her with small provisions, so she will live for a short time to think over what she has done, and then starve to death."

I swallowed my sobs. "Show me."

We stood in the *megaron*. It was crowded with men. Tiresias stood amongst them, before his king.

"What is it now, Tiresias?" Creon asked.

"You must heed my warning," Tiresias answered, staring at the place my uncle's voice came from.

"Get on with it," Creon ordered, waving his hand.

"Apollo has told me that your resolve to dishonour your nephew sets another plague on Thebes."

Everyone in the hall cried out.

Creon rose from his throne and approached the seer. *"No, no, that can't be right. I am no murderer, no kinslayer like Oedipus!"*

"No, you are not. You are far worse. You hold yourself above the laws of the gods. So the gods will send a plague. The altars and sacred hearths are fouled by the birds and beasts who feed upon the dead that linger outside our walls by your command."

Creon held his head in his hands, his shoulders stooped.

Tiresias rested one of his gnarled and bony hands atop his shoulder. *"You must be a better man than your predecessors. All men make mistakes. Admit yours, and you can cure the plague before it devastates the city once more."*

"How?" Creon grasped the seer's bony shoulders.

"Free your niece from her tomb, deliver the last rites to the bodies you exposed. Thebes will be clean of sin once more."

"Of course, of course," Creon nodded, rushing from the halls.

We followed him out of the halls, out of the Cadmeia, out of the gates and onto the field. We passed dogs and birds picking at the corpses of fallen Argives. He stopped at the edge of the plain where the body of Polynices' lay, torn by dogs. I could not look at it.

Creon quickly muttered a hurried prayer. We watched as he darted about the field, collecting fallen branches, twigs, broken shafts of arrows and spears, and scattered them around what was left of my brother, piling a mound of Theban soil around it and setting it alight. A hasty burial to soothe a guilty man's conscience.

Having completed Tiresias' first task Creon made for the living tomb he buried my sister in, racing across the bloody plain. He did not stop until he came to a familiar rocky place. The Sphinx's pass. When I realised that this was where Creon had left my sister to die, my stomach lurched, thinking of how I had been in that very same place not so long ago.

The Sphinx's cave was no longer walled up, the rocks piled before the entrance had been loosened. Creon scurried up to the cave pausing to stare at the scattered rocks, his face warring between outrage that someone had defied him and relief that someone had thought to save his niece.

From within the cave came a voice, a low wailing echoing among the rocks. The smell of damp earth was overpowering after the long rain of the night before.

Creon hesitated at the entrance, staring at the cave in horror. He entered, the glow of his torch bouncing off the many facets of the rocky walls. His wail made the hair on the back of my neck rise, not just at the raw pain I heard, but the way it reminded me of my father's when he found my mother. I went to follow him but paused at the entrance, taking a deep breath as I steeled myself for the worst.

Nothing could prepare me for what I saw inside.

It was Antigone, a fine linen noose around her neck.

I covered my mouth as I cried out, the shock sending me to my knees. As I fell to the ground, we were in the Fate's chamber again.

Apollo loomed above me. I rose unsteadily to my feet to face him.

"And this is what is fated to happen next?"

"Yes." He settled his hands on my shoulders and turned me to face the *Moirai* as they worked. "See? They measure the threads of Fate as we speak. The deaths of your sister and your cousin are yet to come."

As we stood watching the *Moirai* at work, a memory of my time in the women's quarters danced before my eyes.

I was much younger, standing on the tips of my toes to work at my loom, my small fingers plucking a pattern from the brightly-coloured wefts.

"Could you tell me one of your stories, Pyrrha? One I haven't heard before?" I called out, pulling this string, now

that string. My pale fingers, white against the crimson dyed thread.

"One you don't know?" Pyrrha said idly she spun the distaff in her gnarled hands.She sat in silence for a few moments, her sure hands drawing out the suspense as well as the wool she was spinning into thread. "Hmmm. I don't suppose you know the one about Artemis' golden distaff?"

"Artemis is a huntress! She doesn't spin and weave like us," I scoffed, pausing in my weaving to turn and look at my nurse.

"Oh, yes, she did." So accustomed to the task of spinning wool, Pyrrha's eyes roved over my eager face while her hands continued to turn the distaff. "She was once a girl like you. She helped her mother with women's work."

Antigone had sat quietly beside our nurse carding wool. But now she looked up, her eyes flashing.

"Artemis is a goddess, not a girl."

"Well, as a young goddess, Artemis helped her mother spin wool and weave, just as you help me." She nudged the kalathos at her feet. "On Olympus, they have baskets of silver with gilded rims and distaffs made of gold. Artemis herself used that distaff each day to spin clouds.

But she was a naughty girl like you and would much rather hunt on the slopes of Mount Parnassus with her brother. One day, when her mother was visiting Father Zeus, Artemis took her golden distaff and broke the spindle from the end. She fletched the golden pole with feathers and fastened a golden arrowhead to its end. She abandoned her work and went out to hunt. She had such fun she did not realise how much time had passed.

When she notched her bow and raised it up high, she saw that the afternoon sky had turned to dusk. Her mother would be back soon. Artemis raced home—she tore the fletching from the end as quick as plucking a chicken, and she knocked the arrowhead to the ground and fixed the spindle back in place. She gathered the clouds around its end just as Leto came in through the door."

Antigone and I had burst into laughter at the thought of a goddess misbehaving. The sound of our laughter echoed dully in that dark chamber, the memory fading before my eyes until only the glittering gold distaff remained.

I blinked and found myself back in the present moment, looking at the ancient distaff of the Fates as they spun and measured the threads of my family's lives.

The woollen thread was Tyrian purple, a precious dye made from the crushed shells of the murex, the colour of royalty. The thread reminded me of Eteocles and his robes. And there, that thread of scarlet that came from the juices of the madder root was like Polynices, the red reminiscent of his face flushed with temper. And there, that thread of white, un-dyed, pure, like my pious sister. If only I could become one of the *Moirai* myself and spin the thread of their lives to change their fates.

But, why couldn't I? What was stopping me from taking fate into my own hands and preventing the worst from ever happening? I had already lost Eteocles and Polynices. I had already lost Menoeceus. But Antigone's fate had yet to play out. Maybe there was still time to change the thread of her fate.

What if I could change the threads that bound me to my sister? What if, somehow, I could convince the goddess to use her magic distaff to spin a new thread of fate, something so glorious even the *Moirai* themselves would desire it?

But how? What material could that thread be made of?

In Pyrrha's story, Artemis spun the clouds for her mother. I didn't think a thread of nimbus would tempt the Fates. I needed to find something miraculous, something of great importance.

A memory struck me like a blow. Only days before, Tiresias had told me of objects of great importance.

"When a sign is powerful enough, that importance, that sense of meaning it conveys, can become fuel for the gods."

I needed to find signs that represented something so important they become worthy of the gods themselves.

I paced back and forth in that dark cavern, struggling to think, the immortals lingering nearby forgotten. I stopped and looked around in the dark.

The god had taken me into the Underworld itself. A place where the greatest heroes and monsters resided. What better place to find objects of great importance than the resting place of such individuals?

I glanced down and found myself gnawing at my thumbnail, the corner had torn and a burst of copper rushed onto my lips. I drew my hand away. I was only a mortal girl, what difference could I make?

But what if a mortal girl like me had the power to change her world?

18

Change Your Fate

looked around me and tried to come up with a plan. I couldn't rush into the Fields of Elysian and start begging heroes for trifles of importance, no, I had to be clever. Clever like Artemis, who waited for the right moment before going off on her own.

In the Underworld, time passed differently than it did on earth. I had time to gather important signs to convince the goddess to spin the loveliest thread ever made and convince the Fates themselves to extend a life.

As I stood lost in thought, I did not notice that my immortal guide had vanished, taking his otherworldly light with him. I glanced up to find the darkness staring back at me.

I spared one more look at the Fates at their work before I let the darkness swallow me whole.

I raced headlong into the dark, praying that my feet would take me where I needed to go. It wasn't long before I realised I was lost.

I sunk down to the ground. I didn't know how long I sat there alone in the gloom, the darkness wrapped around me like a heavy cloak.

I closed my eyes and listened to the staccato of water dripping on the stones below—*drip, drip, drip*. The whistle of a breeze passing through the twisty caverns. The huff of my own breath. The tempo of my own heartbeat.

As I tried to still my racing heart, I felt something brushed up against my side.

My eyes snapped open.

Something was prowling around me, coming ever closer. I felt the trail of feathers dance across the skin of my arms. Something I had felt before.

The creature came to a halt before me. I found myself staring into a familiar set of eyes.

It was the Sphinx.

"What are you doing here?" I asked her, not wanting to disturb whatever else prowled in the darkness.

"You have need of me."

"I do?"

"You cannot look into the flames for help here. That will only work for you on the earth, where gods speak to you in visions and dreams. Here, in the Underworld, we can be more direct."

"You are not a god," I pointed out.

"Gods and monsters," she amended, sitting back on her haunches to delicately lick at a paw. "While I cannot show you the past, or send you hints like the god, there is one thing I am well-known for." She smiled sweetly at me.

"Riddles," I answered, drawing myself upright. "Will your riddles help me find the signs I need?"

She nodded. "You are no longer on the mortal plane, but the land of gods and monsters. The materials you collect here will have great magic."

"What's the first riddle then?" I asked.

She resumed grooming herself in response. Though I

longed to shout my frustration at her, I waited beside her, listening to the far off cries of the souls of the Underworld.

Her voice rang out in the dark cavern. "Answer me this: Blessed with abundance, pride was my folly and a punishing blight made me childless. Who am I?"

I thought back to my childhood in the women's quarters and the stories Pyrrha told us. I thought of famous mothers, but so often the mothers in Pyrrha's tales were the mothers of heroes. Who was a famous mother made famous for the loss of her children?

Then, I remembered the story of Niobe. A proud woman, Niobe refused to honour Leto, the mother of Apollo and Artemis, boasting that she was more deserving of honour for she had given birth to six sons and six daughters. Leto was enraged and begged her children to avenge the slight against her honour. With their twin bows, the gods struck down all of Niobe's children and their mother turned to stone in her grief. Her stone sat atop Mount Sipylus and weeped when the snow melted down her rocky face.

"Niobe!" I replied.

The Sphinx smiled her inscrutable smile. While I had answered her riddle, I did not know how it would help me find the signs I needed. I stood and paced as I thought aloud. "Niobe is infamous for her pride, and how the gods punished her for it. She was turned to stone and weeps for all eternity." I whipped round to face the Sphinx. "Will I find what I need in Niobe's tears?"

The Sphinx nodded.

"But how can I collect tears? Won't they trickle through my fingers?" I wondered aloud. "I need to find signs of great meaning, of great magic, to make my magical thread. Niobe's tears will have great importance to the goddess who struck down her children. But I need to find more than signs that are meaningful to Artemis alone." I paced back and forth in thought, the Sphinx's eyes tracing my path. I stopped in my tracks. "I need to find other signs that are important to my family, my journey here. Niobe's tears are the first but I will need to find more. Right?"

I turned to the Sphinx. She did not reply. Instead, she shook out her hair and rose to stand on her four lion's legs and unfurled her wings. Looking over her shoulder at me, she gestured towards her back.

I took a step back.

"You want me to get on?"

She nodded.

I hesitated. The Sphinx was a monster—how could I trust her? Yet, her riddles were meant to help me on my course. I had to take this chance.

I strode over to her and clambered onto her back, my fingers finding purchase in her long curls. Without a word, she took flight with a great clap of her wings. We soared out of the cavern to sail over the Underworld, its various rivers snaking out below us. We passed the Fields of Asphodel, the Plains of Elysian, and banked lower and lower. My hands clenched in her mane of curls as we made our descent into the abyss. Tartarus, a dungeon of torment and suffering for wicked souls and the prison for the Titans.

The Sphinx landed at the mouth of the abyss. This was where the wicked were punished for their crimes on earth. She wandered over the black rocks, and I followed in her wake, walking among the cliffs, their peaks resembling their counterparts on earth. Finally, we came to a peak that had the rocky appearance of a woman, water trickling down her face into a stream that poured into the abyss below.

It was Niobe.

To make an otherworldly thread to impress the Fates themselves, I needed to gather otherworldly materials. The tears of a grieving mother must be one of them. I looked around me for the safest path up to the transfigured woman. I scaled the black rocks until my fingertips were worn and bleeding, until at last I was at the peak.

I reached out to touch the trickle of water running down her face and wondered how to collect it. I cupped my palms underneath the stream but the water only trickled between my fingers. I looked down at the Sphinx, who had curled into a ball and gone to sleep.

Niobe had six sons and six daughters and boasted how she was more blessed than Leto who only gave birth to two children. Leto had sent her children to slaughter Niobe's. Niobe was frozen with grief, her unending tears rendering her useless, unmoving. It was only after the bodies of her children had laid unburied for nine days that Zeus turned them to stone and buried the children with their mother.

I turned around me and noticed the other rocky formations atop the cliff face, sprawled at the feet of Niobe like fallen bodies. I was standing on the remains of her children. I looked about me and noticed how the steady flow of water had eroded the stone over time, how it began to flake and crumble, the remains of Niobe now mingled with that of her children and her own tears.

I reached below me and gathered pebbles wet from the stream and placed them in the pouch that hung at my waist. I had found the first of my materials.

Carefully, I climbed down the cliffs and nudged the Sphinx awake. She stretched her paws out before her, her haunches rising in the air and her tail curled and twisted like a serpent as she stretched and yawned. She opened one eye and gazed up at me.

"Where to next?" I asked.

"Follow me."

She leaped to her feet and unfurling her wings she soared ahead of me and I followed. We made our way across the dark rocks until we came to a pool of still, fetid water.

In the centre of the pool, something bobbed slightly. As we were too far away, I couldn't make out what it was. The Sphinx turned her back to me, indicating with a jerk of her chin that I should hop on.

I climbed atop her back and we soared over the pool to get closer to the strange object. But it wasn't an object at all. It was a person, a man, submerged in the lake up to his chin. His head hung listlessly to the side, as his mouth drew close to the water he jerked his chin up, creating ripples across the still lake. He groaned piteously. A withered tree stood on the edge of a rock overhead, a single, ripe fruit hung from its twisted limbs. A pale arm stretched out from the water towards the fruit hanging just out of reach.

The Sphinx soared closer and I pulled on her hair, not wanting to go any closer. We were in Tartarus, after all, the place where the wicked were sent for punishment. Whoever this man was, he had done something *bad*.

"Would you stop that?" the Sphinx snapped at me.

I quickly let go of the matted locks of hair I held in my hands.

"Who is that?" I asked her, afraid to speak too loudly and attract the man's attention.

"You tell me." She cleared her throat. "Answer me this: A table is laid for twelve guests but the banquet remains uneaten. Who is the host?"

I thought back to my travels, and the recent banquet I had attended at Mycenae. But Atreus had only laid out a feast for one. I thought back further, to a vision at a campfire, a pale hand reaching out from within a cauldron and the voice that called to me from within it.

"The son of Zeus himself, was welcomed on Olympus. As a man, he walked among the gods. But in his age, he became jealous of his divine family and wished to prove that the gods were not all knowing. To repay them for their hospitality, he invited them to a well-ordered feast in his own home."

The voice from within the squat cauldron of my vision echoed in my mind. A feast held for the Olympians themselves in those very halls.

I stared down at the man in revulsion.

"Tantalus," I whispered.

Tantalus, the son of Zeus who offended his father and all the gods alike by serving his own son to them.

"Yes. Punished for all eternity for his impious feast to go thirsty and hungry forever."

"But he is surrounded by water, there is fruit just overhead," I protested.

"Yes, he sees the objects of his desire, so close but forever denied to him."

"That's cruel."

"Yes. But it was also cruel to chop up his own son and cook him."

I shuddered. She was right—he deserved to be punished for what he had done, punished for his plan to make fools of the gods themselves. Yet, seeing the punishment enacted before me made me pity the cursed man.

His story was the start of my travels throughout Hellas, no doubt I had to collect something of importance from him. But what? My first thought was to reach for the fruit that hung above him, but now I knew it was part of his punishment, I could not take it.

I looked around that still lake and tried to think. I couldn't collect the lake water, it would trickle through my pouch. But maybe I could snap a twig from the branches.

"Can you swoop down by the tree?" I asked the Sphinx.

She nodded once and soared lower, the tips of her wings brushing against the withered tree as she circled around it. I leaned over and tried to grasp at one of the reaching branches but it slipped through my fingers.

The Sphinx circled the tree again and again as I tried to grasp one of its limbs. I looked down and was relieved to see that Tantalus was not watching us, his eyes remained closed. He must be too exhausted from his effort to stay afloat. I shuddered and focused on my task.

On our third flight around the tree, I grasped at a withered branch and a twig snapped off in my hand. I opened my clenched hand to see the dry stick in my palm, a green shoot emerging from its tip. I opened the pouch at my waist with one hand and with the other I tucked the twig inside.

The Sphinx smiled and we took off, leaving that fetid pool and the man trapped within it far behind us. We crossed the barren rocks until we came to a plain of grass, waving silently like the sea.

The Fields of Asphodel. The place where mortals go after death. As we drew closer, I saw pale forms tucked away in the long strands of grass, waving to and fro, in eerie silence.

The Sphinx landed in the midst of the tall grass and I dismounted. Before I could even turn to her, she had taken off again, leaving me in the Fields of Asphodel alone. She flew overhead and I followed, moving deeper and deeper into the fields until I worried that I would lose myself and join the hoards of pale, still figures.

I heard a whistle overhead and looked up. The Sphinx hovered above me, her wings beating a breeze my way. She jerked her head, indicating that I should follow. I moved through the tall grass, my eyes fixed on her figure above me. I stumbled and crashed to the ground and when I looked up the Sphinx was gone.

The tall grass swayed around me as I felt a panic grip at my throat. I closed my eyes and listened for the beat of her wings but all I could hear was the rush of wind throughout the grass.

I was lost.

I pushed through the tall grass and listened out for the Sphinx but was met with an oppressive silence. Yellow grass parted before me like curtains when I began to hear another sound, a low hissing. I froze. The grass waved around me as I stood still, listening for that strange sound. Again, I heard it.

Hisssssss.

Then I heard the Sphinx call out to me.

"Answer me this: I came from afar to settle in your land. To become king, I slayed what I would later become. Who am I?"

The hissing grew louder as the creature drew closer, the Sphinx's carelessly called-out riddle my only aid. Thoughts took flight within me, and I remembered a story Pyrrha had told to me long ago. The story of the founding of Thebes.

"This story, like so many, begins with father Zeus. Zeus looked down on the world from his seat on Olympus to the kingdom of Tyre, where he spied a beautiful maiden.

Enflamed with desire, Zeus descended to earth in the form of a great bull and approached the maiden while she was out playing. The maiden climbed atop the bull's back and he swam her out to sea.

Zeus did not carry off just any girl, but Europa, the daughter of Agenor, the king of Tyre himself. Stricken with grief, Agenor ordered his son Cadmus to seek his sister.

Like so many before him, and many after, Cadmus went to Delphi to seek the wisdom of the god. In his search for his beloved sister, he came to our city through the words of Apollo. The god of prophecy had told him to follow a young cow to a deserted place and when she stopped to rest upon the grass he was to build his city's walls.

Sure enough, Cadmus spotted a heifer and he and his men followed her to our land. He fell to his knees in thanks and ordered his men to find a spring so that they might pour libations to Zeus. But the spring was guarded by a mighty serpent sacred to Ares, a terrible beast with three rows of teeth dripping with venom.

As Cadmus' men came stomping through that sacred spring, the serpent darted out, striking down each man with its deadly bite. Impatient, he set out for the spring himself, his spear in his hand.

Finally, he found the spring but also the corpses of his friends. He fell to his knees, his head in his hands, his spear forgotten, keening their loss. But there, in the corner of his eyes, he saw movement. The serpent coiled its body back upon itself, ready to strike.

Cadmus reached for his fallen spear and hurled it at the beast." Pyrrha leapt from her perch on her stool and mimicked throwing a spear as we laughed. *"A hit! But not a fatal wound. Enraged now, the serpent reared back, its triple jaws dripping venom, and struck."* She ducked. *"Cadmus leapt away and reached for his shield, bashing at the beast. He rolled towards his spear, still embedded in the serpent's flank, only to tear it out and plant the spear down its vile throat.*

Cadmus looked up and there stood Athena! The bright-eyed goddess bade him to collect the serpent's teeth, to plow the ground and sow the viper's teeth. These were to become seeds of men.

Cadmus put the yoke upon his own back, plowed the dark earth, tossing the teeth into its depths. They sank into the earth with a hiss. The earth began to stir and from the ground grew spears like trees, gripped by hands attached to armed men. No sooner had these men risen from the earth did they fall upon each other, jabbing and striking, dealing fatal blows until only five remained.

Together, Cadmus and the five sown men founded the city of Thebes."

I opened my eyes. Cadmus came to Thebes to found our city all those years ago. He fought and slayed the serpent of Ares. But what of the second part of the riddle? What did Cadmus become?

The hissing drew closer and I squeezed my eyes closed once again, willing myself to remember. Again, Pyrrha's voice drifted from the past.

"Would you like to hear another story about Cadmus? Or are you too old for my stories?" my nurse asked.

"Never too old for your stories." I smiled at her, settling at her feet.

"The serpent, you may remember, was sacred to Ares. When the war god learned his sacred beast was slain, he went to Cadmus and demanded a year of service from him to pay recompense. Cadmus agreed. At the end of his year, Ares gave Cadmus a gift, his daughter Harmonia.

Harmonia, the daughter of Aphrodite, was the most beautiful woman Cadmus had ever seen. The marriage was celebrated in the Cadmeia and all the gods came as guests. Cadmus gave his wife a robe and necklace as a gift. The necklace was forged by Hephaestus himself. Cadmus received the necklace from the divine smith in good faith, he did not know the evils it contained.

For you see, Aphrodite was Hephaestus' wife. Her affair with Ares was a great shame for him. He hated the daughter of his wife and her lover. So he cursed the necklace of his own making, a necklace of glittering emeralds."

"What of the curse? What happened to her?" I leaned forward in my seat.

Pyrrha sighed. *"There are a couple of stories in between but the necklace cursed Harmonia and all her children. Cadmus,* recalling the mighty serpent he had slain, wondered if the cause of his family's misfortune was his deed so many years before. 'If the gods want to punish me for slaying that snake, then snake I should be!' And his body lengthened and scales sprouted to cover his tender flesh." Pyrrha reached out in front of herself, continuing, "Cadmus tried to call out to his wife but the words died on his tongue, speaking only in hisses. Harmonia, beholding what remained of her beloved husband, called to the gods above. 'Take me too, take me too!' She shed her mortal form so she could be with her husband, forever."

"That's so sad," I sighed. "Must all curses end with deaths or some terrible transformation?"

Pyrrha looked at me and said, "Ismene, life ends with death. And transforms us on the way."

I opened my eyes.

Of course. Cadmus was cursed to become a serpent himself, the same creature he had killed to found his city.

I listened out for the hissing and instead of shying from it, I approached it. I crouched down and parted the grass in front of me to reveal two serpents entwined together. Both were deep black, but one had a band of bright green about its neck. That must be Harmonia and her necklace.

But how would I collect it? I watched the snakes for some time as they twisted around one another. I rose to my feet and took a step backward and heard a soft crunch.

I looked down and gasped. Beneath my feet were two snake skins. I had crushed one, but the other was intact. I could see from the slight green sheen around the neck that it belonged to Harmonia. Heaving a sigh of relief, I lifted the skin and placed it in my pouch.

I stepped through the tall grass, my eyes on the distant figure of the Sphinx soaring ahead. I seemed to travel through that sea of grass for ages until the grass ended and I stood on the shore of a riverbed.

Across the water, the land was bathed in warm sunshine and lush groves, the echo of laughter stretched across the riverbed. That shining place must be the Elysian Fields, the place where good souls went after death. I longed to wade through the bright water surrounding that land. I took a step forward and remembered.

The Elysian fields were surrounded by the last river of the Underworld, the river Lethe. Lethe was the river of forgetfulness and those who crossed to Elysian must first drink of its waters to be relieved of the painful memories of their life. I couldn't risk going into that water, not if one small sip could make me forget my purpose.

The clapping of wings echoed above me and I looked up. The Sphinx was circling overhead. She dove and landed at my feet.

"Are we going there next?" I asked her. Maybe she could fly us across.

She followed my gaze across the river and shook her head. "That is not the place for you or me," she said. "A place in Elysian must be *earned*."

The longer I looked over at Elysian, the more it tugged at my heart. I tore my eyes away to face the monster at my side.

"Well, what next?"

The Sphinx still gazed across at the splendid place, a wistful expression on her monstrous face. She, too, seemed to have to tear her gaze away. "Answer me this: The one who

came from afar, what must he create from what he destroyed
to rule over his new land?"

The Sphinx had mentioned one who came from afar in
her last riddle. Cadmus, he destroyed the serpent of Ares to
rule over Thebes.

"Create from what he destroyed?" I murmured, turning
back to look at the tall grasses of Asphodel. I thought back to
Pyrrha's stories of our city's founder. He had slain the serpent
and sown its teeth into the earth and up sprouted men. The
Spartoi, the Sown Men! The five families who advised the
king of Thebes. But how would I find one of the *Spartoi* here?

It was as if the Sphinx had read my thoughts.

"I think you will find your answer over there." She nodded
her head and took off into the air before I could turn.

A figure sat on the riverbed just south of me, his posture
relaxed. He seemed to be waiting for someone.

Something in the set of his shoulders, the way his head
was thrown back to soak in the light dancing off the water
sparked recognition in me.

It couldn't be.

I ran down to him and burst into tears. The figure sitting
on the banks of the River Lethe was a ghost. The ghost of my
cousin Menoeceus.

I approached my cousin cautiously, as if any sudden
movements would dissipate him like smoke.

Without opening his eyes, Menoeceus called over to me.
"Finally. I've been waiting for you."

I crossed over to him and sank to the riverbed beside him,
as close as I could be without actually touching him, afraid
that if I brushed against him there would be nothing there.

Menoeceus opened one eye to peer at me and nudged me with his shoulder. He was solid.

I choked back a sob and threw myself at him.

"I'm sorry. I'm so sorry. I tried so hard to stop the war, to stop the prophecy from happening."

Menoeceus patted my back. "Some things are fated to happen." He placed his hands on my shoulders and looked down into my face. "But you can still change other things."

A shiver ran down my spine at the urgency in his voice.

"I can?"

"I *know* you can. Keep on your path, Ismene. Follow the Sphinx's riddles and once you have collected everything, you must find the goddess."

"Artemis. But how can I find her?" I held onto his arms, afraid to let go.

"Heed the Sphinx's counsel but be wary around her. She will tell you what you need to know but do not put your trust in her beyond that," he warned, his eyes fixed on my face. "Don't despair. You are doing all you can." He smiled. "But before you go off to finish your quest, I have something for you." He reached for his collar and withdrew a leather cord that hung beneath his tunic. Tied to the end of the cord was a single tooth. It was as pale as ivory and slender as a needle.

The serpent's tooth.

"Take it. After this, there is one last sign you will need." He pulled the cord over his head and pushed it into my hands. I opened the pouch at my waist and tucked the serpent's tooth inside.

"Thank you." I threw my arms around him once more and held him tight. He held on just as tightly. I didn't want to say goodbye. Not yet. Not ever.

"Remember, you have to collect one more sign and then you must find the goddess."

"What is the last sign? How will I find it?" I asked.

"The riddles of the Sphinx will tell you," he answered. His eyes drifted behind me to where the shores of Elysian waited for him.

I grabbed his arm. "No. Not yet, please."

He placed a hand atop my own and gently pried my fingers loose. "It is time."

We stood together and approached the shores of the River Lethe. Menoeceus turned to me for the last time and hugged me close.

"Goodbye, Ismene."

"Goodbye."

I let go of him and he stepped into the river, wading across its shining waters.

He did not turn back.

19

THE LAST SIGN

I let the tears dry on my face as I waited for the Sphinx to return.

Soon enough, I saw her circle overhead and dive to meet me. She sat on her haunches and faced me.

"Do you have something to say to me?" I asked her, wiping furiously at the tears that ran down my face, bracing myself for another riddle.

She nodded. "War and destruction will find you when all your father's shadows come to light."

"That isn't a riddle," I protested. "You're repeating what the Pythia said to me. How is that supposed to help me?" I recalled Menoeceus' words from moments ago.

Heed the Sphinx's counsel but be wary around her. She will tell you what you need to know but do not put your trust in her beyond that.

Why was the Sphinx refusing to help me, now that I was so close to completing my task? Menoeceus said not to trust her but she brought me this far. Why would she sit back and watch me fumble my last sign?

"You need no riddle for this last task," she replied. She turned her back to me and stalked away into the long grasses of Asphodel. "The answer is right before you." Her voice was swallowed up as she disappeared within the waving grass.

The answer was right before me? I turned to Elysian. Perhaps she meant for me to go there? But she said one had to earn a place in Elysian, that one could not simply cross onto its shores.

Perhaps she meant for me to go back into the Fields of Asphodel, but who knew how long it would take for me to travel through the fields of grass without losing myself within its depths?

I threw myself to the ground with a great cry of exasperation. I knelt there on the banks of the River Lethe and tried to think. I closed my eyes and listened to the rush of the water. But then, I picked up another sound, a faint voice crying out in the distance.

My eyes snapped open.

I turned my head, following the voice until I saw a figure stumbling ahead of me. He was scrambling at the river's edge. I stood and raced over to the figure, thinking that he was drowning. As I drew closer, I saw that he was bent towards the river, trying to cup its water in his palms. But every time he brought his cupped hands to his lips, the water disappeared and he cried out in anguish.

He wanted to drink from the River Lethe to forget some great trouble. But the man was being punished by being denied what he desired the most.

I took a step back, dismissing the man in front of me as just some other lost soul when a twig snapped beneath my feet.

The man turned from his pursuit to face me. "Who's there?" he called out.

I was standing right in front of him but he could not see me.

His eyes had been gouged out.

I stared at the figure in alarm, realising too late who the blind figure must be.

The ghost of my father was standing before me.

I stood in silence for some time, the lapping of the water upon the shore the only sound.My father stumbled to his feet and stepped towards me, his arms reaching out before him like a child learning to walk for the first time. After spending so long with the blind seer Tiresias, I went to his side to offer him my arm. His hand fumbled up my sleeve to land on my shoulder and I led him to a rock where we could sit.

"Who are you?" he repeated.

I struggled to find my answer. I thought of all the different identities I had assumed in the last three months, ready to assume any identity but my own. I had been running from myself for so long I no longer knew who I was, I no longer knew my place in the world.

"A friend," I answered.

"And what friends can a man expect to find in the Underworld?" my father asked. "I haven't been dead for very long but even I know that I am being punished for the way I lived my life."

Hadn't been dead for very long? I frowned. I had not seen my father since I was a child, which was more than ten years ago.

"What is it?" he asked. He stiffened and shifted away from me. "Do you know me?"

"I know you. You are Oedipus. King of Thebes."

His shoulders sagged at the sound of his name. "King no longer."

"That is true. You haven't been king for eleven years. The people were told you had died of the plague. If you haven't been dead for very long, what have you been doing all this time?" Maybe if I knew more about the man I had come from, I could figure out who I was meant to be.

Oedipus ran a hand down his weathered cheeks before he spoke, a familiar gesture I had seen my brothers make. Something they must have picked up from him when they were younger. I felt my heart splinter within me at the sight.

"I wandered throughout Hellas, trying to atone for what I had done. I wandered for years trying to find a place to rest, but I was often driven out. I settled in a grove in Colonus sacred to the Furies. It was an oddly fitting place for the man I had become to die. This angry, bitter shell of a man would rest in a place sacred to hatred and revenge." Anger twisted his features as he spoke.

"Why would you be angry?" I asked him.

He faced me with a scowl. "I thought you knew who I was. Kinslayer. How could I ever find peace?"

I pushed off from the rock and paced, trying to fight against the anger I felt rise within me. Once I had controlled my anger, I paused to face him. "I know who you are. King, father, saviour of a city."

"What are you talking about?" he snapped.

"You found Laius' killer and you ended the plague on your city. You saved your people."

He leaped to his feet to face me. "*I* am Laius's killer. *I'm* the reason Apollo plagued my city in the first place."

I stepped towards him and took his hands in mine. "But you didn't know that. Once you did you set things right. You saved them."

He pushed me away from him, dropping my hands from his. "You don't know what you are talking about." He turned away from me.

"I do. I am a Theban myself. Our city has been safe for years. But now it is under siege. Your sons wage war against one another."

He whirled around, shouting, "Good! They city doesn't deserve to stand any longer. Let them raze it to the ground!"

"How can you say that! Think of your people, think of your daughters," I shouted back at him.

He froze. He turned around to face me. I did not shy away from his scarred face. I noticed his jaw clenched in anger as we spoke about our city, now his jaw slackened in surprise when I mentioned his daughters.

"Daughters." He stepped towards me hesitantly. "What do you know of my daughters?"

I fought to speak against the lump forming in my throat.

"I know them well."

"What are they like?" he asked.

I struggled to speak. Moments ago, he became enraged at the mere mention of my brothers. But seeing the way he softened when my sister and I were mentioned nearly broke my heart in two. I cleared my throat. "Antigone is talented and clever. She weaves so beautifully you would have thought Athena herself to have created her fine tapestries. She cares for her sister and looks out for her brothers despite the animosity that has grown between them."

"And Ismene?"

My heart did break to hear the sound of my own name spoken by my long-lost father. My name was a prayer on his lips. I only wished I could provide the solace he sought.

"Ismene tries her best. She isn't as clever or as talented as her sister but she loves her family just as fiercely and she will do anything to save them," I spoke through tears.

My father was quiet for some time as he took in my words.

"Do they...do they know the truth about me?" I heard his own heart breaking as he asked the question he feared the most.

"They know their father saved their city and they miss him every day. They are proud to be the daughters of such a great king."

He sobbed at my words and sank to the ground. I went to him and put a hand on his shoulder.

"They wouldn't be so proud if they knew what I had done," he gasped through his tears.

I drew back. "What have you done?"

"There was a prophecy. An oracle from the Pythia. She said that my grave would be a site of victory for the city in whose territory it lies. I could have returned home to Thebes and let my body offer protection to my city, my family. But I had become so twisted with hatred, a cursed old man whose crimes have doubly cursed the ones I loved. I vowed I would never return."

"What are you talking about?"

"The god said that where I chose to rest will reward my friends and punish my enemies. I chose to rest in Colonus." He gestured to the empty clearing around him. "All I had those long, lonely years was my hatred. I had forgotten what

I had left behind, what still needed protection." He stepped towards me and grasped my shoulders, placing his face close to mine. "You want to save Thebes? Go to Colonus and retrieve my bones. Lay them to rest in Thebes so that I can protect my daughters."

My breath caught in my throat at his words. He drew in closer.

"Can you pass a message to them? To my daughters?"

I nodded, tears streaming down my face.

"There are some advantages to being dead, for the dead have the power of foresight. I have seen flashes of my children's lives. Tell them I am proud. Tell Antigone, for too long she has taken up the sorrows of others, making their grief her own. No more. She should be comforted as she comforts others. She should have the life she deserves."

"I will tell her," I whispered.

His hands tightened on my shoulders. "Tell Ismene, guardian of my house, she has left safety behind to challenge fate and try to save this family. I had tried the same and failed. Let the Fates destroy what is cursed and rotten in our family. My daughters are the only light in all my shadows, and they will continue to shine."

I could feel the sobs try to break free from my throat but I kept them inside, trying to be strong for my father.

"Go." He pressed a kiss to my forehead.

I stood still, my head bowed, not wanting to watch him head back to the waters of the River Lethe to retreat towards the water, reaching for the oblivion. When I lifted my eyes, I was surprised to see the figure of my father still looming before me.

"But, before you go…" As he spoke he put a hand within his torn *chiton* and withdrew something, I couldn't see what he clutched in his clenched fist. "I wondered if you might take these with you? I've held onto them for so long, reaching for them to prick my fingers and remind myself of my sins. I think I would like to let go of them now."

He stretched out his arm. I placed my cupped palms beneath his closed fist and I watched his face as he passed his burden onto me. The years melted away, his stooped spine straightened, his hair darkened. He passed a hand over his brow and when he removed them, his eyes had been restored, eyes that were the same shade as my own. He looked at me in wonder and smiled. I smiled back at the man my father once was, the man I had seen in my visions.

Then, he turned from me to head towards the shores of the river Lethe and the water did not shy away from him then but bore him across to Elysian.

I looked down at what he had placed in my hands and gasped. Cupped in my palms were the pins my father had plucked from my mother's body to blind himself with. The pins were the representation of his guilt and shame. I knew that they must be my final sign. Gingerly, I placed the pins in my pouch.

I had collected all the signs. It was time to change fate.

20

OUT OF THE SHADOWS

I made my way through the tall grasses of the Fields of Asphodel, my own laboured breathing the only sound to reach my ears. As I moved deeper and deeper into the fields, I realised how lost I was.

The tall grass waved in the slight breeze all around me. The grass had grown so high I could only see a small stretch of what lay overhead. I pushed through and occasionally caught sight of one of the dead, standing stock still, their face devoid of any colour. The sight chilled me to my bones.

After some time, I looked up, expecting to see the Sphinx circling overhead, but all I saw was darkness. I gripped my pouch tighter to my chest, its precious contents giving me strength. I *had* to find my way out of here.

But how? And once I got out of the Underworld, how would I find the goddess? And once I found her, would she agree to help me to use her golden distaff to make my otherworldly thread with the signs I had collected? The signs held great meaning to me and my journey, but they were not formed of flax or wool. If she didn't agree to help me, how could I spin rock and snakeskin and gold pins to make thread?

I sank to the ground, weariness overcoming me at last. I clenched my teeth in desperation, gritting them so hard that I half-expected my teeth to crumble to dust. Had I just wasted more time on another useless journey? I clutched the pouch, suppressing the urge to toss it away in anger.

No, I had not wasted my time. I was on the right path. I just had to keep following it.

A gust of air stirred my curls and I looked up to see the Sphinx circling. She did not call out instructions as she had before, she simply continued to soar above me.

I looked around, looking for a sign, a hint—*anything* that would help me find my way.

I looked up again and the Sphinx was gone.

I had a sudden flash of my first vision of the Sphinx atop the rocks, her feathers stiff with gore and fresh blood still dripping from her paws. I gulped. What if she had decided not to help me any longer? What if she had remembered her liking of human flesh? I closed my eyes and saw the bones littered around her cave. I opened my eyes once more. I stood still, willing my beating heart to quiet. The grass rustled all around me, something was there, waiting for me. I was too afraid to move.

Something that felt like a cool, dry fingertip drew along my skin and I leaped out of the way. I spun in a circle looking around for whatever had touched me. It must have been one of the shorter lengths of grass brushing up against me. I shuddered all the same.

I looked around frantically, the grass seemingly growing taller all around me, until I felt as if I was as tiny and as insignificant as an ant. I thought of the grey, listless spirits trapped within the fields and swore I would not join their ranks.

Now was not the time to cower in fright. I straightened my spine and faced my fears. I would not let the Sphinx make a meal of me.

"What, no riddles for me now?" I called out to the darkness.

The Sphinx laughed, the sound like the grating of bronze against stone.

"The end of woes will come when the descendants of the Ismenian serpent restore worship of the gods." Her voice echoed all around me. I could not pinpoint her direction.

Menoeceus had told me not to trust her, yet her words struck true with me. I knew they were important but at the same time, I knew she was not speaking of how I could get out of the Underworld. Instead, she was giving me a clue, *at last*, on how to help my family.

But to help them, I had to find my way out of here first.

The descendants of the Ismenian serpent. Could she mean the serpent that Cadmus slew and took its teeth to sow the founders of my city?

"Do you mean the *Spartoi*?" I called out into the darkness. There was no reply save for the waving grass all around me.

The Ismenian serpent. How did I not know that the serpent shared my own name? It was not a coincidence.

I knew now what I needed to do. I must use the signs, the bones of my father and the assistance of one of the *Spartoi* together to save what was left of my family.

I stepped forward to part the grass before me and spotted two eyes glowing in the darkness. Before I could retreat, the Sphinx leapt straight towards me, her needle sharp teeth going for my throat.

With a cry, I threw myself backwards and rolled out of

the way. The Sphinx landed in the spot where I had been only moments before, her claws extended to pierce the earth beneath her. She whipped her head towards me and snarled.

I stumbled to my feet and ran, the pounding of the Sphinx's paws against the earth and the beat of her wings accompanied the fierce beating of my heart.

A great weight knocked into me from behind and I felt a sharp pain in my shoulder. I cried out.

The Sphinx had pinned me to the ground. I dared a glance over my shoulder and flinched. Her face was inches away from my own.

She leaned closer, her fetid breath warm against my face.

"Love of your family and nothing else will destroy you."

She opened her mouth wide, her teeth dripping with saliva and my blood, her eyes fixed on the rapid pulse that fluttered at the base of my throat. I longed to close my eyes and give in.

But her words made me pause. I looked her in the eyes. "If love of my family and nothing else will destroy me, you will not."

With a scream, the Sphinx threw herself away from me, her wings beating furiously behind her. The great grass bent all around us and the listless ghosts turned as one to stare in our direction. Their blank eyes fixed on the Sphinx and my own blood trickling down her chin.

Pyrrha had told me of heroes that spoke to the dead. How the only way to get the attention of a ghost was with blood. The ghosts had paid no heed to us before but now, with my blood bright and glistening on the Sphinx's face, they had all their attention focused on her.

They shuffled forward, their colourless hands reached for her, grasping at her feathers, the stiff tufts of fur, the Sphinx cried out as the ghosts leaned in to lick the blood from her face.

I dug my fingers into the earth until my fists were full of dirt and I reached for the wound on my shoulder, packing the earth into the punctures so the ghosts would not spot the blood there.

The Sphinx cried out as ghosts swarmed around her. I could no longer see her. Scarcely daring to breathe, I rose to my feet and stepped backwards until I was swallowed by the tall grass once more.

When the ghosts were no longer in sight, I began to run. The blades of grass whipped against me as I rushed past but I did not slow down until I had left the final cries of the Sphinx long behind me.

Finally, the Fields of Asphodel were silent once more.

I sank to the ground and grabbed for my pouch, opening it to gaze at its contents. I smiled.

I would use the signs, the bones of my father and the aid of one of the *Spartoi* together to change fate, save my family and maybe my kingdom, too.

I had found my path. Now all I needed was to follow that path out of the darkness.

And who had brought me out of the darkness once before?

I closed my eyes and kneeled in supplication.

"Apollo," I called out.

The waving grass stood still, the absence of that light breeze causing goosebumps to crawl up my arms.

"Apollo," I called out again. "Help me." I bent my head and waited for the god's familiar voice to tell me what to do next.

The voice never spoke.

Tears gathered on my lashes to fall upon the grey earth of the Underworld. Of course, he hadn't come to help. What did I expect? He told me I would fail.

I clenched my hands in frustration and felt something warm brush against my palms. I opened my eyes.

There, cupped in my palms, was a beam of light thin and stretched out like a line of thread. I reached for that thread of light until it danced between my fingertips and watched, amazed, as it stretched through the ghost-filled fields pointing the way out to the land of the living.

I grinned. The god had given me a path of light once more.

"I thought you said I couldn't change my fate?"

Don't make me regret helping you, the voice replied in my mind, its presence a familiar friend in that dark place.

I grasped the light in my hands and made my way out of the Underworld.

The light of the god blazed among those shadows who had lost the light. The Sphinx did not turn up again. I found myself missing her company—to journey through the Underworld with a companion was one thing, to do it alone was another completely.

I was struck by the silence of this place of the dead, pierced by a wail or a scream. I kept my eyes focused on the light and kept going, past the listless ghosts and trembling shades.

When Cerberus, the three headed hound of Hades, stalked by, the light dimmed and I felt myself dim as well, the light of the god protecting me from the beast's sight. Standing beneath those triple rows of teeth, I was glad of the god's favour then.

After scaling the dark rock of the Underworld, I emerged to the land of the living. I felt as if the shadows of death clung to me still and I fought in vain to shake them off. I stumbled out from the darkness of the Underworld into the moonlit night. I had emerged from an opening in the earth and found myself in a grove. Cypress trees trembled in the night breeze, their leaves limned with silver.

I gulped in the fresh night air, a welcome respite from the sulphurous air of the House of Hades. I stepped through the cypress trees that stood sentinel around me and looked around, my surroundings glowing in the moonlight. I noted the sloping ground, the light air and realised I was on a mountainside.

I sat upon the dew soaked grass and waited, twirling the threads of light between my fingers. The god would come and aid me.

The trees rustled around me. The thread of golden light flared in the night air and went out.

I sat up in the sudden darkness, fear making my blood run cold.

The woods were watching me.

The back of my neck tingled. I could feel the weight of its gaze settle on my shoulders like a heavy woolen cloak.

A glowing figure stepped out of the trees, a pair of silver does followed close behind them.

"I saw your light—" the figure began, but fell silent when spotting me sitting on the damp grass. "You are not my brother. Why do you carry his light with you?"

I had expected one god to aid me and another had arrived. The one I had been searching for.

Artemis.

21

Into the Light

Artemis, the Huntress, Queen of Beasts, stepped out from the shadows of the cypress trees, the white armed goddess glowed sliver, as if she was bathed in moonlight. The immortal goddess looked around the clearing, a furrow in her brow.

"I followed my brother's light here, but you are not him. Who are you?" she repeated, her fingers tightening on the bow she gripped in her hand.

I scrambled to my feet, tugging my *chiton* straight. "I am Ismene. I am favoured by your brother," I replied.

The goddess arched her brow. "Why has he led you here to me?"

"I need your help." I stepped closer to the goddess, kneeling and grasping at her knees in supplication.

"None of that," the goddess scolded, using the tip of her bow to raise my chin to look her in the eyes. "What do you need of me, girl favoured by my brother?"

As I looked into her eyes that shone like the moon above us, my words died in my throat. I swallowed and tried again.

"My nurse told me stories of you, *Aristo*, best of the immortal gods. She told me that you are *Chryselacatus*, of the golden distaff. I spent most of my life in the women's quarters, spinning wool to thread and weaving and dreaming of the virgin goddess with her golden distaff. Please, can you use your distaff to spin me a thread so wondrous even the Fates themselves will covet its beauty?" I reached for my pouch and showed her its contents: the tears of Niobe, the sustenance of Tantalus, Harmonia's necklace, the serpent's tooth and my father's shadows.

The goddess peered into the pouch. "Ah, you have brought me signs of great importance. But they are signs of great importance to *you*." She stepped back.

"But look!" I cried, raising my offering higher. "I have brought you the tears of your enemy, too!"

"Yes, you have." She placed a finger on her chin in thought. "It's not enough, but..." I felt the hope shine from my face. "But I will accept it as payment as a favour to my brother." She reached down and snatched the pouch from my grasp.

I tried not to cry. I had worked so hard to gather the signs, and they all held such great meaning to me. It wounded me to hear that my hard work was not enough. I let go of the pouch and watched the goddess sling it over her own shoulder. She reached behind her and withdrew her distaff wrought of gold.

"Please," I asked, "what will you spin to make thread? Will you spin the clouds like you did with your mother?" I tried not to let my worry colour my voice. I feared a thread of clouds would not be enough to tempt the Fates.

The goddess smiled at me. "Surely, your nurse told you. But maybe she didn't know *all* the tales about me. I haven't spun clouds since I was a girl. Now..." She reached into the air, her hand bathed in silvery light. She made a fist and I watched in amazement as the light bent into her grasp. "Now, I spin moonlight."

I sat in awe as Artemis gathered moonlight in her hand and wrapped it around the conical end of the distaff, turning it until the moonlight gathered in shimmering strands of light. The goddess worked in silence for some time, the stars coming out from behind the dark clouds that hung overhead to watch her progress.

Finally, she gathered the delicate length of moonlight in her hands and passed it to me. It weighed nothing in my hands, glittering faintly as I passed the thread through my fingers. The Fates would covet this for their own.

"Thank you!"

The goddess raised a brow. "There is no need to thank me. You have paid for my help." She shook my pouch and the sound of its contents jingling filled the clearing. One of the silver deer that flanked her side stretched its neck to nibble at the pouch. The goddess snatched it out of the way with a laugh. She scratched the animal behind the ears and turned to leave. I threw myself at her feet and grabbed at her ankles.

"Wait!" She couldn't leave yet.

The goddess did not look amused. "What else do you want?" She sighed.

"Can you help me find the Fates?"

"I could," she replied. I waited for her to go on. She rolled her eyes in exasperation. "I could once you have offered something in payment."

I spread my hands out in front of me. "I have nothing left to give," I protested.

She nodded. "There's your answer then."

"Wait! Please, give me some time to think."

The goddess tapped her foot. "Go on."

My thoughts raced, trying to come up with something, anything, that a goddess would find worthy. The help of a goddess would not come cheap—I would have to give up something else dear to me, something that a goddess would value. What else could you offer a god? Inspiration struck me like one of Zeus's lightning bolts.

"What about a vow?"

The goddess ceased tapping her foot. "I'm listening."

"What if I were to vow to remain unmarried, a maiden, like you?"

A moment before, the goddess stood across the clearing from me. Now, she stood so close, her face was inches from my own.

Artemis's lambent eyes bore into mine. "A vow is no light thing to make," she said. "You know what will happen if you break it."

I did. I knew the stories of men ripped apart by their own hunting dogs, of the goddess' own nymphs transformed into beasts. If I were to break that vow, she would not be lenient.

But I had nothing else to offer. I gulped. "I know."

Artemis smiled. "Good. Now, say the words."

I took a breath, glancing at the animals that flanked the immortal facing me and wondering if they were once girls that broke a vow. I looked down at the moonlight spilling from my hands and knew what I had to do.

I tucked the thread of moonlight inside my *chiton* and held my arms out in front of me, my palms facing upwards, the posture of a worshipper before their god making an offering. I closed my eyes. "I vow to remain a maiden for the rest of my days."

I opened my eyes to see Artemis smiling down at me. "Alright." She jerked her chin, indicating I should follow.

I went to her side and the goddess took my hand.

We ran in the moonlight, the does leaping and bounding beside us. I was giddy from the ramifications of my vow and a laugh tore from my lips. Together, the goddess and I raced down the mountain until we came to a small opening in the rock. Artemis stilled. I came to halt beside her, panting from exertion.

"Here is your entrance. Follow the path and you will find the Fates." The goddess threw up an arm and the clouds obscuring the face of the lovely moon parted and a beam of silvery light shone into the crevice. "Remember your vow."

"I will," I replied.

Artemis raced off into the trees, the does following close behind her.

I took a deep breath and descended into Hades once more.

I followed the path of moonlight deep into the earth, that beam of light growing weaker and weaker the further I descended until it faded to nothing. I expected the darkness of the Underworld to overwhelm me but I could see lights flickering ahead. I headed in that direction until I could see the source—the flickering flames of torches that danced across the cavern where the *Moirai* did their work.

I stood in the shadows for a while, mustering my courage and watching the three figures as they ambled around. Pyrrha had raised me on stories of them and I felt like I was watching old acquaintances. There was Clotho, spinning the threads from her distaff. And there was Lachesis, who judged the length of each thread and the lives they represented, holding her measuring rod aloft. And there, her face shrouded by the mantle pulled up over her head, was Atropos, gleaming shears clutched in her hand that she used to cut lives short.

Great lengths of threads of every colour stretched throughout the cavern like the web of a great spider. Occasionally, Lachesis would reach out her arms to take hold of one and inspect it. I held my breath as I watched her stretch out a length of thread and measure it against the rod in one hand, the other hand she used to gesture to Atropos. She then pinched the thread near the top of the rod and nodded to her sister. Atropos took out her shears and the sound of the blades closing around the thread echoed throughout the chamber like a thunderclap.

I jumped and clapped my hands to my ears with a squeak of alarm. Three heads turned towards me in unison.

"Who's there?" Clotho called out hoarsely, her distaff spun in her hands.

"Who's there?" Lachesis cried shrilly, brandishing her measuring rod like a weapon.

"Who's there?" Atropos whispered, her shears glinting in the torchlight.

I stepped out of the shadows.

"Who are you?" Clotho snapped.

Who are you? Who are you? Her sisters' voices echoed.

Lachesis glanced my way and reached behind her to grasp a thread. As soon as her fingers touched it, I felt a tug on my heart.

"Here she is," Lachesis called to her sisters. She peered at the thread and squinted towards me. "The little princess of Thebes."

I cleared my throat. "Yes, I am a princess of Thebes. I am Ismene."

"We know that," Lachesis replied, tossing the thread of my life over her shoulder like it meant nothing. I winced at the feeling. But then, I noticed that clinging close to mine was another thread.

"And who is that?" I asked, pointing at the thread that clung to my own.

Lachesis glanced down. "Oh, that? Some lives are entwined so closely together, their bonds so strong that they keep getting caught together. It's a big nuisance, it is." She sighed, trying to untangle the two. I felt another tug in my chest.

"And whose life is bound so closely to my own?"

"Don't you know?" Lachesis asked, surprised. She tugged and tugged at the string until it came loose from my own and she held it up for me to see. A thread of white.

"It's your sister's," Atropos whispered from behind me.

I jumped. I didn't realise she stood so close to me. Her face was still hidden in the shadows so I couldn't make out her expression. But her voice sounded amused. I suppressed a shudder.

Antigone. Of course, her life was so closely bound to my own. Before I had left the Cadmeia months ago, we had never been apart. I felt a sharp pain in my chest the longer Lachesis held the two threads apart.

"I'm glad you brought it up," Lachesis mused, taking out her measuring rod from beside her. My blood ran cold. No, it couldn't be time. Ice crept through my veins as I watched her measure the thread of my sister's life and pinch the thread. "Just about time."

Atropos began to brush past me, raising the shears in her hands. I grasped at her arm. Her head jerked back and the hood fell from her face. I was expecting something hideous but her face looked exactly the same as her sister's. I dropped my hand from her arm. Atropos placed the blades of the shears on either side of the thread, the blade so sharp I could see the fibres of the thread began to break.

"Wait!" I shouted. The three women turned and stared. "You don't want to cut that thread short."

"Yes, we do," Lachesis snapped. "Look at it, so frail and thin. It's liable to snap on its own anyway."

"What if we made it stronger?"

The three women paused.

"What do you mean 'stronger?'" Lachesis asked, cocking her head to the side.

"You said it yourself, the thread is too thin. If we were to reinforce it with another thread, it would hold longer."

"And what," huffed Clotho as she stood from her stool, "is wrong with my thread?"

"Nothing!" I held up my hands. "It's just, you've been using the same wool for so long, I thought you might like something new."

"Something new?" Clotho frowned.

"Something new?" Lachesis scoffed.

"Something new?" Atropos considered.

"Yes, something new. I went out and asked the goddess Artemis herself to spin you something special."

"Artemis?" Atropos repeated.

"Artemis," Clotho spat. "And what makes her distaff better than mine?" She gestured to the ancient distaff of ash wood sitting atop her stool.

"Well, it is made of gold," Lachesis said.

"And what did she spin for us?" Clotho asked.

I smiled at her. "Something wonderful."

I reached within my *chiton* and withdrew the length of moonlight. It glittered in the cavern like polished silver.

The *Moirai* gasped, all three eagerly reached for the thread. But I held it out of reach.

"Is this worthy of the *Moirai*?'

"*Yes,*" they replied as one.

"Can you use it to reinforce that thread? To extend that life?" I tried to keep my emotions from colouring my words. But surely, they could see the love that blazed from my eyes as I looked at the representation of my sister's life.

"We could," Lachesis answered, taking hold of the thread of Antigone's life once more. But as she drew it closer, I saw that it had become tangled with my own. "But if we were to reinforce that thread, we wouldn't be able to separate it from your own any longer. The two of you would be bound together."

"We are already bound together."

Lachesis continued speaking as if I hadn't interrupted her. "The two of you would be bound together for life. Her death would be your own."

"Please. I'd do anything for her."

I held out the length of the moonlight. Lachesis plucked it from my grasp and gazed down at the thread. The light emanating from the thread cast the cavern in a silvery glow, so that the three sisters began to shimmer like the goddess herself atop the mountain. Lachesis' eyes reflected the unearthly light. After an eternity, she looked up, her eyes meeting my own.

"So be it." She took the thread of Antigone's life entwined with mine and ever so gently, she passed the thread of moonlight to her sister Clotho. "Bind them together."

Clotho nodded, taking up the threads in her gnarled hands. The threads came apart in her hands to reform as one mass. She spread it on the cavern floor and laid the head of her distaff upon it, turning until it was covered by the glittering fibres. She strode over to her corner and withdrew a drop spindle. After taking a seat upon her stool, she swiftly propped the distaff between her knees and tied one end of the fibres to the spindle and then let the spindle fall, the threads of my life and my sister's life twisting with moonlight as the spindle twirled and fell.

I watched Clotho at work, a heavy feeling in my chest. The gravity of what I had done threatened to overwhelm me. I was binding my life to Antigone's, a reckless thing to do. But if I didn't extend her life with my own, I would lose her forever.

Finally, the spindle ceased spinning. The new thread was complete. It shimmered silver and gold, three threads bound together by the Fates themselves.

"Thank you."

"Do not thank us, girl," Atropos said. "You have done a dangerous thing."

"I have done a noble thing," I protested.

Clotho shrugged. "Dangerous, noble. What's the difference?"

Perhaps she was right. Often the bravest acts were reckless ones. I just hoped this desperate act would save my sister.

My task done, I left the *Moirai* at their work and tried to find my way to the land of the living once more. This time, I did not need to ask the god for aid, a golden light acted as my guide as I made my ascent. After climbing in the darkness for ages, I found a small opening in the rock. I climbed out into the still night air.

     ❋   MEAGAN CLEVELAND   ❋

I had emerged into a grove of ash trees, the home of the *Meliae*, wood nymphs. Pyrrha's tales taught me that the *Meliae* were created from the blood of Ouranos, deposed by his own son the Titan Cronus. But when those drops of blood fell upon the earth it also gave birth to monsters: the Giants and the *Erinyes*. The Furies.

The words of my father echoed in my mind.

I found my place to rest, a grove in Colonus sacred to the Furies. It was an oddly fitting place for the man I had become to die. This angry, bitter shell of a man would rest in a place sacred to hatred and revenge.

I had exited the Underworld at the grave of my father. My father had also said his bones would offer protection to whatever city possessed them. He had ordered me to retrieve his bones and lay them to rest in Thebes so that he could offer protection to his daughters.

I stumbled through the grove until I found a grave, a monumental *sarcophagus* made of limestone and intricately painted. Holding my breath, I approached the *sarcophagus* and, with all my strength, I shifted the lid to reveal the contents within. The bones of my father.

I was seized with fear. Even though his ghost had given me his permission, I found it very hard to bring myself to rob the grave of my own father.

I closed my eyes and thought of Thebes besieged, of Haemon and Antigone and even treacherous Creon. They were all that remained of my family. And I had said time and again I would do *anything* to save them.

I held my breath for a moment and let it go in a rush. Trying not to think too hard on it, I laid my travelling cloak out on the grass and then bent into the *sarcophagus* to withdraw the bones of my father. Carefully, I placed them onto my cloak and wrapped them up. I tied up the bundle and rose to my feet.

"What now?" I murmured to myself.

"Now you try to save Thebes."

I whirled around. Apollo leaned against a tree, grinning at me.

"I thought you wanted me to fail?"

Apollo stood straight and walked over to me.

"I gave you three months to try to find the source of your family curse and break it, or else you would go into my service. I gave you the chance to change your fate, to save your kingdom and your brothers. Your brothers are dead and today, your three months are up."

My heart sank at his words. I couldn't go into his service now, not when I was so close to saving my sister. He was right, I was too late to save my brothers. But it wasn't too late to save Antigone. I noticed that he had omitted one thing.

"But I found the source of the curse. The whole point of my travels was to find out the curse of my family. I learned it was my father who had cursed our family and Thebes by becoming a kinslayer. I learned this before my time was up."

Apollo smiled. "Not one to admit defeat so easily? You're right, you did discover the source of the curse before your three months were up. But you did not break the curse before your time was up."

I glared at him, his skin glowing as brightly as the sun in the gloom.

The sun!

"We made that bargain as the sun was setting. Look around us." I waved at the groove of ash trees. "The sun hasn't risen yet. I have until sundown to break the curse."

His eyes narrowed. "I could just keep you here until the sun rises and sets and our bargain has come to an end."

"You could," I agreed, stepping closer to him. He sucked in a breath at my audacity. "Or you could help me."

"And why would I do that?

"Because of our new bargain."

He raised a brow. "And what bargain is this?"

"That if you allow me to complete my task, I will vow to go into your service."

He froze and the breeze that shook the leaves in the trees overhead stilled as well, as if the world was also holding its breath.

"You vow to go into my service? You won't try to fight me?"

"After sunset, I vow to go into your service."

The wind picked up and the limbs of the ash trees shook and their leaves rustled, the sound like a cheering crowd.

The god grinned. "Alright. We have a bargain. I will allow you to finish your task. Where to next?"

I gestured to the bundle at my feet.

"I need to return the bones of my father to my family tomb."

"How?"

How indeed. I bit at my thumbnail as I thought. I must have tore the skin for the copper tang of blood rushed into my mouth. My last memory of blood surfaced in my mind, the memory of the Sphinx's bloodstained face and the ghosts that tore her apart.

"When I was in the Underworld, time ran differently and I was able to cross great distances quickly. If we were to enter the Underworld, would we be able to take a shortcut to Thebes?"

Apollo nodded.

"Alright, let's go." I lifted the bundle in my arms and set off to find the entrance to the cave.

We travelled through the Underworld once more and exited a cave to find ourselves in a monumental tomb.

"It worked," I breathed, looking around in wonder. "Why, exactly, did it work?"

"Two reasons," Apollo replied. "It is believed that all caves lead to the House of Hades. The land of the dead. And your ancestors had the brilliant idea of carving into the rock to make caves of their own to house the remains of their royalty."

"My family," I said. I lingered in the shadows, not wanting to walk into the chamber that acted as my family tomb.

"And the second reason?" I asked, rubbing at my bare arms for warmth.

He paused and turned around. "This is a place of death." He nodded to the cave. "Places of death have power."

"Why?"

"Places, like people, have memories." He felt the earth beneath him, gathering it in his fingers and blowing the brittle dirt towards me. "This place remembers death."

I shuddered, uneasy to be physically in this place that held the remains of the dead. This was the tomb of my parents. I had no memories of them while they were living, and I disliked the idea of my only memories to be of their remains.

Especially the remains of my mother. While I could not remember Jocasta the person, to me she was an ideal. The perfect mother, the perfect wife, the perfect queen. I was afraid that if I stayed in this place too long, that fragile image would be shattered.

I looked around furtively, as if my mother would rise up out of her *larnax*, a *sarcophagus* made of clay. I hated the word *sarcophagus*, it literally meant flesh eater. I couldn't bring myself to look at the box that swallowed up what remained of my mother.

You should look. An all too familiar voice whispered in my mind.

"You are right beside me. Please speak aloud," I snapped at the god who lingered at my side.

He chuckled. "You should look. It isn't as fearsome as you think."

I stood beside him, my spine as straight as a spear. Apollo settled his hands on my shoulders and brought his lips close to my ear. I shuddered.

"Look." Carefully he turned my body until I was facing the *larnax*.

The *larnax* was intricately painted. Typically, *larnakes* are painted with processions of women, their hands raised to their heads in the traditional gesture of mourning, a mirror to the rituals that took place at the time of burial.

But my mother's *larnax* was different. Instead of mourning women, my mother's *larnax* depicted a Sphinx flanked between two palm trees. The monster who had terrorised our kingdom now acted as the guardian of my parent's tomb. I thought of my last memory of the Sphinx, her face smeared with my blood, being overrun by ghosts. I tried to shake the memory from my mind.

I stepped closer to the *larnax* and placed my hand atop it.

"Now that you've seen your mother's *larnax*, it's time to see your father's." Apollo spun me again until I was facing another *larnax*, almost identical to my mother's, however the Sphinx painted upon its side bore a man's face. "If you were to look into your mother's *larnax*, you would find her bones. Your father's, on the other hand, is empty."

"Not for long, it isn't." I broke free from the god's grasp and pushed aside the lid of the *larnax*. As the god had said, the *larnax* was empty. I slung the bag from my shoulder, laid it on the ground and ever so carefully lifted out the bones of my father and placed them within his family tomb. As I laid the last bone inside the *larnax*, a gust of wind blew through the cave, the sound like a sigh held in for far too long. I moved the lid back into place and stepped back. My father's ghost had said his bones would lend protection to the city where they laid. Now I had some protection to offer my family.

I straightened and faced the god.

"I'm ready to save my family."

"Not yet, you're not," the god replied. He stepped around me, his gaze appraising. "You can't confront your uncle looking like this." He picked at my worn and dirty travelling clothes, my hair falling out of its ribbons.

He snapped his fingers and though I could not see the changes he had wrought, I felt the difference. For the first time in what seemed like weeks, I felt clean.

I stretched my arms out in front of me and inspected my hands. There were no crescents of dirt under my nails, no marks or blemishes on my bare arms. I looked down and saw the god had replaced my simple *chiton* with one befitting a woman of my status, its edges embroidered with golden thread. I reached up to touch my hair and wasn't surprised to find my shorn hair had grown back to its original length to spill over my shoulders in neat curls. A diadem sat atop my head and gold bracelets and necklaces clinked when I moved.

"I guess I look the part now?" I looked up, expecting a quip from the god.

But he was gone.

I would have to go alone.

22

ᴄ͟Thebes ᴅDestroyed

Standing at the entrance to my family tomb, I could see the Cadmeia in the distance. All I had to do was cross a battlefield to get there.

I steeled my shoulders. I wasn't the same girl who had snuck out of the women's quarters looking for adventure all those months ago. I had faced the trials set against me and emerged victorious. I had faced the gods and the Fates themselves. I accomplished what I had set out to do.

As I stepped out of the tomb, I could feel something brush my cheeks. I looked up to see what looked like snowflakes drifting down to settle on my hair, my clothes. But the flakes did not melt when they met my skin. They left a black smudge upon my exposed flesh, a stain upon my clothes.

It was not snow. It was ash.

I looked to my city. Once the Cadmeia sat atop the *acropolis*, nestled within the famed seven gates. Now the Cadmeia looked sadly down on fallow fields mired with blood, the famed gates a smouldering ruin.

I crossed the battlefield. Corpses lay all around me, my eyes darting around to see a flash of bronze, the red flow of blood, the spray of dark earth churned by the horses. There was a man pinned to the ground with a spear, a grim echo of my own friend Theron's death. There were cut down limbs and exposed throats empty of their lifeblood. The carnage was not too different from what I had seen at the Sphinx's pass after Tydeus' attack. Except this time the ground was littered with dead Argives and not Thebans.

I looked away.

I passed dogs and birds worrying at the corpses of the fallen Argives, discarded weapons littered the plain. Black arrows protruded from the narrow space between armour and skin, the barbs of arrows deeply embedded in tender throats. As I grew closer to the city's walls, I saw abandoned siege ladders laying broken amidst fallen rocks, arms and faces peeking from underneath the rockfall.

I watched as a chariot exited the gates and rumbled across the field, its wheels grinding dead men as it passed. Blood spattered the gleaming gold of the chariot. As he thundered past, the charioteer tore spears from corpses and collected them in his cart. They were already preparing for the next battle.

Gorge rose in my throat but I fought against it. I needed to be composed for the reunion with my uncle. I had seen the effects of the war in my visions and I knew he was close to breaking. His strength was fleeing from him as his mind splintered and broke for good. I needed to show strength and wisdom where he showed weakness and madness.

The charioteer wheeled to the right and came straight towards me. I watched impassively as the driver reached for one of the spears and pointed it at me.

"Who are you? What are you doing here?" he barked, his face obscured by his horsehair helmet. But I recognized the voice of one of the sons of *Spartoi*.

I hesitated to answer. For so long, I had been running away from who I was, who I had feared of becoming. I had been a servant, an aristocratic boy, a servant and then a daughter to a wandering seer. When I had left, I didn't know who I was. But now, I was sure.

"I am Ismene, princess of Thebes. I have come to give counsel to my uncle."

The charioteer took me inside the city gates, past weary warriors slumped at their posts, past mourning families and past row upon row of bodies waiting to be taken outside the city's walls and put to rest in their family tombs. As we passed the biers, I was alarmed to see some of the bodies still moving.

I grabbed at the arm of the charioteer. "They are not dead."

He looked down at his arm, bemused and followed my gaze to the bodies laid out on biers, still living but on the brink of death. He shrugged. "They will be soon."

I glared at him. "They are not warriors, but women and children. What happened?"

The charioteer let out an exasperated sigh. "We don't know. A sickness overcame the city. It's almost like—" he began but cut himself off, too afraid to say the words aloud.

My eyes widened in understanding. "As if the plague had returned," I finished.

The charioteer grunted his assent and jerked his head, indicating that we move on.

But I couldn't leave my people just yet. I trailed among the sick, wiping at their brows and murmuring prayers with them.

The charioteer was growing impatient. I nodded to him and began to rise, to stop avoiding the confrontation with my uncle. But something was tugging at my skirts. Someone was clutching at my skirts.

I looked down and with alarm I recognized the hand that gripped the embroidered hem of my *chiton*. Hands I had known all my life, hands I had watched work at the loom and spin wool, hands that wiped away my tears and comforted me to sleep.

"Pyrrha." I bit back a sob, crumpling to the ground beside her.

When I was growing up in the women's quarters, Pyrrha was my parent, my teacher, my guardian. She was my bard, telling me stories about our city, its people sown from the serpent's teeth, the home of a god. While the rule of Thebes seemed uncertain, the only sure thing in my life was Pyrrha's love. I had taken for granted that she would be safe from the tragedy that befell my family.

My beloved nurse seemed to have aged decades since I had left, her body shrunken, her hair no longer threaded with silver but completely grey. She looked up at me with eyes glistening with fever.

"Is that you, my love? Have you come home?" Her voice was so soft I could barely hear it but my heart knew her words.

I grasped at her hand and kissed it. She took in a breath and began to wheeze.

"I'm home," I told her, smoothing her brow. I was alarmed by the heat that rose from her skin, signs of the fever that tried to take her life. The Fates would not take her too, not yet.

You know what to do, the voice of the god echoed in my mind.

I did. The last plague had been sent because the king had offended the gods. It was time to let the current king know the error of his ways.

I raised Pyrrha's hand to my lips and kissed it. I placed my forehead against hers. "I will be back soon. I know how to lift this plague."

"Of course, you do. You will end the plague and save the city. Just like your father."

Tears gathered in my eyes and began to roll down my cheeks.

Pyrrha brought a quivering hand to my face and I leaned into her familiar palm. "You are just like him, you know. You will do anything to protect your family."

"Yes," I replied. "I will do anything."

With the image of my suffering people blazing in my mind, I walked beside the charioteer and into the *megaron*. The *megaron* was crowded with men. Tiresias stood amongst them before his king. The king sat slumped on the stone throne, a hand cast before his eyes as he listened to the complaints of the *Spartoi*.

Heads turned my way as I strode into the hall, the murmurs echoing throughout the room fell silent. All that could be heard was the snap of embers as they drifted from the central hearth.

As we drew closer, I heard my uncle ask the seer, "Tiresias, tell me. Has Apollo plagued our city a second time?"

Tiresias cocked his head, considering the question. But instead of answering, he turned his head in my direction.

"What is it now?" Creon sighed from his seat on my father's throne, my brother's throne.

No one spoke.

Creon dropped his hand from his face to peer around the hall. He gaped when he saw me, rising from his chair in a rush, only to falter and come to a halt before me.

"Jocasta?" he asked, astonished.

"No," I replied, hoping my voice sounded steadier than I felt. "Ismene."

"Ismene?" He came closer until he stood before me. "Where have you been?"

"I was sent on a quest."

Creon laughed darkly. "A quest? There has been talk that you defected to Argos, to aid your treacherous brother." He began to pace around me, a lion closing in on its prey. But didn't my uncle know that it was the lioness that did the hunting?

"I have been to Argos," I replied. The crowd began to whisper at this, thinking that I had confirmed the rumours. "I have been to Argos, Mycenae and Corinth, too."

Creon stopped in his tracks. "Corinth?"

"Yes." I stepped closer to my uncle, leaning towards him so that I could whisper into his ear. "I know *everything*."

Creon stumbled back. His fevered eyes searched mine, sweat dripped from his hairline to streak down to his chin. His face darkened. "You know *nothing*," he hissed.

I turned from him, my gown billowing around me. "I was sent on my quest by the Far-Shooter himself."

The murmurs throughout the crowd swelled, Creon raised his hands, trying to control the crowd's outburst, but they did not heed him. I raised an arm to point at my uncle. The hall fell silent.

"What would the god want with you?" Creon demanded.

Tiresias stepped forward. "The shining god has chosen your niece as one of his own," he began. Creon took a step backwards. "She is Manto. A seer in her own right. The god allows her to see the past, the present and the future in the flames."

Creon blinked and sputtered. "Ismene? A seer? She hears the god's will?"

Tiresias nodded. "Yes, the god speaks to her directly."

"What did the god tell you?" Creon demanded.

"The Far-Shooter bid me to give you a warning. You must be a better man than your predecessors."

Tiresias cocked his head as he listened to my voice. I had been raised to believe that a woman's voice was too weak to give great pronouncements. I had foreseen Tiresias say these words to my uncle in that dreadful future shown to me by Apollo.

But I had changed the future. I took that famous seer's words and spoke them myself. He knew. And he was proud, a bright smile shone on his face.

My uncle began to laugh. "You must be going senile old man," he barked at the seer. Tiresias bristled at the insult. "And you," he said, turning to me, "you expect me to believe the god sent you, a *girl*, to order me?"

I raised my arms and the flames that sat in the central hearth flared up behind me. The crowd drew back.

"I have looked into the fire and Apollo has shown me the future in the ashes. Apollo has told me, it is you, your resolve to dishonour your nephew, that sets another plague on Thebes."

Everyone in the hall cried out. Creon rushed at me, violence written in his features. The flames danced around me and he drew back. "No, no that can't be right. I am no murderer, no kinslayer!" He dropped his voice so that only I would hear. *"I am not like Oedipus!"*

I gazed at him. I had entered Hades itself and faced monsters and survived. The fury of one man did not scare me. "No, you are not. You are far worse. You hold yourself above the laws of the gods. The gods have sent a plague in response."

Creon held his head in his hands, a fevered shine to his eyes.

Tiresias left his place in the corner to approach him and rested one of his gnarled and bony hands atop the king's shoulder. "It is true."

Creon shook himself from the seer's grasp.

The crowd began to whisper amongst themselves. Creon cast a wary eye over the growing dissent. He straightened his back and turned to the seer once more.

"All men make mistakes," Tiresias began. "Admit yours and you can cure the plague before it devastates the city once more."

"How?" Creon asked.

"That is not for me to say," Tiresias replied and nodded his head in my direction.

Hesitantly, Creon turned to me.

"Lay the bodies you have desecrated to rest and Thebes will be clean of sin once more," I ordered.

"Of course," Creon replied through gritted teeth.

"And one more thing," I called out and my uncle paused. "You will release my sister."

Creon froze. "She is a criminal, she acted against my laws—"

The flames rose up behind me. "And you have acted against the laws of the gods! You must release her. The gods demand it!"

"You demand it," Creon hissed.

I stepped towards him and grabbed a fistful of his royal robes. I pulled him closer to the fire.

"Shall I show you what will happen if you refuse?" Creon tried to pull back but I held fast, bringing his face closer to the flames. I watched him start as he saw figures take shape in their depths. His eyes grew wide as he watched the future unfold before him.

The flames showed our family tomb carved from the mountains themselves, but the wide entrance was blocked by row upon row of heavy stones, placed there to keep its occupants inside. A living tomb for the king's rebellious niece.

A figure rushed to the blockade and scrambled to remove the stones until one by one they fell to the ground around him.

Creon drew in a breath beside me. The figure in the flames was Haemon.

Haemon stepped through the entrance and was swallowed by the shadows. Soon, the figure of Creon scurried up to the cave, pausing to stare at the scattered rocks.

From within the cave came a voice, a low wailing echoing among the stone. Creon stared at the cave in horror.

He entered the cave, the glow of his lamp bouncing off the many facets of the rocky cave. He stood in shock at the scene that lay before him.

It was Antigone, a fine linen noose around her neck. Haemon had his arms flung around her waist, clinging to another one he loved who had been taken from him.

"Haemon!" Creon gasped, reaching for his son. "Haemon, come away, come away with me now. I came to let her go. I was too late, but you will be alright. Just come with me."

Haemon knocked his father's hands away. He did not utter a word in reply. He simply drew his sword and leaned his full weight upon the blade. It buried itself in his chest, halfway to the hilt. One arm wrapped around Antigone.

Creon crumpled before him, his mouth gaping open. He reached out for his son with a trembling hand but withdrew it, wrapping his arms around himself he rocked back and forth, murmuring his son's name.

My uncle at last tore himself away from me, his face gone pale. He stared at the flames and then back at me.

"This is the future?" he whispered.

"This is the future if you do not heed me now," I replied. I stepped closer to him. "We have lost enough of our family as it is. Please, Uncle, let me try to salvage what remains."

Creon drew back as if I had struck him. His mouth gaped open but no words emerged. Finally, he came to his senses.

"Fine. Fine." He turned away from me and shouted, "Bring me my niece!"

I reached out and placed a hand on his arm. He glanced at me in annoyance.

"No. Bring me to her."

Creon led me to the rooms where Antigone was being held before he enclosed her in a living tomb. He ordered the sentries at the door to let us in.

As I moved to brush past him, he grabbed at my arm, hard. "Don't think that you can take the throne from me," he snarled.

I stared pointedly at his hand until he let go.

"It is yours to rule," I replied. "But remember, Uncle, that the gods are watching you. And I am their voice on this earth."

23

FATE AVERTED

I stepped into the small room to face my sister at last. I had been gone so long I lingered a moment at the threshold before entering. In my mind's eye, I still held the image of my sister hanging from the noose, that sad fate that had awaited her before I met with the *Moirai* and made a bargain to extend her life.

Antigone's head turned towards the door when she heard it creak open. She looked at me in shock, rising to her feet to stand before me. Soon, her shock gave way to another emotion.

I don't know what I expected. Perhaps I thought my sister's face would be a mirror to my own, her face shining with the gratitude and relief that shone upon my face, happy to be reunited with the person who mattered the most to me. I expected gratitude, relief and love.

I did not expect anger.

There was Antigone, standing directing in front of me. She looked *furious*.

"Are you mad at me?" I croaked.

After all this time, after all I had been through, all I had given up, I did not expect to be met with such a reaction.

But then again, sisters were anything but predictable.

"Of course, I am mad at you!" she exploded. "You've been

gone for months! I thought you were never coming back." Her voice broke and she sank to her knees, the heels of her palms pressed to her eyes.

I approached her. "I'm here now. Don't cry."

"I'm not crying," she retorted, furiously wiping the tears that gathered in her eyes. She wiped at her face for some time, until finally: "You left me."

Guilt wrapped itself around my throat. "I had to."

She nodded her head in agreement. "You had to," she repeated. "I know that. It's just..." She took in a deep, shuddering breath. "It's just I didn't think of how it would feel to be left behind."

"Oh, Antigone." I sank down beside her. I longed to put my arms around her. But I knew if I did, she would shrug me off. I wrapped my arms around myself, a mirror to my sister's posture.

Antigone peered at me. "You know what? I always thought that if one of us was going to be left behind, it would be you. Not me."

"I always thought that, too," I admitted. "Until the god."

"Until the god."

We sat in silence for a few minutes, thinking of our shared past.

As a child, Antigone was my guiding light. When darkness stirred up all my fears, when the image of monsters from our nurse's stories etched themselves onto the backs of my eyelids like figures etched on the slip of clay pots, it was Antigone who was my comfort. In times when fear struck me, I found myself reaching towards my sister.

I had never considered that I brought her the same comfort.

This time, when I went to put my arms around her, I knew she would accept my embrace. I reached for her hand, twining ours together the way we so often had when we were girls.

"I'm back now," I whispered.

"I didn't think you were coming back."

"I know."

"I had a plan."

I drew away from her to look her in the eyes. "I know about your plan. What were you going to achieve by killing yourself?"

She stared stonily back at me. "If I killed myself, he wouldn't be the one killing me. I would be the one in control for once."

I sighed. "Well, you don't have to worry about that now."

"I don't? You mean he isn't going to bury me alive?"

"No, he isn't," I snapped.

She pushed away from me, leaping to her feet. "He will eventually! I am not going to stop until our brother is at rest."

I rose with her and grabbed her hand, forcing her to stand still. "No, he won't."

Antigone dropped her hands from mine and scowled. "Yes, he will! Your work was for nothing. You can't sneak me out of here. I won't stop obeying the laws of the gods, I won't."

"I know," I replied calmly. "But you are wrong. He won't punish you because he must obey the laws of the gods now, or suffer their wrath."

Antigone paled. "What do you mean?"

"Come on, Antigone. You must have seen the bodies piled *within* the city walls. Apollo has sent another plague on Thebes for Creon's folly."

Antigone clasped a hand to her mouth in alarm. We had both grown up fearing the plague. The news that it had returned was a waking nightmare.

I placed a hand on her shoulder. "I told Creon all this. The only way to lift the plague is to bury the fallen Argives outside the city."

Antigone let her hand fall. "And you believe he'll do it?"

"He must," I replied. "The god commanded it."

Her eyes narrowed. "I thought you commanded it?"

"We are one and the same," I said. The dimly lit torches outside the door blazed, the light reaching over the threshold door like grasping hands.

Antigone leapt away from me. "Ismene," she breathed. *"What did you do?"*

"I can't believe you did this," Antigone said as we made our way out onto the battlefield to give funeral rites to the fallen Argives at last. "You got Creon to see sense. I can't believe he allowed this desecration to go on as long as it has. Even our enemies deserve the rite of burial."

We walked onto the field, trying not to stumble upon the uneven ground of the battlefield until at last we came upon the body of our brother Polynices.

After days on the battlefield among carrion birds and dogs, he was unrecognisable, save for the tattered lion skin cloak, his sword with a sphinx carved into the hilt, still stained with Eteocles' blood.

We stood over the body in silence for a moment. Then, I softly muttered a prayer to Hecate of the Crossroads and Hades to hold back their anger at being denied their rites.

Antigone had brought a small vessel of water with her and I used it to wash our brother. I poured the purifying liquid on his skin and watched the dirt and blood smooth away while my sister strode about the field, collecting fallen timber of broken siege engines and broken shafts of arrows and spears, scattering them around what was left of our brother, and piling a mound of Theban soil around it. She pulled me back and she set the mound alight.

As we watched the flames consume what was left of Polynices, Antigone worried the hasty burial wouldn't appease the god's anger. But I knew the god was pleased.

The flames rose higher and I tried not to cry. After everything I had done, I had not saved my brothers.

Staring at my brother's pyre, I realised that I never could have prevented his death. Not just because the gods willed it, but because my brother's hatred would not let him consider any option but war. It was not for me to stop the bloodshed. My brothers had the power to stop it and save so many lives but they allowed their greed and anger to destroy a city.

Though I could not prevent my brothers from fighting till the death, I had still managed to save my brother's soul.

While we stood there, the fire blazing around us, our uncle caught up with us, his retinue following close behind him. He viewed the funeral in silence. He would not punish us for doing something he had come to do himself.

The retinue went about the field lighting their own small pyres for the other Argive dead until the field was alight like a sea of flames. And as the Argives were laid to rest, Thebes was safe at last.

Antigone and I stood in silence, watching the flames flicker across the field. I needed to tell her what I had done, how I had bound her life to mine, but I didn't know how to begin.

It was her who began to speak first. "I know what you are thinking. What do we do now? No, please let me finish." She turned to me as I opened my mouth to speak. "I can't stay here. I can't be hidden away in that room any longer, left to be forgotten. I don't want to be cursed with a purposeless life forever. I need a purpose, Ismene." She looked over her shoulder, her eyes meeting my own. "And so do you. Let me go and find my purpose. Let's find our purpose together."

I smiled.

"I was hoping you'd say that."

"You were?" She raised an eyebrow. "Any ideas about where we should go?"

"As a matter of fact, I do."

Antigone and I spent the next few days preparing to depart Thebes. The city itself was stirring once more, like a sleeping giant rousing awake. The sick who had been laid out on biers ready to transport to their mass grave began to heal once the Argives had been laid to rest and the gods had been appeased.

Our own beloved nurse was one of the first to heal, her eyes no longer bright with fever. I made up for all the time I had lost with her, making sure she was whole and hardy for our upcoming journey. Of course, Pyrrha would come with us.

This time, I did not try to squeeze myself to fit into that small life I led before. I had grown too much and seen too much to revert to my former self.

I walked among the halls of the Cadmeia, not as a servant, not as a boy, but as myself. I was Ismene, princess of Thebes and Seer. The *Spartoi* sought me out to ask the god's wisdom and I gave it gladly. Those who were in the hall for my confrontation with Creon called me Manto. They didn't need to know that the words from my lips were my own and not sanctioned by the god. But I could sense Apollo was pleased.

Antigone lingered close by, the *Spartoi* turning to her for guidance as well. Though she was not chosen as the god's own servant, she had become a hero in her own right for standing up against the king to uphold the laws of the gods. We had come so far from being the silent, decorative sisters of a boy king.

I looked towards my sister and could feel the bond of moonlight that bound us together.

By binding my fate to hers, I had saved more than just Antigone's life. That terrible vision of Antigone swinging from a noose had also contained the horrific death of our cousin Haemon as well. Antigone was alive and well and Haemon was not driven to his desperate act of defiance against his father. I had seen the relief in Creon's eyes that his remaining son had been spared but the bond between them was broken beyond repair.

In those busy days where Thebes sought to rebuild itself, Haemon came to find me. He lingered behind the *Spartoi*, a smile playing at his lips. After my crowd of querents had dispersed, he approached.

"What?" I asked.

"I was just thinking of something Menoeceus told me when we were in Delphi."

Menoeceus. I could have saved him as well. He was closer to me than my brothers had ever been and his death had made a hole in my heart I feared would never be filled.

"What did he tell you?"

Haemon and I walked along together through the Cadmeia and out into the courtyard. A playful breeze tugged at my curls, my skirts. My cousin looked out at the mountains that ringed our city, the blue sky reflected in Lake Copias. He took his time to answer, the memory a good one, but painful because of who he had shared it with.

"It was after the chariot race. He told me you were upset about how Tydeus had killed his wounded horse. Menoeceus said he told you that you shouldn't have come because the real world was too much for you. And you replied that maybe it was time for the world to change."

He tore his eyes from the sky and turned to me then, his eyes shining with tears. "You did just that, Ismene. You changed the world for the better." His voice was thick with emotion. He grasped my hands in his. I turned my head, my failure to save my brothers ready to spring from my lips.

Haemon tightened his grip on my hands. "I know what you are going to say. You are going to say you failed. That you couldn't save Eteocles, or Polynices or Menoeceus. But you saved Thebes. You saved Antigone." He took a deep, shuddering breath. "You saved me."

I gripped his hands just as tightly. "I know."

"You don't," he said quickly, pain flashing across his features. "You don't know what I planned to do if my father harmed Antigone—"

"I know," I repeated. "I saw both your futures. That

Antigone was fated to die by her own hand, and your death would follow swiftly afterward."

Haemon exhaled, a weight on his shoulders seemed to lift as I spoke the words aloud. "You really did it," he breathed in wonder. "You changed fate."

"Yes."

"But there was a cost?"

"Yes," I repeated, softer.

"What was the cost?"

"I made a deal with the god. I vowed to go into his service if he allowed me to save what remained of my family."

Haemon was silent for a moment. "Then, I will do the same."

"What?"

"I will go into his service, too. I wouldn't be here if not for you, if not for him."

"How will you go into his service?" I asked.

Haemon smiled. "I will build a temple for the Far-Shooter. A temple along the rushing waters of the Ismenos river."

"What will you call this temple?"

"The Temple of Apollo Ismenios. Its priests will serve an oracle who will look into the fire to know the god's will. That is," he said as he turned to me, "if you would be our oracle."

I smiled.

"Of course."

I stood with Haemon, discussing the plans for the temple while the sun set and bathed the sky in streaks of red and orange.

Later, he waved in farewell and left me alone. I approached the city gates and the sentries gladly waved me through. I trod across the former battlefield and kept walking until I reached the burial chambers of the *Spartoi*. I halted before the monument tomb and sat upon the grass and called out softly to my friends.

"Dorylas, Theron and Chromis. We never got the chance to properly meet but I was hoping it wasn't too late to introduce myself. You knew me as Ismenos, a son of the *Spartoi*. One of you. My name is Ismene, a daughter of Oedipus, our former king. I am not who you thought I was, but I hope you still consider me one of you."

A breeze stirred the blades of grass all around me, the gust of air playfully tickling at my hair and clothes.

I smiled. I took this as their agreement.

"You were the first friends I ever had outside the palace," I continued. "Tomorrow, I am taking my sister to Delphi, along the same path that we took together. I'll be thinking of you three all the while."

I sat with the ghosts of my friends for company and waited for dawn and the start of my journey to arrive.

We left Thebes at dawn. We crossed the fields that were so recently churned by the soldiers and their steeds. Tufts of grass poked from the blood soaked earth, the land's attempt to heal itself. We marched across the fields of war towards the mountains, the air thinning as we rose higher and higher into the clouds.

We made frequent breaks to accommodate Pyrrha. She had recovered from her illness but was still a shade of her former self. All the same, she seemed glad to be going on an adventure with us.

Finally, we stood upon the slopes of Mount Parnassus, the golden rocks dotted with towering pine trees, the sky suspended above us like a great bolt of cloth stretched over the heavens.

There was no sound save for the wind rushing through branches, the gurgle of the Castalian spring.

Antigone whispered into the silence. "So, are you going to tell me where we are now?"

"Not yet," I whispered back. I took her hand and we continued to climb. I gestured for Pyrrha to go on ahead of us, and she winked in reply. Soon, our nurse disappeared behind a shield of golden rock.

Grasping Antigone's hand in mine, together we passed the jutting stone to reveal the sun blazing down upon the sanctuary nestled into the mountain. Antigone gasped. The sanctuary of Apollo was bathed in the light of the setting sun.

I turned my back to the sanctuary to face my sister.

"Do you remember saying how nice it would be if we could go to Delphi? Well, we're finally here, together."

We marched towards the sanctuary nestled in the mountains. But instead of going up the Sacred Way and towards the temple, we headed for the Castalian Spring.

There, sitting by the trickling stream was the Pythia. She stood and waved us over. I almost didn't recognize her when she wasn't wreathed in smoke. She seemed formidable from her seat on the tripod, but here in this open space, I could see that she was just a girl, like me. A girl favoured by the god.

She stepped forward and embraced me.

"You did it!" she spoke into my ear.

"I did it," I repeated with a smile.

The Pythia turned to my sister. "I've heard you wanted to meet me for some time."

Antigone stared. "Who told you?"

The Pythia grinned. "Who do you think? The god himself."

Antigone blushed.

Pyrrha ambled over and sank into the grass with a sigh. We all took a seat beside her.

"So, now that you've met me, is there anything you'd like to ask me?" the famous oracle inquired.

Pyrrha nudged my sister with her elbow and Antigone reddened with embarrassment. "I'm not sure. Do you mind if I think about it a little?"

"Of course," the Pythia agreed.

Antigone turned to our nurse and the two of them whispered furiously about what they would ask while I watched on with amusement. They were more than welcome to ask me for a prophecy, but they longed for the novelty of asking the most famous oracle in all Hellas.

"The most famous for now," my companion amended.

I laughed. "I forgot you could read my mind."

"Not read your mind so much as sense what you will say before you say it." The Pythia reached down to tug at the strands of grass beside her, twirling the green shoots between her fingers as she appraised me. "And are you ready to become another famous oracle?"

"I doubt I could ever be as great as you."

"You will be great. Your people will turn to you in times of crisis to come."

"I don't know how many crises I can take," I muttered. "I barely made it through the last one."

"You do yourself a disservice by belittling your achievement," The Pythia replied.

"It doesn't feel like an achievement. I did the impossible and changed fate to save my city and my sister. But there were so many I couldn't save. I don't know how I can face something like that again."

"You can and you will face it."

I sighed. "You're right. I will use the skills I have gained on my travels and the god's favour to continue to protect my city as long as I live."

"I know you will."

We sat in silence, gazing at each other, two halves of the same coin. Both servants to a great god, both burdened with the futures of so many lives.

"I know what to ask," Antigone called out.

I rose to give Antigone and Pyrrha privacy to ask their questions of the oracle.

I walked along the sacred spring and turned to look at the golden mountain rising above me into the clouds.

When I had first met her, the Pythia was such a mystery to me, a figure to be feared as well as revered. Now I must step into a similar role and I had no doubts that I had the strength to do it.

After weeks spent in the sacred city with the oracle as our guide, our friend, we departed from Delphi to make our journey home. We begged our nurse to tell us a new story, for old time's sake.

Mischief twinkled in our nurse's bright eyes. "A new story, you say? I think I've told you all I know."

"Go on! I am sure you're holding out on us," I replied.

Pyrrha raised her hand to her chin in thought while Antigone and I struggled not to laugh. "Have you heard the tale of the cursed king?"

We shook our heads.

"Well, this king had a daughter. She used her visions to save a kingdom, end a war and reunite her family." As she spoke, tears gathered in her eyes and rolled down her cheeks. She reached for our hands.

Antigone smiled. "I think that may be your best story yet."

I raised my hand to my chin, a mirror of Pyrrha's movements moments before. I shook my head. "I think it was much too short."

Antigone, Pyrrha and I laughed together that bright afternoon. The last afternoon the three of us would spend together.

Soon, we came to a crossroads, one path led home to Thebes, the other to Corinth. I made for the path to Thebes but stopped when I didn't hear footsteps accompanying my own. I turned. Antigone lingered at the crossroad, her gaze turned towards Corinth.

"What are you doing?" I asked. "Aren't you coming home with me?" My voice broke on the word home.

Antigone faced me. "Remember what we talked about when we buried Polynices? I need to find out who I am. It's

my turn to have an adventure. The adventure starts here."
Her smile blazed as brightly as the sun above us.

"Your adventure starts here," I agreed. I rushed towards her and embraced her.

As I stood watching my sister and our nurse head to Corinth to meet with our grandmother, it did not feel like goodbye. After all, our lives were bound together, I would always feel her with me in spirit.

24

THE ROAD HOME

When I arrived back in Thebes, construction of the Temple of Apollo Ismenios was underway. The temple lay outside the city's walls to the southeast, built upon a hill that bore the same name as the river flowing alongside it.

That evening when I had arrived home, I went to see the temple.

Though it was still undergoing construction, I used my power as a seer to see the temple as it would be once it was finished. The painted marble columns were bathed golden in the setting sun. Statues of Athena and Hermes would flank the entrance to the sanctuary. I took a deep breath and crossed the threshold.

Inside the temple, votive offerings would glitter in the firelight, statues and tripods crafted of bronze. I gazed in wonder at what my cousin would accomplish.

"You must be so pleased with yourself," I muttered in that sacred space.

You could say that, the god's voice whispered in my mind.

"You set out for just me and you ended up with Haemon and priests and a temple, too."

Who said I set out just for you?

I froze.

"You knew?" I whispered.

Of course, I knew. I am the god of prophecy, after all. I knew you would try to change fate and I let you, knowing that you would go into my service, and your cousin, too.

"Are you sure you're really Apollo? Not Hermes? You are more of a trickster than I thought you to be."

The god's laughter rang in my mind. *You should have known as well. It was right there all along.*

I thought back to my first meeting with the Pythia in the Temple of Apollo, her face wreathed in smoke and the life changing words that fell from her lips: *"You will tend the holy house of Lord Apollo the far-shooter when all is ruined by fire and the God of War. War and destruction will find you when all your father's shadows come to light."*

"You will tend the holy house of Lord Apollo the far-shooter when all is ruined by fire and the God of War," I murmured.

You see? You were destined to go into my service no matter the outcome of your family war.

I felt anger rise within me. "Then why bother to make a bargain with me? Why go through any of this if you knew how it would play out?"

Ismene. You should know by now. It isn't enough to simply know the future—you must encourage things in the right direction. I couldn't force you into my service, could I? I needed you to think it was your own idea and let you come to me as a willing servant.

I bristled at his words. "Couldn't force me? You are the catalyst that drove me to this."

Like I said. I encouraged things in the right direction.

As I stood and fumed, a figure stepped out of the shadows. A familiar handsome face grinned down at me.

"You had to come and gloat in person."

"And?" Apollo spread his arms, gesturing to the ghost of splendour around him. "What do you think of our temple? Do you approve?"

I smiled despite myself. "Our temple?"

He nodded, his smile gleaming in the torchlight. "You see it as it will be, don't you? One of the greatest oracles in Hellas." He nodded towards the altar that held a ceremonial fire and then gestured towards me. Together, we walked over to look into the flames.

"This will be the altar of Apollo Spodios. Apollo, God of Ashes." He preened as he spoke aloud our epithets for him. "Look into the fire. What do you see?"

The flames rose to dance in the darkness and then banked until only the embers glowed in the darkness.

I rolled my eyes and leaned in to gaze at the embers. In their depths, I saw myself, seated on a great stone, issuing prophecies to querents, much as the Pythia at Delphi. The sight tugged at the thread of fate I had created for myself. For all his talk of how it was destined to happen, I knew this was the right course. Earlier this year, I was a foolish princess, imprisoned by her own ignorance, despairing of ever being able to live a life that would make a difference. And here I was now, watching a future unfold where I had the power to enact change for the better.

"You seem pleased." I could hear the grin in Apollo's voice.

"I am," I replied as I turned to him. "But not because of you."

His face sobered. "Because of who, then?"

"Because of me. I achieved all this, I fought against fate and the gods themselves to save the rest of my family, my city. And I will continue to do so through this position you created for me." I smiled at him. "I spent so long with a heavy heart, despairing that all I loved would be destroyed. But now my heart will be light because I know I will remain here to protect my city."

Apollo nodded. "Thebes is in your hands now." He reached out to clasp his hands around my own. "If you ever have need of me, look to the flames and you will have your answer."

The embers snapped and sparked, little lights danced all around, suspended in the darkness like small stars. And the god disappeared.

I resumed my tour of the temple, seeing the temple how it would be in the years to come. In the *adyton*, a great stone would sit where I would dispense my prophecies.

I thought long and hard of what I would be called. I couldn't call myself a Pythia, there was only one of those and she was tied to the site where Python had been slain.

My temple was also built around a slain serpent, Ismenion. I toyed with the name but ultimately decided on Manto, the name the people of my city had already begun to call me. Manto would act as the seer of this temple, a name that acted as a reminder of the journey that brought me here and tied me to another famous Theban seer.

Statutes of women would stand along the walls of the temple to act as guardians of the sanctuary. My own face would be carved in stone, a permanent fixture to protect the city of my birth. While I would act as the oracle, each year a boy from the sons of the *Spartoi* would be chosen to act as my priest. Haemon himself would take the role at first and pass it along to another Theban youth in a year's time.

Outside the temple, a fountain gurgled happily. The spring that fed it was that same spring that was sacred to Ares, where Cadmus had slain the Ismenian serpent and sown its teeth to make his citizens.

A sob escaped my throat as I took in all that Haemon would build, all he would do, because I had the bravery to try to fight fate and save the lives of those I loved.

GLOSSARY

Acropolis: The citadel or fortified part of an ancient Greek city. The *acropolis* was typically built upon a hill for defensive purposes. Literally means "high city."

Adyton: The most sacred space of a temple, located at the deepest space of the temple structure.

Agora: The city centre and marketplace. A place of assembly for citizens to talk politics and trade.

Alastor: An epithet of Zeus, avenger of evil deeds.

Apollo: Greek god of prophecy, plague, archery, civilization, music, poetry and medicine. Apollo is the son of Zeus and Leto, and twin brother to Artemis.

Artemis: Greek goddess of the hunt, archery, childbirth and the moon. Daughter of Zeus and Leto, twin sister of Apollo.

Athena: Greek goddess of wisdom, war and craft. Athena often bestowed her favour on heroes, the most famous of which are Odysseus, Diomedes and Tydeus. Daughter of Zeus and Metis.

Astragaloi: Knucklebones. A game played in ancient Greece in which the bones were rolled to divine answers to questions asked by the players.

Aulos: A wind instrument

Cadmeia: The palace complex and administrative centre of the ancient city of Thebes. Stationed on the *acropolis,* the *Cadmeia* was named for Cadmus, one of the legendary founders of Thebes.

Chiton: A tunic fastened at the shoulder worn by both men and women in ancient Greece.

Chresmographeion: A shaded space for querents to wait for an audience with the Oracle of Delphi.

Chryselactus: Epithet of Artemis, of the golden distaff.

Crete: An island to the south of Greece in the Aegean Sea. Crete was the home of Minoan civilization who were notable for their trade by sea. The Minoan civilization was named for the legendary King Minos, the father of Ariadne, who was famed for sending Athenian youths to their deaths in his labyrinth.

Delphi: A sanctuary on the slopes of Mount Parnassus, *Delphi* is sacred to the god Apollo. The oracle of Apollo is situated here, as are the *Pythian Games*.

Demeter: Greek goddess of agriculture

Dionysus: Greek God of wine, theatre and madness

Epinetron: A ceramic covering placed over the knee for working the hand loom

Erinyes: The Furies. Greek goddesses of vengeance.

Exedra: a raised, stone platform

Fresco: A wall painting painted on wet plaster, a typical decoration of Minoan and Mycenaean palace structures

Hades: Greek god of the Underworld, Hades rules over the dead

Harmatodroia: Chariot race. One of the athletic contests of the Pythian games.

Hera: Greek goddess of marriage and married women. Hera is the wife of Zeus and queen of the gods.

Heraion: The temple of Hera in Argos

Hermes: Greek god. Hermes is a trickster, messenger, guardian of travellers and guide of the souls to the Underworld. Son of Zeus and Maia.

Himantes: Strips of oxhide wrapped around the hands and knuckles that served as boxing gloves

Ismenos: A river that flows to the east of Thebes named for the son of Melia and Apollo

Isthmus: A narrow land bridge connecting the Peloponnese to mainland Greece

Kalathos: A ceramic basket, used to store unspun wool

Kapeloi: Traders

Kithara: A seven-stringed musical instrument

Kore: Literally means 'girl' or 'maiden' in Ancient Greek. A statuary type depicting young women. *Kore* statues also served as grave markers.

Kouroi: Literally means "boys" in Ancient Greek. *Kouroi* are also a type of statuary depicting young men. *Kouros* statues also acted as grave markers in Archaic Greece.

Kylix: A broad rimmed Greek vessel meant to hold wine

Lake Copias: Lake of Thebes in the Bronze Age. This lake no longer exists in the present time.

Larnax, larnakes: A sarcophagus made of clay, typically painted with protective figures or burial scenes.

Lekythos: A tall thin ceramic pot used to hold oils

Mantis: A seer

Meliae: Wood nymphs

Megaron: A central hearth. The *megaron* was a social, ceremonial and religious centre of the Mycenaean palace structure.

Moirai: The Fates. Three beings who spin, measure and cut the threads of mortal lives. The three Fates are named Clotho, Lachesis and Atropos.

Neis Gate: One of the 7 Gates of Thebes. One of the distinctive features of Mycenaean palaces and cities was that they were fortified, which means they were protected by defensive walls. A large defensive wall with 7 gates was said to have surrounded the ancient city of Thebes.

Omphalos: Literally means 'navel.' A stone representing what the Greeks believed to be the centre of the world. Located in the sanctuary of Delphi.

Oracle: A figure who can see the future thanks to the powers of the god Apollo. The most famous oracle was the Oracle of Delphi.

Parabates: The man who stands beside a charioteer in their chariot who protects the driver from danger

Parados: The first choral passage in Greek drama sung as the chorus enters the orchestra

Peplos: A large, square cloth fastened at the waist, this folded cloth was worn by Greek women and girls

Petasos: A broad rimmed hat worn by travellers

Pithoi: *pithos* singular. A large ceramic vase in which necessities such as olive oil, wine, barley, wheat, olives and figs were stored

Promanteia: Privilege. The right to go before the *Pythia*. The right of *promanteia* was often gained through donation by wealthy men or kings.

Pronaos: The vestibule.

Pygmachia: Boxing match. One of the athletic contests held at the Pythian Games.

Pythian Games: Athletic, musical and poetic contests held every four years at the sanctuary of Delphi

Pythia: The name given to the Oracle of Delphi, often a young, unmarried woman

Python: The serpent who guarded the sanctuary of Delphi, child of Gaea the earth goddess. Python was slain by Apollo.

Pyxis: a small box

Sacred Way: The processional road through the sanctuary of Delphi which leads to the temple of Apollo

Sarcophagus: Literally means 'flesh eater'

Segma: Signs or portents. Symbols with meaning used to divine the future.

Skene: A tented backdrop behind the stage in a Greek theatre. Origin of the English word *scene*.

Smintheus: An epithet of Apollo the mouse god. Some scholars attribute this epithet to Apollo the god of plague, as it was believed that plague was spread by rodents.

Spartoi: The Sown Men. Refers to the mythological story of the founder of Thebes. Cadmus came to Thebes from tyre and slew the Ismenion serpent and sowed its teeth into the earth to become his citizens. The Five aristocratic families of Thebes are said to be descended from the Sown Men, the first citizens.

Sphinx: The legendary monster with the face of a woman, body of a lion and the wings of an eagle. The famous *Sphinx* terrorised Thebes by asking travellers to the city riddles and devouring those who answered incorrectly.

Spodios: Ashes. Epithet of Apollo of the Ashes referring to his temple of Apollo Ismenios where the future is divined from fire.

Stadium: A racetrack. The location of the footrace held in the Pythian Games.

Stoa: A covered walkway or portico for public use

Strigil: A blunt blade. Greek athletes would rub oil into their skin and use the *strigil* to scrape away dirt and grime from their skin.

Thebes: An ancient Greek city in the region of Boeotia. Thebes was founded by Cadmus, a prince of Tyre who came to Greece in search of his missing sister Europa abducted by Zeus.

Theopropoi: Querents. People seeking an audience with the Oracle of Delphi.

Theoria: An act of observance

Xenios: Epithet of Zeus, protector of strangers

Zeus: Greek god of thunder, justice, hospitality. Zeus is the king of the Olympian gods.

Adrastos: The king of Argos. Father of Argia, father-in-law to Polynices and Tydeus. One of the Seven Against Thebes.

Amphiaraus: One of the Seven Against Thebes. A seer.

Antigone: Daughter of Oedipus and Jocasta, sister of Antigone, Eteocles and Polynices. Princess of Thebes.

Apollo: God of prophecy, plague, archery, civilization, poetry, medicine and the sun.

Argia: Daughter of Adrastos, wife of Polynices. A princess of Argos.

Capaneus: One of the Seven Against Thebes led by Polynices.

Chromis: Son of the *Spartoi*, Friend of Ismenos.

Creon: Brother of Jocasta, father of Haemon and Menoeceus and uncle to Antigone, Ismene, Eteocles and Polynices. One of the *Spartoi*.

Dorylas: Son of the *Spartoi*, Friend of Ismenos.

Eteocles: Son of Oedipus and Jocasta, brother of Antigone, Ismene and Eteocles. Prince of Thebes. Son-in law of Adrastos and husband to Argia. One of the Seven Against Thebes

Theron: Son of the *Spartoi*, Friend of Ismenos. The king of Thebes.

Haemon: Son of Creon, brother of Menoeceus. A prince of Thebes.

Hippomedon: One of the Seven Against Thebes

Ismene: Daughter of Oedipus and Jocasta, sister of Antigone, Eteocles and Polynices. Princess of Thebes.

Ismenos: The name Ismene goes by when she is masquerading a boy on the journey to Delphi.

Jocasta: The queen of Thebes. Wife of Oedipus, sister of Creon and mother of Antigone, Ismene, Eteocles and Polynices.

Laius: Former King of Thebes, first husband of Jocasta.

Manto: Daughter of Tiresias. The name Ismene goes by when she is masquerading as a commoner on her travels with the famous seer.

Menoeceus: Son of Creon, brother of Haemon. A prince of Thebes.

Merope: Queen of Corinth, wife of Polybus and mother of Oedipus

Oedipus: The king of Thebes. Husband of Jocasta and father of Antigone, Ismene, Eteocles and Polynices.

Parthenopaeus: One of the Seven Against Thebes. Son of the hero Atalanta.

Polybus: King of Corinth, husband of Merope and father of Oedipus.

Polynices: Son of Oedipus and Jocasta, brother of Antigone, Ismene and Eteocles. Prince of Thebes. Son-in law of Adrastos and husband to Argia. One of the Seven Against Thebes

Pyrrha: Nurse of Ismene, Antigone, Polynices, Eteocles, Haemon and Menoeceus

Theron: Son of the *Spartoi*, Friend of Ismenos.

Tiresias: The famous wandering seer.

Tydeus: One of the Seven Against Thebes. Son-in law of Adrastos and brother-in-law of Polynices.

$\mathcal{A}$CKNOWLEDGEMENTS

Thank you to the Classics Department at the University of Guelph. To Dr Padraig O'Cleirigh, Dr Andrew Sherwood, and Dr John Walsh—not only did you teach me about the languages, history, literature and art of Ancient Greece and Rome, you shared your passions and made a lasting impression. To Padraig O'Cleirigh for spreading his genuine joy for languages and poetry. To Andrew Sherwood for driving me to do my best and encouraging me to speak up for myself. And to John Walsh who persuaded me to change majors to Classics.

Thank you to my fellow Classics students for growing and learning with me and forging memories together.

Thank you to the faculty, grad students and administration at the Classics Department at the University of Western Ontario. To my cohort for being the group of friends I needed, to my professors for their guidance, and to the administrators for their kindness and support. Special thanks go to Dr Kelly Olson whose classes made me rediscover my love for Classics at a time when I feared I would lose it forever. Your Women in Antiquity course changed my life.

Thank you to the friends I made at the Conventiculum Lexionise for demonstrating how welcoming and kind Classics can be.

Thank you to the friends I made over Classics Twitter—to Liv Albert from "Let's Talk About Myths Baby" for listening to me talk about Thebes and for the podcast that made Classics a safe space for me again. Thanks to Brittany Beverung, otherwise known as Artistfully, for bringing my characters to life and for sharing her art.

Thank you to Dr Stephanie Larson for sharing your knowledge about Thebes. I appreciate all the time you took to answer my questions and for recommending further reading on Thebes.

Thank you to Dr Roger Lipsey for permitting me to use your translations of Delphic oracles in this book.

Thank you to my friends and coworkers at Indigo North London for reigniting my love of books. Big shout out to the Kids Team for making all the long holiday hours fun. To Chloe Marenette for reading more than one draft of this book, for creating the first piece of art for *Riddles of the Sphinx* and for all our clandestine talks around the bargain kids books about publishing, YA and writing. Chloe I will always appreciate your never failing enthusiasm and support. To Nicole Bolin for being my number one hype person, for the shared memes and twitter comments and secret notes by the kids cash. Nicole, I am so glad to have a supportive friend like you.

Thank you to Yin Chang and the 88 Cups of Tea podcast community. I am happy this community helped introduce me to incredible writers like Christiana Ducette and Jeanne Rodrigue. Thanks to Christiana for being my first ever beta reader, and to Jeanne for beta reading and being the Queen of Nanowrimo. Jeanne you make every April, July and November the best months ever.

Thanks to my dear friend Jen Puchalski for doing NanoWrimo together with me and keeping me accountable when I wrote the first draft of *Riddles of the Sphinx*. Thank you for the years of friendship and support.

Thanks to my friends at David's Vacation Club Rentals for their enthusiasm about my book.

Big thanks to Kate Cimafranca for being my fairy godmother of self-publishing. You shared your knowledge with me when I needed it most.

Thanks to KB for being an extraordinary editor. KB, thank you for your kindness and patience and for making *Riddles of the Sphinx* the best it can be.

Thanks to Holly Dunn for creating the most amazing cover. I am so thankful we got to work together.

Thank you to my best friend, Jen Colclough, for our long phone calls workshopping our writing, for the memes and jewellery hauls and for sharing our deepest fears. Here's to being writers together.

Thanks to my family for always being my biggest fans. To Mum, Dad, Amanda, Andrew, Melanie and Allison for listening to my stories. To Nan and Grandad for always believing I could do it.

And to Richard. Thank you for always believing in me, supporting my dreams and pushing me to be a better person and a better writer. I love you.